# IT COULD ONLY HAPPEN TO MISS SEETON . . .

"Why," Chief Superintendent Delphick wanted first of all to know, "was Miss Seeton on that bus, anyway?"

"Her umbrella," muttered Brinton, still not entirely believing it himself.

"Did you say—?" Delphick broke off to answer his own question with a sigh. "Her umbrella—yes, that figures."

"She'd put it up, because it was raining so hard. So she wasn't seeing so well, with the wind driving rain right in her face, and her brolly sheltering her *and* blocking her view, of course—and the coach wasn't the usual Plummergen shuttle. So naturally Miss Seeton didn't recognize it."

"Naturally," said Delphick, "she wouldn't, armed with her umbrella and all set to stir up trouble . . . But why didn't somebody tell her she'd made a mistake?"

Brinton sighed. "It could only happen to her, couldn't it. Nobody told her, because nobody knew . . . before they set off. For France."

*Miss Seeton Books From The Berkley Publishing Group*

*Heron Carvic's Miss Seeton*

# MISS SEETON
# CRACKS THE CASE
## HAMILTON CRANE

BERKLEY BOOKS, NEW YORK

MISS SEETON CRACKS THE CASE

A Berkley Book / published by arrangement with
the author and the estate of Heron Carvic

PRINTING HISTORY
Berkley edition / April 1991

ISBN:0-425-12676-5

A BERKLEY BOOK ® TM 757, 375
Berkley Books are published by The Berkley Publishing Group,
200 Madison Avenue, New York, New York 10016.
The name "Berkley" and the "B" logo
are trademarks belonging to Berkley Publishing Corporation.

PRINTED IN THE UNITED STATES OF AMERICA

10  9  8  7  6  5

# chapter

## ~1~

As the courier's watchful eyes spotted the very last of her charges coming into distant view, she heaved a great sigh of relief and turned to give the driver of the air-conditioned coach a brisk thumbs-up.

"About ruddy time, too," muttered the driver, switching on the ignition and thumping his foot hard down upon the accelerator. "Fine start to the week *this* is, running over an hour late," and a heartfelt chorus of agreement erupted from the crowd of irate passengers behind him.

"Are we going to leave them behind, after all?"

"Serve them right if we do!"

"Making us late like this . . . never catch up . . . spoil the whole trip . . . selfish . . . hardly what we expected . . . "

They must have known that they'd kept everybody waiting; yet even the impatient gunning of the engine and the polite but agitated gestures of the courier failed to increase the walking pace of the latecomers. They moved with a strange, irregular gait, close together, and the taller of the two women—bony in form and equine of feature—seemed to be supporting the other, a dumpy little body who appeared to have developed a limp.

They had been checked off the courier's clipboard list long before their feet were anywhere near the coach's bottom step. And it took a real effort for the young woman in the crisp uniform to smile in greeting.

"Miss Nuttel, Mrs. Blaine—we were starting to worry about you! Still, here you are, better late than never—but is everything all right? Mrs. Blaine, you look . . . "

1

"Ricked her ankle," explained the human crutch, as she prepared to assist her patient up the steps. Mrs. Blaine paused, favouring her with a reproachful stare.

"Sprained it, Eric. It's far more uncomfortable than just ricking. If you'd cut my shoe off as I asked you, I'm sure it would have swollen like a pumpkin. And how I'll manage once we're home, I just don't know . . . "

Erica Nuttel shook her head. "Had to be able to walk," she pointed out in the tone of one who has repeated herself several times already. "Too heavy for me to carry, and can't walk the streets in bare feet."

The courier glanced down at what was visible of the feet of Mrs. Blaine, but could see very little difference, if any, in size. "You'd better leave your shoe on," she suggested, "until we can get you to a doctor." But Mrs. Blaine shook her head. Her black-currant eyes creased in reminiscent pain.

"If only we'd managed to find the herbalist," she said with another reproachful look at her companion. "Eric was so sure she could remember where, but it's been such a long time since we were last in Winchelsea. I kept saying we must have taken a wrong turning, but . . . and if I could only have applied a suitable poultice—though I'm afraid it's going to be far too late—"

"It certainly is!" came an angry voice from the doorway above, where a small crowd of curious passengers lurked in an attempt to find out why even now, with their companions safely restored to them and the engine of the waiting coach ready to roll, they were stationary still. "How much longer are we going to hang about here? We ought to have been in Rye over an hour ago!"

"I'm sure we'll catch up without too much trouble, if we hurry things along as best we can right now." The courier glanced up at her grumbling charges with a wide, artificial smile and wondered whether she sounded as phony as she felt. "If you'd all please get back to your seats, so that Miss Nuttel and I can assist Mrs. Blaine up the steps . . . "

She reflected briefly that it was as well this pair of late arrivals had not always been so tardy. By being first—aggressively so—in the queue when the allocation of seating was made, Miss Nuttel and Mrs. Blaine had managed to secure the prime position behind the driver. Indeed, they had positively rushed to stake their claim on the one place where the view ahead was unobscured by plastic antimacassars fastened over high-backed headrests.

Such triumphant ownership of this particular seat would make it an easy matter to deposit Mrs. Blaine and her ankle, whether ricked or strained or pure imagination, in safety—and with luck it wouldn't be very long before the two women were their own responsibility once more and not the courier's. From what she'd overheard them saying, they were local people—strange, perhaps, that locals would take a tourist trip on such a glorious day, but tastes differed—and wouldn't, in Rye, be more than half-a-dozen miles from home. A village with a fruity name, she reflected— might it be Appledore? No, that didn't sound quite right, though it was something similar, she thought . . .

The bright May sunshine sparkled on the plate-glass windows of Lilikot, Plummergen home of Miss Nuttel and Mrs. Blaine—who have long been known to village humourists as The Nuts, though only in part because of their vegetarian lifestyle. The windows of Lilikot always sparkle, for they are cleaned far more often and with more enthusiasm than those of any other house in Plummergen: The Nuts appreciate fully their fortunate situation directly opposite the garage in the main—virtually the only—street, an excellent vantage-point for the observation of all local comings and goings, and thus the origin of many an enthralling scandal.

Miss Nuttel, and the friend known to herself as Bunny and to Plummergen wits as the Hot Cross Bun, perform what many might consider a public service in the dissemination of gossip, rumour, and wild surmise. Though often the grain of truth becomes buried under a mountain of inaccuracy, there may remain an element of fact among the monstrous fictions which will enter Plummergen folklore, there to be not so much fossilised as fermented. Like yeast, the original seed expands mightily—and persistently—to result in glorious legend, long-lasting unto the third and fourth generation.

It may seem strange to some that there are those in Plummergen who do not approve of the great public spirit demonstrated by The Nuts in saving many of their neighbours the price of a local newspaper—a paper which, moreover, is edited in Brettenden, a town six miles distant. Too often what is observed from the vantage-point can have more than one possible interpretation— and thereby many a tale may hang, and many a character, as well. Yet the majority of villagers understand well the limitations and accuracy of the intelligence system, and can adapt or select their responses as seems fitting, while others may choose to ignore the gossip, or to remonstrate, or attempt to set up their own counter-rumour. Few people in Plummergen remain untouched by rumour . . .

Which has of recent years been brought to focus, more than once, upon the new owner of Old Mrs. Bannet's cottage at the south end of The Street. Flora Bannet lived to be ninety-eight, bequeathing Sweetbriars to her second cousin and god-daughter, Miss Emily Seeton. Miss Seeton was glad to retire from her London flat and her nosy neighbours to the country, little realising that Plummergen could leave Mrs. Perrsons and her ilk far behind in the nosiness stakes. For Miss Seeton, her inheritance came as a welcome delight, a chance to have a proper home; and she was determined to enjoy herself to the full.

She was kneeling now in her sunlit garden, a small fork in her hand, loosening the earth around the roots of what she knew to be weeds, and wondering why the illustrations in *Greenfinger Points the Way* could not be more accurate in their depiction of the good and the undesirable in floral life. As a former art teacher, Miss Seeton thought accuracy very important. One should only draw what one sees; and, conversely, what one sees ought to be recogniseable from what some other one has drawn.

Yet it is in her depiction, not of what her artist's eye sees, but of what her artist's mind senses as the truth behind sight, that her artist's abilities are most valued—and valued by the police, who have found her in the past to be of such help that they now pay her a modest retainer for her services. Their calls upon her time and talents have given The Nuts much cause for speculation; speculation to which Miss Seeton, as a true gentlewoman should, remains utterly oblivious. She keeps herself politely to herself, and while being friendly to all has chosen long ago not to become too closely involved in the affairs of others.

The fact that the affairs of others—often criminal affairs— tend to become closely involved with Miss Seeton is something to which she has been able, surprising though it may seem, to close her mind: she considers her life to be routine and uneventful, not knowing that in some quarters she is considered a catalyst, a stirrer of hornets' nests—the misguided missile, as someone in authority once called her. The newspapers, national and international, describe her as the Battling Brolly; yet somehow Miss Seeton still manages to regard herself as peacefully retired and placidly resident in Plummergen, that most English of villages in Kent, that most English of counties, where nothing out of the ordinary ever occurs . . .

• • •

"I hope you all enjoyed your visit to Winchelsea," said the courier, as at last the coach was under way, "and that you remembered to take a good look at the tree in the churchyard which marks the spot where John Wesley preached his last open-air sermon in 1790." Dutiful murmurs with an undertone of guilty shuffling greeted this pious wish. The courier cleared her throat, and continued:

"We're now driving along the Royal Military Road towards Rye, which I'm sure you'll find a fascinating place."

"If we have long enough there to find out," muttered a disaffected voice from the rear of the coach. Miss Nuttel, bridling, tossed her head; Mrs. Blaine's black eyes vanished in a scowl. The courier ignored them all as she went on:

"The name Rye means *at the island,* and comes about by a misreading of the original Anglo-Saxon which would have been pronounced *at ther eye,* where *eye* was the word for island. Which Rye is, as you can tell as we drive along—we're right at sea level here, but as you look upwards and ahead you can see how steep a hill it's on . . ."

More sounds of disaffection from the rear. The Nuts, in their front seat with the windscreen view, congratulated themselves and gazed dutifully at the sight they had seen several times before.

"Rye has a colourful past and is full of interesting buildings with historical associations—"

"Is that where the Rye House Plot happened?" came an interruption which did not unduly surprise the courier. On every tour there was always at least one person, usually an enthusiastic American, who had studied English history and enjoyed the thrill of fitting places to facts. This time, though, the facts weren't quite right.

"I'm afraid not," replied the courier, kindly. "We're in Sussex here, and Rye House is north of London, in Hertfordshire, a few miles from Broxbourne. The derivation of the name is probably the same, though." She cleared her throat and went back to her commentary. "Now, in *this* Rye, you'll be able to see many fine examples of various early styles including brick, stone, and timber. Perhaps the finest timber-frame building is the Mermaid Inn, which was a famous smugglers' headquarters and where the notorious Hawkhurst Gang used to sit in the bow windows fronting the street, drinking to their success—"

"Smugglers?" came a query from behind. "Pirates?"

"Highwaymen!" came another suggestion.

"No highwaymen around these parts," said the courier with a

smile, as she pressed on with her commentary. "The Hawkhurst Gang were one of the worst bands of smugglers in the country in the eighteenth century. They murdered people and tortured informers, and fought pitched battles with rival gangs. They were said to be able to muster five hundred men within an hour—far worse than any highwaymen," she concluded with relish, hearing her audience shudder with gleeful terror.

Then she heard an outburst of real terror: a curse from the driver and a screech of brakes, cries of shock from The Nuts as they were thrown forward with the impetus. Across the road, in front of the coach, a dark blue car had turned, and stopped. Dead. Blocking the road completely . . .

And, giving the lie to her recent words that there were no highwaymen associated with that part of the country, two masked figures with shotguns appeared and made menacing gestures at the driver through the windscreen.

"Turn round!" she gasped, as passengers in the front began to exclaim in fright and those at the rear demanded to know what was happening. "Reverse—get away!"

"There's another car blocking my tail—I can see it in the mirror," the driver told her, and swore. "Looks like they want me to open this door—and I'm no hero. Those guns could do a deal of damage, shooting through glass . . ."

Above the horrified protests of all those who were not riveted with fear or startled into silence, he pressed down the pneumatic lever. With a sigh and a rubbery thud, the coach door folded open.

And one of the ambushing figures, shotgun in hand, with the other covering from outside, climbed the steps, stood beside the driver, and gave the traditional command:

"Stand and deliver! Your money—or your life!"

# chapter

# -2-

"REMARKABLE," SAID THE chief superintendent, with what in a weaker man might have been regarded as a sigh. Sergeant Bob Ranger looked up from his notebook, from which he was trying to transcribe his shorthand. Practice in his case did not make perfect: he knew what it said, true enough, but there was more than a suspicion that this was only because he made a point of writing up his notes as soon as possible after making them. Memory, he felt, had perhaps too large a part to play in his work: suppose one day he should be hit on the head and suffer amnesia? Where would that leave whichever of his colleagues had to take over his caseload?

Then he remembered how marriage to Anne Knight had given him access at all times to the most devoted of professional nursing care, and he smiled. His superior looked at him quizzically.

"My words are not intended to amuse you, Sergeant Ranger. They are intended to prompt a spark of curiosity, a query as to what it is I am talking about. Curiosity should be the good detective's watchword at all times."

Bob removed the smile and substituted an air of alert interest. "Certainly, sir. You were talking about something, as yet unspecified, being remarkable. I was simply waiting—politely—for you to enlighten me as to what that something might be."

He closed his notebook, folded his arms, and tilted his head slightly to one side, the perfect pupil in the front row, eager for Teacher to begin the lesson. Very few schoolchildren, however, stand six foot seven in their socks and play football for the police eleven. Bob looked rather comical, and Delphick had to laugh.

Then he sobered, and sighed more obviously this time. "I had in mind the monumental growth of paper work in this office," he said, regarding his overflowing in-tray with a thoughtful expression. "No matter how hard I work—you as well, for that matter—"

"Thank you, sir," murmured Bob.

"—the evidence always seems to suggest that we spend all our time in idleness. Blink but an eye, and the in-tray which was almost empty Friday evening is full again, and the week barely begun. I swear that the files must multiply when we're not looking."

"Or they creep back across from the out-tray," suggested Bob, "and change their appearance with intent to mislead."

"Personation, you mean? Not an altogether common crime nowadays—in Scotland Yard, unheard of, to my knowledge." Delphick shook his head. "Time to tackle the next batch, I suppose, if you'll only stop chattering long enough to let me get down to some honest work."

"Sorry, sir," Bob said, not sounding it in the least. Delphick chuckled briefly, then reached for the topmost file of an unsteady heap.

When the telephone rang, Bob looked up with alacrity from his perplexing pothooks and wondered if he was to be spared any more of the struggle by the call to action. He kept his eyes on the chief superintendent's face, and from Delphick's sudden frown and exclamation knew that the call had indeed come.

He listened with dismay to the accessible half of the ensuing conversation; he knew enough about the recent crime wave to be able to supply the inaudible half without too much difficulty. He looked at the heap of files on Delphick's desk and guessed that it would grow a great deal higher before it began to diminish.

His guess was correct, although it hardly needed the instinct of a detective to make it. "We'll be right there," concluded Delphick briskly, "and you'd better let us have your files on all the other occurrences, as well. Unless it's a copycat crime, I think you're right—it's our friends again. And this time they really have killed someone . . . "

He hung up the receiver and turned to Bob; but there was no need to explain. His sergeant said at once: "The Sherry Gang, sir?"

"The same. Everyone kept saying that they'd go too far some time, or get it wrong—and now, they have. A fatality. I don't suppose they intended it to end like this, but someone has died, and it's entirely due to them." His face hardened. "Any death is bad news, Bob, but this—this sick preying on the elderly, taking advantage of people who are alone in their declining years, when they ought to be treated with respect and left their personal dignity—" He slammed shut the file he'd barely begun to read, and dumped it back with irritation on the top of the tilting heap. But he utterly ignored the Pisa-like result, though there was an ominous slither and rustling noise before they had left the room. "I didn't like the sound of them when we first heard about them, and I like it still less now they've become responsible for someone's death. They'd better not try any *we didn't really mean it* when we finally catch up with them, because that's about the worst defence for the worst kind of killing I've heard of in a very long time."

"Let's hope that's what we manage to send them down for, then," said Bob, who agreed entirely. "What happened? The usual, I suppose, but—man or woman dead? And how?"

"The usual. How exactly they got into the house on this occasion, nobody seems to know just yet—but it's sure to have been the usual."

"Meet someone in the town laden with shopping, offer them a lift home, be ever so helpful when they're trying to cross a busy road," enumerated Bob, who'd heard the sorry tale more than once in recent weeks. "Weasel their way into the poor old soul's house under the pretence of being just a good neighbour, get pressed to stay for a bit of a chat and a cup of tea. You know, sir, I think somehow that was worst of all, putting the dope in the drinks the grateful victim had gone to the trouble of making."

"Denying them even a modicum of dignity," Delphick agreed. "At least once they switched to suggesting a little drink from a bottle of sherry they *just happened to have* with them, it took away the cheap nastiness of it, somehow. It's still a wicked way of robbing anybody—using gratitude to take advantage like that— but it's not quite so sick, if that's the word I want. Maybe somebody's begun to develop a bit of a conscience about it all."

"Or maybe they found it easier to disguise the taste of the sedative in sherry," said Bob. "Either way, you've got to hand it to them—it's a clever plan."

"Very clever, and very simple—planned by a pretty good amateur psychologist, too. Understanding how people, and the older generation especially, like to give thanks of some sort for an unexpected kindness. Exploiting the way so many old folk either can't, or won't, spend money on those little luxuries their Victorian consciences still tell them they ought not to enjoy. And sherry's respectable to the most maidenly of teetotal aunts. They wouldn't have much difficulty in persuading their mark, poor soul, to indulge in a little tipple . . . but this time they overdosed on the sedatives, and the poor old chap died."

"Ugly," said Sergeant Ranger.

"Very ugly," said Delphick. "He was found this morning by his Home Help. She's still very shocked, but had enough of her wits about her to be able to give a fair description of what's missing—all his treasures, of course. Even his medals, she said. Went right through World War One without a scratch, and ends up choking to death on his own vomit. Not the nicest way for someone who risked his life for his country to lose it, Sergeant Ranger . . . "

"No, sir," said Bob. "Not nice at all," and his face was as grim as the chief superintendent's. He could not help thinking of his own, adopted, maidenly aunt Miss Seeton (known ever since a tricky moment in a case involving witchcraft and a sinister, thug-patrolled cult called Nuscience to himself and Anne as Aunt Em) and her own trusting, open nature. Any stranger who offered to help her home with her shopping would be more than welcome to a cup of tea and a slice or two of cake; too easy to slip something into that cup, or persuade her to sip a little sherry . . .

Miss Seeton was not sipping sherry at present, nor did she have any plans to do so: her mind was sufficiently confused as it was without adding to her problems. She was about to set forth to the shops, and what in happier times past had taken a matter of minutes—the leaving of her cottage and the closing of her front door—now seemed to take forever to achieve. So very kind of Chief Superintendent Delphick—so gratifying for him to be doing well in his career, he having been only a superintendent when they first met—to think of her as he'd done, and of course it was setting a good example to others as well as accommodating the wishes of the chief constable of Kent, but there were times when the security system which had been installed was really more of a burden than the benefit she'd been led to believe it would be.

Besides, living so quietly in the country as she did, she really had no need of any such protection: against what was she being protected? If she ever returned to live in London, perhaps there might be some sense in sirens and bells which would erupt into life if anyone tried to break in; or if she lived in a large and obviously expensive house likely to contain anything worth the efforts of any burglar. Rytham Hall, for instance, right at the end of Marsh Road—such a lonely spot, and the Colvedens must have a great many heirlooms and antiques—she would certainly suggest that they ought to think about having a burglar alarm put in. But Sweetbriars was a cottage, not a stately home, and she herself not an aristocrat, but a retired teacher of art. Her little knick-knacks, while of sentimental and some practical value to herself, could never interest the criminal classes any more than she, Emily Dorothea Seeton, could be of interest to them . . .

It had been in just such innocence that Miss Seeton had reluctantly accepted Delphick's offer to hurry through the installation of the burglar alarm, such innocence that she failed to understand how she might be at risk from the heavies of the gambling syndicate in whose affairs she and her brolly had become embroiled not so long ago. The chief superintendent, worried that she might suffer a repeat performance of a past criminal incursion into her cottage, had arranged with his colleague Superintendent Brinton of Ashford to have a reliable security firm install a suitable system as a matter of urgency; the explanation best understood by Miss Seeton being that the chief constable was having a campaign to encourage householders to help protect their own property, in this way saving the police both time and money.

The argument had, as he'd known it would, appealed to the conscientious nature of Miss Seeton, and she had come, slowly, around to the idea that she was being used as what might be called, inelegantly but she could not think of a better term, a guinea pig. Or perhaps a market research project, she wasn't entirely sure— but whatever she might be, in the eyes of the police, she felt it now her duty to make full use of the alarm system so that when she told other people about its merits she could truthfully say that she found it helpful. Only she didn't . . . or rather, that was hardly the first adjective which sprang to mind. Complicated . . . . vexatious . . . time-consuming . . .

Wearing her distinctive cockscomb hat she stood now in the little hallway, with her basket beside the telephone on its table, and studied her instruction leaflet yet again. She felt guilty that she had not been able to memorise all the contents properly by now, but somehow she never felt that in a matter as important as this she ought to rely on her memory alone. She had pressed *Tet* and the green light had come on. She had turned the oddly-fashioned key in the lock of the main alarm box on the stairs. The next

stage must be to turn the same key in a different lock—the one
set in the jamb of the front door—and then to be sure to lock the
front door in its usual fashion as well.

Miss Seeton sighed, then reproached herself. She shook her
head, put down the leaflet, picked up her basket, took the key
to that extra keyhole in the door and turned it, stepped out
of the door and pulled it firmly closed, then locked it with her
own familiar key. She sighed again, with relief, and prepared to
set off down the path.

It was another glorious day, with a sparkling sun high in the sky
and the only visible clouds far off on the wide Kentish horizon.
Spring in the Garden of England, breathed Miss Seeton, savouring
the perfumes of—of whatever flowers Stan had so kindly planted
in her borders. Although autumn might be her favourite season of
the year, on such a day as this she did not find it hard to see why
poets celebrated the spring. She smiled at the thought of how her
colleagues at that little Hampstead school would have teased her
for carrying her umbrella with her—

"Oh, how annoying!" With all the worry of the oddly-shaped
key and the green *Tet* light and the final locking of the front door,
she had left her umbrella behind. She could see it now, in her
mind's eye, clipped on the wall over the drip tray, beside the table
she'd been so careful to pick up her basket from: she'd put on her
hat, collected her basket, and been so preoccupied with the alarm
system she'd forgotten her brolly. Such a thing had hardly ever
happened to her before. "Old age, I suppose," murmured Miss
Seeton, hurrying back up the path to her front door and hunting
for her key. "Although I wouldn't have thought—they have done
me so much good in the past—but maybe one can only hold nature
back for so long—yet it's impossible to deny that physically, at
any rate, they continue to keep me in excellent shape," musing
on the exercises she studied in *Yoga and Younger Every Day* as
she rattled her key in the lock.

The bells and sirens exploded all about her into the normally
peaceful Plummergen air. "Not again!" pleaded Miss Seeton,
knowing that there could be no restoration of silence until she
had attended to the main box halfway up the stairs. The bells and
sirens continued to jangle her nerves as she made for the switch—
*exploded* certainly wasn't too strong a word for the experience, she
told herself as she turned the right key in the lock and everything
went quiet. Those dratted bells—a kind thought, but nevertheless
a nuisance—surely they could be made a little quieter, not so, so

noticeable, so intrusive. Miss Seeton was sure that when she finally emerged from the door of Sweetbriars, a crowd of Plummergen residents would be clustering outside her gate with offers of help. So very kind of them, but irksome that her own carelessness should cause them all to interrupt whatever they had been doing to attend her little mishap.

But to her surprise, when for a second time she emerged from the cottage and, her umbrella and basket safely in her grasp, made her way down the path, there was nobody in sight at all. Not even PC Potter, who had been so prompt to ask her if everything was in order on the first few occasions when she'd made the same foolish mistake . . . . Nobody, as far as the eye could see.

Yet Miss Seeton, instead of wondering where everyone might be, uttered a silent word of thanks that her blushes on this occasion had been spared, and headed for the shops without arousing a quiver of curiosity.

# chapter

# -3-

SCOTLAND YARD—OR rather those members of it with whom Miss Seeton was most closely acquainted—stood grimly in the neat little parlour of the terraced house formerly owned by an old soldier. Formerly, because he was now dead.

"Yes, feel free to call it murder," invited the police doctor, after Delphick posed the question. "Whoever nobbled him is responsible for letting this chap die, whether they meant it to happen or not. He lay on the ground and choked to death—so why did he vomit? Shock after his fall—so why did he fall? Nothing obvious here to trip him up, no shiny lino with rugs to slip on, no rucks in the carpet or bits of nonsense on the floor to catch his feet—so, maybe a sudden dizzy spell? But his Home Help says he was the fittest old chap for his age she's ever known, and she's worked with 'em for long enough to be a good judge. And I'd agree with her; he's on the list in my group practice, but I can't say I've ever had him coming in for a consultation. Maybe he's seen one of the others, but . . . "

"But," supplied Delphick, "considering the almost-full bottle of sherry on the table, added to the fact that the house has been ransacked—in a manner with which we're all too accustomed in recent weeks, unfortunately—it would be a fair assumption that it wasn't an accident or some health problem that might have caused him to lose his balance."

"It wasn't," said Dr. Hallingbury. "Call it murder, and you won't be far wrong. But," he added, as he could see the next question coming, "don't ask me to say yes or no to the sherry lot until I've had a chance to do a proper check that the poor old chap's been drinking the horrible stuff. It might just be some ghastly coincidence—I want to be sure—but off the record I think you can assume it was, unless you yourselves turn up any evidence to the contrary."

He nodded a brisk farewell to Sergeant Ranger, who was busy in the background making notes, and pulled a battered soft hat from his pocket, clapping it on his bald head with an explanatory, "The sun. Gives me hell every year—comes of having what little hair's left round the edges ginger, and pale skin to match. Hang on to *your* hair, young man, while you can—life's a misery without it."

Before Bob could reply, Dr. Hallingbury was gone, with an instruction to have the late Regimental Sergeant Major Brent delivered to him for autopsy as soon as possible, "So that I can confirm what we think we already know. But it's as well to be certain which villains you're chasing . . . "

Delphick gazed round him at what remained of the home of RSM Brent. It was clearly the room of someone with military training: a place for everything and everything in its place—only everything wasn't anymore, according to Mrs. Pelham.

"If he was such a fit old boy, how come he needed a Home Help?" Bob Ranger suddenly wanted to know.

Delphick looked at him. "He may well have been fit, but as you yourself said, he was old, or heading that way. We're half a century and more beyond the end of World War One: even supposing he lied about his age, as so many of those poor devils did, he can't have been much under seventy-five. And by then you're beginning to lose your friends. It's not so easy to make new ones. You can go for days without talking to anyone except the milkman when he takes your money, or people in shops—which is exactly what the Sherry Gang didn't need to have explained to them. They knew it, and exploited it."

A bleak look flickered across his face, then was almost gone when he continued: "Someone to talk to, that's often all these old folk need—and besides, he'd recently lost his wife, they tell me. I've no doubt your wife—" Bob was observed to grin in a fond, embarrassed fashion—"intends to train you well, so that when she's busy in the evenings and you're hoping to toast your toes by the fire, she'll have you toasting your own muffins and not dying of starvation before she gets back from work. But RSM Brent wasn't the generation that knows anything about this women's lib that's come on the scene in the last few years . . . "

Which Mrs. Pelham was quick to confirm, when Delphick and
Ranger spoke with her. Several cups of well-sugared tea and the
chance to have a little weep into her handkerchief had settled her
initial shock, and she was able to talk brightly to the detectives
about "her old man" and his habits.

"Ever so friendly, he was, and polite with it, never missed saying thank-you before I went, and giving me a bunch of flowers
out of the garden, not that we're supposed to take presents but
you'd never get him to see it, returning thanks for a favour, he
called it, and honest as the day is long. Break his heart, it would,
to know they'd gone poking and prying about his things, never
mind poisoning him, and all because he was such an old-fashioned
sort, tip his hat to you in the street and always open doors, which,
believe me, you don't always find in this job. Some of them treat
you like nothing better than a servant, not that I expect them to
fall on their knees being grateful because, after all, they pay for
it, don't they, but it never hurts to be polite . . . "

She broke off with a choke in her voice as she recalled how
being polite had done more than hurt Regimental Sergeant Major
Brent. Her eyes began to fill with tears again, and she fumbled in
her pocket. "Oh, dear . . . "

"Mrs. Pelham," Delphick said quickly, "you've been very helpful in supplying the local police with a list of what you believe to
be missing. But if you wouldn't mind going over it again with
my sergeant here—a double check, just to be absolutely sure—
now that you've had time to catch your breath, as it were. You
might just remember something else—or be able to enlarge on
the understandably brief descriptions you first gave . . . "

It was a heartbreaking list over which Delphick and his sergeant
pored: the treasured accumulations of a lifetime, gone, probably
for good, as the detectives feared only too likely. "No need even
for a fence," grumbled Ranger. "Pop along to the nearest street
market, no questions asked. It makes me sick, sir. His wife's photo in a solid silver frame, and they'll chuck the picture out with
the rubbish as if she'd never mattered in her life at all. Ghouls,
that's the only word for them. I wish we could catch them, but
we just don't seem to be able to get a lead on them. Too canny to
leave prints on the bottle of sherry, and they seem to be practically
invisible except to their victims, who're all too upset to tell us
anything useful. Could be almost anyone, from the descriptions,
and the IdentiKit even looks like almost anyone."

"We never supposed it was going to be easy, Bob. That's precisely what they've relied on all this time—their very ordinariness. One middle-aged woman, one younger woman, one in-between-age man—could be the boyfriend of one or other of them, perhaps. That much the few neighbours who've seen anything at all have agreed on. One or both of the women make the first contact, and the man follows along and helps shift the stuff out of the house into a small, dark van while the poor old soul is presumably asleep inside. When the victim wakes up, he or she is too upset and muddled to give any coherent picture of what they looked like—"

Delphick broke off, and slapped his hand on the table so that Bob jumped. "Old people—picture—IdentiKits—we're idiots for not thinking of it before, Bob."

Ranger was there as quickly as the chief superintendent. "Her, you mean, sir. For not thinking of her—Miss Seeton. But it wasn't rightly our case before, was it?"

"True enough. But, since it is now, we'll call on the good services of MissEss as soon as we can. I won't ask her to draw poor Brent for us, unless it's absolutely necessary, but I'd love to get her talking to some of the other victims—the set-a-thief-to-catch-a-thief principle. They'll look on her as someone exactly like themselves—"

He broke off as Bob spluttered, turning it too late into a cough. "Yes, I know, Sergeant, that to you and me and the world in general, Miss Seeton is far from being exactly like anyone else. But I'm willing to bet that's not how she sees herself. *She'll* think she really is like them, and they'll treat her that way as well, with luck. She won't be as intimidating as someone official. The uniform's bound to make them nervous, even when they've done nothing except been taken advantage of and made to feel a bit foolish . . . but she'll know how to talk to them to save their pride and, if we're lucky, one of her sketches will produce something to give us a lead on these crooks."

"It's a good idea, sir," said Bob, regarding his chief with some awe. "In theory, that is. Honestly, I can see why you're so keen on it, but . . . "

"But you can't help wondering what hornets' nest will be stirred up by having her umbrella poked into it?" Delphick laughed. "Forget it, Bob. I know how things never turn out the way anyone expects when Miss Seeton is involved—but it can't possibly be asking for trouble if we simply send her to talk to a few old people and draw a few sketches, can it? If I know her, she'll jump at the chance of furthering the cause of justice. All we'll have to do is explain the cheap and sneaky method they've used to steal from old age pensioners, and we can safely leave it to Miss Seeton's sense of duty to take it from there."

It was an inspired plan. "At least it doesn't sound like any syndicate effort," Ranger murmured, thinking of some of the large and sinister concerns against whom the Battling Brolly had waged genteel warfare. "Just three people—which hardly counts as big-time crime, does it?"

"It didn't," Delphick corrected him, "but it does now, because it is. Murder is no small-time stuff, Sergeant, and we both know it. In any case, you needn't worry about Miss Seeton taking on more than she can handle—I'm fast coming to the conclusion that she bears a charmed life. For which we should be thankful, Bob, and leave her to live it in her own . . . " It was rare for the Oracle to be pressed for words. But anyone, Bob thought, would find it hard to describe Miss Seeton succinctly: her quality was, well, it was—

"Unique," Delphick produced after a lengthy pause, and echoed Bob's own choice. "Her own unique way of life—the quiet tenor of which we from time to time have to disturb, as we're going to on this occasion. But Miss Seeton will understand, I'm sure, and think it goes with the territory of the retainer we pay her. I'll telephone and tell her I'm sending you down with a car to collect her—"

He regarded his sergeant with an amused air. "Yes, I know what you're thinking. But I'm not suggesting you turn up in Plummergen in a Panda car with the blue light flashing at full throttle. What I had in mind was more in the nature of a private visit from a family friend, dropping in after a duty· call on his in-laws. Does a man need an excuse to talk to his wife's parents? Take Anne with you, if you like."

"Well, sir, I'm not sure about that. She hasn't been in her new job long enough to start asking for time off—but it's a pity she can't." He grimaced. "The way that village gets the wrong end of the stick about Miss Seeton, they'll be convinced she's been nicked for something or other. Half of 'em already suspect her of practically every crime in the book, and when they see her driving away with me . . . "

"Try to make it look convincingly casual," Delphick told him. "We owe a lot to Miss Seeton, and the least we can do when we're using her services is treat her nicely. I know she'll insist it's no bother to ride her bicycle to the station and catch a train, but I'll point out that it'll take too long. Which is partly true, of course, although I consider it important not to act as if we're taking her too much for granted . . . "

Bob Ranger grinned. "Be honest, sir. That's not the real reason, is it?"

The Oracle hesitated, then almost grinned back as he replied: "Well—if you bring her up to London by car, we can be reasonably sure that, when she's supposed to be in a certain place at a certain time, she will be."

Sergeant Ranger, remembering some of the gyrations of Miss Seeton on occasions past, added under his breath the rider, *"Deo volente."* Because with Miss Seeton, you could never be entirely sure . . .

# chapter

# -4-

MISS SEETON WAS not entirely sure that the main street of Plum-mergen—The Street, as it was known with prosaic civic pride—was usually so quiet at this time of day. Apart from Tibs the tabby (the worst-tempered cat in Plummergen, plump and smug and belonging to PC Potter's little girl Amelia, who alone had any control over the creature) there was not a living soul in sight. Everything was so very peaceful, indeed, that Tibs had set herself down in the sun in the middle of the road, a striped lazy form with a glossy coat and eyes shut, weary from the effort of basking. Miss Seeton tutted and clicked her tongue at Tibs, who twitched the tip of her tail and would not open an eye.

"You foolish creature," chided Miss Seeton. "If you lie here too long, you will be run over. Or you will be responsible for a serious accident, should a car try to drive around you and hit one of the trees. Wake up, do," and with the tip of her umbrella she gently prodded the tabby in her well-covered ribs.

Tibs raised her head and blinked up at Miss Seeton, then uttered a little growl, flattened her ears, and lashed her tail. Miss Seeton, who had controlled an entire classroom, was not intimidated by one fat tabby, especially one whose life could be in danger. "Wake up and move, you silly cat," commanded Miss Seeton, and poked at Tibs again in a more assertive manner. "I won't let you stay here, so you need not adopt that attitude with me."

The voice of authority, crisp and compelling, penetrated the wilfully deaf feline ears. With a long, leisured stretch and an impertinent yawn, Tibs grudgingly bestirred herself to move to the side of the road. She would sunbathe somewhere else, far

20

removed from umbrellas and those who wielded them; she glared over her shoulder at Miss Seeton as she stalked slowly away, and the uttermost tip of her tail jerked in an angry, twitching little dance.

Normally, the sight of Miss Seeton—concerning whose true character the villagers were hotly divided—dallying in the centre of the main road with a cat (a cat, moreover, notorious for her spiteful nature) would have given rise once more to those deeply-rooted suspicions of her held, among others, by an entire generation of schoolchildren, who had fixed it well in their heads that she was possessed of remarkable powers. The escapade which had led them to this conclusion could have been simply enough explained, if any of them had cared, or dared, to ask; but their parents had already sown the seeds of acceptance of Miss Seeton's supernatural gifts long before that momentous visit to the seashore, and from that day in certain houses Miss Seeton's name was mentioned only with furtive crossing of fingers, or a backward, wary look as if she might lurk in some corner ready to pounce.

But there had been nobody in The Street—nobody behind net curtains, afraid of missing out on any item of gossip—nobody to see at all.

"It seems rather strange," murmured Miss Seeton. "Early closing day, perhaps? But today is Tuesday. Would it have been changed without my remembering? Surely not—at least, I suppose Martha may have told me and it slipped my mind, but . . . In any case," with a firm shake of her head to settle her wandering wits, "how silly of me, for nobody closes early in the mornings, and it can hardly be eleven o'clock yet." She glanced at her wristwatch, a sensible silver mounting fastened by a neat leather strap. "Well, just after," she admitted, "but still nowhere near afternoon. I wonder whether there is some interesting programme on the wireless which is keeping everyone indoors? And if that is the case," she brightened, "I shall finish my shopping so much sooner, then I may return to the garden and remove some more of those wretched weeds . . . "

There was indeed something of interest on the wireless: the eleven o'clock news from the BBC. The News came almost every hour on the hour during the day, and so those people who first heard it at six were able to warn others to be sure not to miss it at seven, and anyone who had listened at seven could barely wait until eight in case more details had emerged.

Not for the first time, a Plummergen resident—a brace of

residents, in fact—was likely to feature in the headlines. Daily
papers were being studied in depth and swapped from house
to house; speculation and surmise were being exchanged at an
ever-increasing rate and degree of inaccuracy. The Press, and
maybe Television as well, were expected any minute, and there
was a general sense of indignation that they had not so far
arrived.

But Plummergen, for once, was not the seat of the action.
Winchelsea and Rye, or rather the road which joined them, had
the best claim to that title. The modern highwaymen—the New
Dick Turpins, as they were called in some journals—had carried
out their latest daring daylight robbery in Sussex, not Kent, and
the Plummergen connection of Miss Nuttel and Mrs. Blaine had
not yet been made.

Their startling experience had left both The Nuts a prey to all
manner of nervous reactions. In Mrs. Blaine's case these had been
manifested in an insistent demand for herbal tea—chamomile for
preference—to soothe her quivering sensibilities, a demand which
the police station was quite unable to fulfil. Mrs. Blaine's frantic, high-pitched and repetitive refusal of the dark brown syrup
tasting of tannin and dashed with milk which passed for tea in
the constabulary canteen had been echoed, with less hysteria and
more aggression, by her friend Miss Nuttel.

"Never touch the stuff," she snapped, "and nor should you.
Coats the stomach, rots the insides—not surprising criminals get
away with highway robbery in broad daylight if the police don't
keep themselves fit. Drink rubbish, and rubbish is what you'll
turn into—"

"Now, that's uncalled for, Miss Nuttel," the inspector was
moved to protest. He'd had a long struggle with himself all the
time The Nuts were complaining their exaggerated complaints:
Nobody had come near them for hours; they'd been shunted into
a corner and simply left there while everyone else was being
looked after. This was hardly the way to treat anyone who'd gone
through all they had so recently suffered . . . It was too much not
to expect the inspector to snap back when something inside him
did. "It's not going to help anyone if you waste everybody's time
in hurling insults when it would make more sense, and be far more
productive, for you to settle down and make your statements and
help us get a line on these characters."

Inspector Furneux had been trying to work out some sort of
line on the robbers for over two hours. He had interviewed all

the other trippers from the stricken coach; he'd left The Nuts until last, partly because Mrs. Blaine's hysterical seizures stopped her saying anything useful, and partly because most of the others were foreigners, and he wanted no accusations of discourtesy to tourists appearing later in the newspapers, which had already turned previous Turpin incidents into full-blown sensations.

But now he felt sorely tempted to be brutal. He thought wistfully of having himself put on a charge—either for boxing Mrs. Blaine's ears or for wringing Miss Nuttel's neck. Nobody would blame him after the amount of aggro they'd been giving him, worse than all the other passengers on the coach put together. And if he went on a charge, he wouldn't have to listen to either of them ever again . . .

He forced himself, with a real effort, to dismiss these glorious daydreams, and returned sternly to the present. If chamomile tea was unforthcoming, and they were positive they didn't fancy the canteen tea, which everybody else had been pleased to drink, might the ladies—gritted teeth just prevented him from using a stronger word—prefer lemonade? There was a small sweetshop and general store just around the corner: he believed that cans of soft drinks were kept permanently chilled in hot weather . . .

"Sugar," said Miss Nuttel, as Mrs. Blaine closed her eyes in a despairing gesture. Furneux noticed this almost normal reaction, and uttered a silent prayer that his luck might be changing. The hysterics seemed to have died down, whether from scandalised shock at his suggestion, or from physical exhaustion, he did not dare guess.

"Bad for the teeth," said Miss Nuttel. "Artificial—no sugar needed if the body balance is right. Plain water'll do, if you've nothing better. Day like this, even tap has to be better than sugar."

Mrs. Blaine opened one black-currant eye in mute protest, but nobody noticed. She wondered whether to throw another fit of hysterics, but Eric was so right, it was a very hot day, and emotion was always exhausting. Mrs. Blaine slumped in her chair and looked as pathetic as possible.

"Water, two glasses, with ice—and quickly!" instructed Inspector Furneux, opening the door of the interview room and venting his feelings in a bellow. Every inch of the corridor hummed and echoed as his command bounced off walls and ceiling and linoleumed floor; the double swing doors to the street quivered; the station sergeant's helmet clattered from its customary hook to the ground, there to roll about in nervous arcs, a residual echo still vibrating round its rim many minutes afterwards, an object of interest to all who saw—and heard—it.

Furneux closed the interview door with a slam that sent flakes of plaster snow drifting from the ceiling down to the table on which his notebook—filled so far with nothing of use from these two nuisances—lay open. He brushed off the snow with an impatient sleeve, and took a deep breath.

"Suppose we begin again," he suggested. "Miss Nuttel—Mrs. Blaine, you're still obviously in deep shock, suppose you just listen quietly until it's your turn? Miss Nuttel, this coach trip you were on. Unusual, isn't it, for someone who lives as close to Rye as you claim to do to take such a rather touristy excursion?"

"No claim about it," Erica Nuttel informed him. "Twelve years, more or less—"

"More, Eric," chimed in Mrs. Blaine, roused from her dumb slumping. "Nearly thirteen years, it must be by now."

"Mrs. Blaine, please!" Furneux barely stopped himself uttering some unfortunate remark about thirteen which would have lost him the small advantage he'd managed to win. "Your turn will come, I assure you. But for now—you'd say you think of yourselves as locals, Miss Nuttel?"

"Not ashamed of it, Inspector." She threw back her head and bridled. "Nothing wrong with living in Plummergen—at least," as a sudden thought came to her, "not really."

"But, Miss Nuttel?" She'd sounded as if she'd like to change the subject; Furneux decided that if he kept her off-balance, he might stand a better chance of making her talk some sense . . . he hoped.

"But what, Inspector? But nothing."

"I hardly think it's *nothing*, Miss Nuttel. You seem to be implying that life in Plummergen isn't what it was twelve or thirteen years ago when you first moved there . . . " With the cunning of a fisherman playing a pike—only in natural history terms it was rather a horse of which Erica Nuttel reminded him—Furneux left the bait dangling.

The bait was taken. Miss Nuttel snapped at it with eager jaws and swallowed it whole. "That woman," she said, and Mrs. Blaine nodded fervently. "Never had this sort of carry-on before she came to live in the village—murders and robbery and kidnapping and drugs and gas and witchcraft and goodness knows what else, not to mention today's effort. More than coincidence, if you ask me!"

Mrs. Blaine nodded again in silent agreement; and Furneux turned pale. "Miss Seeton," he breathed. He'd wondered why the name of Plummergen, that little village just across the county border, had sounded so familiar—notorious—to his ears; he thought he'd left the interviewing of The Nuts till last because he'd· recognised them as troublemakers—but not so, he now realised. As soon as it learned where they came from, his subconscious must have been trying to protect him. He knew—everyone knew—about Miss Seeton. Superintendent Brinton from nearby Ashford, in Kent, had waxed eloquent about her, one inebriated evening at some inter-county bash: the papers didn't know the half of it, he'd said. "Battling Brolly? Boomerang Bomb, they ought to say. Never know where she's going to turn up or what she's going to do when she does—nor does she, if it comes to that. If there was some logic to what happens when she's around, you wouldn't worry so much, because you could make some sense of it all—but even she can't do that, most of the time; she's a law unto herself. Just be thankful she's stayed out of your hair so far," he'd warned Inspector Furneux, and thankful the inspector had been.

He should have known it was tempting fate . . . But there was still hope, he thought. "You're not seriously accusing Miss Seeton of being one of the, the highwaymen, are you? Surely her age, apart from anything else—"

He had no idea how pleading his voice now sounded. Gone was all the stentorian command, the air of interrogation. The very thought of Miss Seeton's possible involvement in this case had shaken him to the depths.

"Wore masks, didn't they? Stockings—and helmets, all the motorbike gear, shapeless, could be anyone inside. Only one of 'em spoke—man's voice—who's to say a woman wasn't at least one of the others?"

"One man," Inspector Furneux noted down; curious, how his hand had begun to shake. Tiredness, no doubt—couldn't be anything to do with this Plummergen news, surely. "One man, possibly a woman. How many others were there?"

"Two, maybe three—hard to tell," said Miss Nuttel.

Mrs. Blaine perked up again. "There must have been at least three of them, Eric, when you start to work it out. Remember? The one in the front car, who had the shotgun and did all the talking. There was that other person with him who collected all our valuables while he kept that poor driver covered—"

"Collector didn't speak," Miss Nuttel remembered. "Odd, not even a mumble. Tried to keep her head down, too—as if she didn't want to be recognised."

"Her?" Furneux needed details and reasons for such a suggestion; none of the other victims of this robbery, or indeed any of the others, had made it. They'd all assumed that the Turpins were male—although, as the Nuts had implied, in these days of unisex costume there was no good reason why they should have been. Then again, there was no good reason why they should not. Levi Strauss had much to answer for . . . "Can you give any particular reason why you thought it was a woman?"

Erica Nuttel looked blank. Bunny Blaine rushed into speech once more: really, now her nerves were feeling better, she was almost starting to enjoy this. Assisting the police with their enquiries—working for law and order—no doubt the newspapers would want to interview her, especially if she could perform well enough to be the star witness. And Eric not saying much would mean . . .

She sat up straighter and could almost hear the flashbulbs popping. "The way she walked, I suppose. And a different shape," she added, but as an afterthought. "We were sitting right in the front—" which didn't surprise Furneux one jot—"and could see everything, much more clearly than anybody else. So we saw her walking about properly, if you understand me, not in the coach squeezing sideways down the aisle, which was all the others could have seen of her. Or him." Star witness, Norah Blaine! And she began composing headlines, and wondering which was her best side for photographs.

"And you'd agree that's what made you suggest a woman, Miss Nuttel? The better view of her—if it was a woman—you were able to have, sitting in the front?" He'd have to check again with the courier and the driver, who'd also been at the front of the coach; but the driver was in hospital with shock and a suspected heart attack, while the courier had fainted three times before collapsing into genuine hysterics. All he'd got from either of them was name, rank, and number, and the medicos hadn't even wanted him to have that much.

"Could have been a woman," muttered Erica Nuttel, with a blush that Furneux at first thought he was imagining. "Hard to tell," she repeated, looking uncomfortable.

She was too embarrassed to admit that she'd spent much of the time with her eyes tightly shut, perhaps on the principle that

if you can't see trouble it can't trouble you. The very thought
of guns, violence, blood . . . Miss Nuttel gulped and closed her
eyes again.

Furneux realised that they weren't going to enlarge just yet on
their suspicions—perhaps they were really as shocked as they'd
made out earlier—and was grateful for the timely arrival of the
iced water, which revived the subdued spirits of Miss Nuttel and
perked up Mrs. Blaine still more. "Let's continue, shall we?" he
urged, striking while the iron was at least lukewarm.

"So, tell me, what were you doing on this trip, anyway?"
he asked again, determined not to let them divert him for a
second time. He couldn't help being suspicious of The Nuts:
so convenient, the swollen ankle (easy to damage yourself just
a little) which delayed the departure of the coach—perhaps to
a time pre-arranged with the rest of the gang? So convenient,
those seats in the front which blocked a proper view of the
robbers from everyone else on the coach. The more he thought
about it, the blacker the picture looked for Miss Nuttel and Mrs.
Blaine. And their paranoia about Miss Seeton—Scotland Yard's
own unlikely secret weapon—could derive from a guilty pair of
consciences . . .

"Won it," said Miss Nuttel, while Mrs. Blaine smirked. "Competition—*Anyone's*, last month."

"Oh. Yes, I seem to recall . . . " Furneux, like many of its
detractors, never actually *read* the notorious newspaper: but when
it was left lying around in the police canteen, he might dip into it—
the odd spare moment, nothing deliberate—and, strangely, could,
if pressed, give chapter and verse for any of the scandals and
exposures it was currently running. "*Anyone's*—yes, of course.
Famous Royal Mistresses, wasn't it? And you won?"

"Historical, Inspector," Miss Nuttel hastened to assure him.
"Perfectly respectable people, king's mistresses—not like some
I could mention. Shady—often wondered how she gets away with
it . . . "

Mrs. Blaine nodded wisely, her plump cheeks puckered in a
knowing grimace. "Not that we're mentioning any names, you
understand, Inspector, but strange things have happened . . . iron
filings, and magnets—no smoke without fire . . . "

Inspector Furneux was speechless. He'd never met Miss Seeton—it was obviously the Battling Brolly they were so busy
hinting at—but he'd heard, and read, a lot about her. The idea
of Miss Seeton setting up as a royal mistress—a latter-day Jane

Shore, or Anne Boleyn, if you were Roman Catholic—was ludicrous. If people could make accusations like that and expect him to take them seriously, they had another think coming.

Or might that be what they wanted? Were they playing a clever double game of their own, to direct suspicion from themselves by acting and speaking so strangely that nobody would dream of taking them seriously?

On the other hand, people who read *Anyone's* were an odd enough lot that he was prepared to believe almost anything of them—connivance with highway robbery not excluded . . .

And Inspector Furneux resolved to get in touch with Superintendent Brinton at Ashford, to learn what he could tell him about the two women who claimed to be Miss Erica Nuttel and Mrs. Norah Blaine.

# chapter

# ~5~

"THE NUTS—YOU *do* mean that pair from Plummergen, don't you?—in league with highway robbers?" Superintendent Chris Brinton spluttered briefly into the telephone receiver and then gave up the struggle. He laughed. The ears of Inspector Furneux, already pink with embarrassment at having had to consult his Ashford colleague on such a remarkable matter as waylaid tourist coaches and shotgun-toting crooks with masks over their faces, turned scarlet. He cleared his throat in a manner that was both apologetic and reproachful.

"Then I was correct in my supposition, sir. That you'd know of the ladies through the, er, Plummergen connection, that's to say." But I'd infinitely prefer you not to make fun of me for asking, came the underlying message, which Brinton could hardly miss.

"Sorry, Harry." He sobered at once. "I shouldn't laugh, but the thought of those two . . . those two Nuts . . . " With a further brief burst of mirth, he coughed, and continued in a voice that barely quivered: "So, having had me explode one fine theory for you, how else can I be of help?"

Well, he'd rung to ask for advice, so he'd better take whatever was on offer. Furneux allowed his tone to become less oppressively formal. "Can you tell me a bit about them, sir? I gather I can rule them out for complicity, but I don't think you can really blame me for wondering. I can't exactly make sense of them; they're an odd pair. Is that why you called them The Nuts?"

"Not just me, Harry. Everyone in the village, from what Potter—he's the local bobby—says. Everyone except Miss Seeton,

29

that is . . . " Trust her never to be like the rest of them. And, though Plummergen might claim the nutty nomenclature derived from the grimly vegetarian stance taken by Miss Nuttel and Mrs. Blaine, there were still two ways of looking at this derivation. They avoided meat and ate nut cutlets (factual nicknaming) or they were crazy to do so (character assessment, and from what Potter said not far wrong, either).

"The Nuts," repeated Superintendent Brinton, with a sigh as he thought of Miss Seeton. "Barmy but harmless—from our point of view, that is. Unlikely to commit any crime worse than slander. According to Potter, they're as evil-tongued a brace of biddies as you're likely to come across in several months of Sundays, though there's always going to be someone like that in every village, I suppose."

"They certainly did a bit of nasturtium-casting at Miss Seeton. Made out they recognised one of the robbers as a woman, which is possible, of course, but hinted that it might be the Battling Brolly, which I find hard to credit, from what I've heard of her."

Brinton exploded again, but whether from mirth or shock at the slander Furneux couldn't tell. He held the receiver away from his ear until the curious spluttering sounds had decreased in decibel level.

"Miss Seeton a highwayman?" gasped Brinton at last, with wild visions before his eyes. "Don't let The Oracle hear you or he'll wash your mouth out with soap—or get that tame giant of his to do it for him. Delphick and Bob Ranger think the world of Miss Seeton, though sometimes I wonder why, the mayhem that woman causes without meaning to. Did I ever tell you about those three police cars she managed to reduce to scrap iron even while she was fast asleep?"

"You did," Furneux informed him with a grin. The superintendent had been purple in the face during the narration, and needed several whiskies to soothe him after the tale was fully told.

"Then, if you know the risks you're running, why are you deliberately asking for trouble by getting involved with the woman? And don't," snarled Brinton, "try telling me it's an indirect association. Everything about Miss Seeton is indirect, and woolly-minded—but catastrophic, nevertheless. Take it from one who knows!"

"I can hardly," pointed out Furneux, "ignore two vital witnesses just because they happen to live in Plummergen and that's where Miss Seeton happens to live. I do understand the problem, sir, but there are these—these damned Dick Turpin types to be caught, and The Nuts do seem to be some of the more noticing witnesses we've had, plus they were in the front seat. Now you've given me the all-clear, I can start to take what they say rather more seriously. Let's face it, we need as much information as possible, and in the nature of things they've more than most of the other passengers to tell us."

"If you want my advice—" began Brinton, then stopped. "Well, it's probably too late now in any case, and what's more it's hardly the usual way for an investigating officer to behave. You'd best ignore it—I'm rambling. But . . . "

"Then what would your advice be, if I decided that I wanted to behave in an unusual investigative manner?"

"To wait until the next time and get all the information you need from *those* front-seat witnesses. Do yourself a big favour— stay away from The Nuts."

"The next time?" Furneux was appalled. "What makes you think there'll be a next time?"

Brinton uttered a scornful snort. "Just use the brains you were born with, Harry. Of course there'll be a next time, and for at least two good reasons. One, it works, doesn't it? Every time! A guaranteed method of collaring a fine and varied haul of swag. Tourists always cart cameras and travellers' cheques and their best jewellery for dressing up on holiday with them. All you need to help yourself is a couple of cars to block the road, and someone who can look menacing behind a shotgun." He paused. "Mind you, most people would look menacing behind a shotgun . . . "

"And the second reason, sir?"

Brinton emerged from his daydream—or was it a nightmare— of Miss Seeton, armed *cap a pied* with pistols and shotguns and the inevitable umbrella. He knew which he'd bet his boots on her causing the most commotion with . . .

"The second reason? I've already told you that, Harry, if you'd bothered to listen. Miss Seeton! Never mind how distant the connection—when that woman's involved, there's bound to be a recurrence of whatever trouble she's involved in, only double. Or squared. Or cubed, or whatever the biggest magnification of anything is. I confidently predict a rash of highway robberies right through the summer—but I won't bother to bet on having Miss Seeton turn up in it all somehow or somewhere. I can guarantee she will. So, don't say I didn't warn you!"

• • •

Inspector Furneux was more unnerved than he might care to admit by the doom-laden prophecies of his Ashford colleague, but, having asked the superintendent for advice, he would have thought himself a fool not to take at least part of it. His subsequent questioning of The Nuts was completed with their signing of the most detailed statements for which anyone could have wished—too detailed, perhaps. Did Norah Blaine's sprained (or ricked) ankle, and her subsequent search for the herbalist, have to be excused and explained by her at such length? But the statements were signed at last, and these troublesome witnesses smuggled by a back-door route out of Hastings police station and into an unmarked car. The driver had his orders to deposit them safely in Plummergen without any of the crowd of journalists and television reporters catching sight of so much as the tip of Miss Nuttel's equine nose.

"Let 'em chatter away all they like to the tourists," Furneux decided. "The Americans'll love it—their pictures in the English papers. They'll buy hundreds of copies to take home as souvenirs. Compensation, perhaps, for having had pretty well everything else pinched. As for the other two, they're the home-grown variety. Only on the trip because of some daft competition run by a newspaper. And we know," he said cunningly, "how the English gentlewoman dislikes seeing her name in the papers. We'll be doing them a favour by keeping a low profile for them . . ."

For there was, apart from Superintendent Brinton's quite understandable pessimism concerning the Seeton connection, an obvious and serious justification for keeping quiet about The Nuts. They had, after all, been star witnesses: Miss Nuttel might have had her eyes closed for most of the time, but the Dick Turpins weren't to know that. As far as they were concerned, the two front passengers had seen them; and could be asked to identify them, masks or not; and were therefore as much of a threat as all the previous front-seaters whose identities were being kept secret. Let their names and even partial addresses be published abroad, and Furneux wouldn't care to take a bet that they might not be in danger . . .

This constabulary regard for their safety left The Nuts in peevish mood. Mrs. Blaine had been eagerly anticipating the sight of her photograph in the papers alongside articles she would deign to dictate to eager newshounds clamouring for audience; Miss Nuttel had been willing, in the interests of law, order, and justice, to do every citizen's duty and speak the truth, which all had a right to know.

But, having been kept until last to be interviewed; and then being taken twice (or was it three times?) through their statements when before he'd gone out to telephone the inspector hadn't paid proper attention; and then being asked whether they mightn't care for something to eat after their ordeal, and having sausage and chips or pie and chips or fish and chips offered to them despite their protests . . . it was a grim-faced pair of Nuts who finally disappeared in the unmarked police car in the direction of Plummergen.

It was a silent journey. Once or twice Mrs. Blaine, with an exasperated air, attempted to break that silence, trying to pass comment—which surely was not an unnatural thing to wish—on all that had befallen the two friends during that momentous Monday afternoon. But every time she opened her plump little mouth, Erica Nuttel would nudge her crossly or—and this would hurt—kick her ankle, which happened to be the injured one. Bunny was not used to such harsh treatment from Eric, and she wasn't sure whether her eyes should flash or fill with tears. While she made up her mind, she pursed her lips and decided to say nothing at all.

Thus it was a silent journey back to Lilikot, and the plate-glass windows seemed to mock the brooding Nuts as they made their weary way up the stone-flagged path to the welcoming front door and the longed-for chamomile tea. Once inside the house, Mrs. Blaine flopped sulkily on the sofa and propped her injured ankle high on a pile of cushions, while Erica Nuttel, with a gruff and indistinct mutter of what might have been apology, busied herself in the kitchen with boiling the kettle (using water drawn from their very own well) and thoroughly warming the teapot before spooning in double the usual amount of herb mixture. "Dollop of honey each, for shock," prescribed Miss Nuttel, reaching for the rustic earthenware jar next to the bread crock. She took mugs from the carved wooden stand, and clattered a tin tray out of the cupboard. "Seaweed biscuits," she added, as a nearby container caught her eye.

Miss Nuttel at last returned to the sitting room with the laden tray and handed Mrs. Blaine her mug and plate. Bunny took them as her due, and still said nothing. For the next few minutes, only a grateful, crunching, busy drinking broke the silence of the sitting room. But it was a silence that was thoughtful . . .

"Another cup, Bunny?" Erica Nuttel gestured towards the fat

brown teapot. "Topped it up well, just in case. Likely to need something extra for our nerves, after the day we've both had."

"What a day!" agreed Mrs. Blaine, as she held out her mug and helped herself to another seaweed biscuit. Really, she felt much better about everything now that she'd had time to catch her breath and take in some proper healthy nourishment instead of those terrible, animal snacks the policeman had tried to force upon them. And Eric seemed in a more approachable mood, too, now that she'd stopped brooding and started talking. Maybe she could be persuaded to explain her extraordinary behaviour in the car.

"There was no need for you to kick me quite so hard," she complained, dipping her biscuit in the chamomile tea and looking hurt. "On top of everything else, I do think that was a bit much. Whatever possessed you?"

"Not to be trusted," said Erica Nuttel, shaking her head with disapproval as she stared down her nose at unseen mischief.

"If you're talking about me, Eric, I must say I don't think that's very—"

"Police driver, Bunny, not you. Probably a spy—finding out how much we know—inspector's orders, mark my words. That change in his attitude to us—too dramatic, about-face—didn't believe us at first, can't think why, then deliberately made us late and kept us back, not allowed to join the others, went on checking and rechecking our statements, far too much of a good thing. Can't believe they normally behave like that—suspicious, all right."

"Oh Eric, that's so true. I noticed as well, but it only started after he'd gone hurrying out of the room like that, didn't it? He seemed a different person when he came back—almost as if," and Mrs. Blaine dropped her voice to a thrilling whisper, "he'd been given new orders about how we ought to be treated."

They stared at each other for a moment. Then Eric said, slowly: "If we're right, only one person likely to have that sort of influence. Getting us brought back in a police car—driver the least likely person for us to suspect—hoping we'd let something out . . ."

Bunny's eyes were bright. "That woman," she breathed in terrified delight. "She knows we recognised her, and she's not sure what we've told the police in our statements so she planted a spy to bring us home—keeping tabs on us. If her game's up, she wants to be the first to know so she can make fresh plans . . ."

"Miss Seeton," said Miss Nuttel, with satisfaction. Mrs. Blaine nodded.

"Miss Seeton! If the police are involved with anyone in the village, she's the one. It's been too easy all along for her to pull the wool over their eyes, pretending she's on their side and so helpful. They refuse to admit she might be acting a part, and so very successfully, as well, because even when we tried to tell them, they didn't believe us. But we were witnesses, Eric!"

"Right in the front seat," agreed Eric grimly. "Bunny—maybe they did believe us. That inspector—he's known all along. Telephoned her for instructions, or to warn her or something. Probably in her pay, buying his silence. Spied on us when we came home, reported back to her later, having to tell her we were too smart for them."

"*You* were too smart, Eric," said Mrs. Blaine with pride. "I never *dreamed*—the police, if you can't trust them, who can you trust? But you were clever enough to suspect the truth— and you stopped me giving anything away!" Almost without a hint of annoyance in her tone did she bring out the final words; but she made a point of rubbing her ankle and wincing, very bravely.

But for once Miss Nuttel was oblivious to her friend: she was too preoccupied, and Bunny quickly realised this. She waited in respectful silence until Eric should speak.

"Bound to guess we're on to her," she said at last, with a jerk of her head in the direction of Sweetbriars further along The Street. "If we'd talked in the car—but we never let anything out. Knows we're on the watch. Hide the evidence, that's what she'll do."

"And without evidence," lamented Mrs. Blaine, "who will believe us? And anyway," as the thought struck her, "who is it safe to tell? The local police are in her pay, so . . . "

Miss Nuttel threw back her head, her nostrils flaring. She looked more like a horse than ever, but a horse with a mission. "Duty's duty, Bunny," she informed Mrs. Blaine in ringing tones. "Even if it's against the grain, the truth has to come out. Don't like the thought of doing it this way, but if they know it's us they'll manage to nobble what we tell them so it's ignored even there."

"Where, Eric? Who? And how?" breathed Mrs. Blaine,

"Obvious, when you think of it." And Erica Nuttel directed a pointed look towards the telephone. "Fight one with another. Police called her, we'll call them. Only—not the local police. Corrupt," she explained, her features twisted in a shocked grimace.

"Oh, Eric, you don't mean—you can't mean . . . "

Eric nodded. "Only thing for it," she said. "Scotland Yard—and," she concluded, "best not to say who we are or how we know. Anonymous, that's how!"

# chapter

## ~6~

THESE WERE BRAVE words—but words are easier than deeds any day. Miss Nuttel found that somehow, even with Bunny at her side to egg her on, she couldn't quite bring herself to pick up the telephone and dial Whitehall 1212. "Might trace the call," she pointed out, "and warn that woman we're on to her. Needs careful thinking about, Bunny."

To which Bunny, as ever, agreed that Eric was so right, and suggested a fresh brewing of chamomile tea to strengthen both nerves and resolve. "And we could take a peek at the Nine O'Clock News on television," she added. "I know that the inspector did his best to keep the journalists away from us, but we *might* just see something about ourselves . . ."

But they did not. Interviews with selected Americans, all enchanted with the unique historical experience they'd undergone in such a romantic setting—some of them seemed almost to believe the tour company had arranged it on purpose—preceded shots of a solemn reporter outside the hospital in which the coach driver, now in intensive care, and the courier sheltered from the media while they recovered: which stern seclusion naturally made them the people to whom everyone wished to speak. Nobody mentioned the Nuts; and the Nuts were disappointed.

They were to a certain extent mollified, however, by the way their telephone tintinnabulated rhythmically into life almost before the broadcast was over. Most of their cronies—indeed, most of the village—had known of their success in the *Anyone's* competition, and knew also which day they had intended to claim their prize: and what a day, thrilled their envious callers, to choose! Plummergen

had become newsworthy—some might say had achieved notori-
ety—more than once in the recent past, mostly due to Miss Seeton
and her innocent umbrella-wielding; but Miss Seeton, to cronies
of the Nuts, was not as yet considered true Plummergen. The
adventure today, however, was different. Miss Nuttel and Mrs.
Blaine had lived in Lilikot for twelve years, and though it might
take a lifetime to be fully accepted, there were some who were
more (partially) accepted into the village than others, by some
villagers.

It was these who clamoured to know why The Nuts hadn't been
on telly like everyone else. How come they had missed seeing the
robbery? Weren't they there, after all? Would it be in the papers
tomorrow, instead? The good name of the village was somehow
seen to be at stake . . .

Yet to all this, Miss Nuttel and Mrs. Blaine could only reply in
mysterious tones that their lips were sealed, and that maybe tomorrow's papers would tell a different story. "Don't want word getting
back to her that we've rumbled her little game," Miss Nuttel said
to Mrs. Blaine. "Best keep quiet until we've got proof—at least
till we've warned the police about her," she added. She sketched a
vague gesture. "Search warrants . . ." she said darkly, and Mrs.
Blaine gave a squeak of horror.

"To think of such goings-on in our peaceful little Plummergen,"
she said, and shivered gleefully. "Oh, Eric, d'you suppose they'll
send someone down tomorrow? But they can't, of course," she
recalled, "until you've telephoned. When shall you ring
them?"

"Too late now," said Eric, peering first at her watch, then out
the window. Yes, as she'd feared: The Street was still empty
of reporters: nobody wanted to know about her—their—shared
and shocking experience of highway robbery. Resentment came
welling up in what passed for Miss Nuttel's soul.

It is possible that, had the reporters eventually manifested themselves, next day's call to Scotland Yard might never have been
made. But nobody came at all; which left Eric, who was beginning
to have doubts about the whole enterprise, a more or less easy
prey to Bunny's blandishments, though she did not yield without
a struggle.

"It's much more expensive to ring in the morning," she tried to
tell her friend, but Bunny refused to consider this important. Duty,
she remarked, was—as Eric herself had said—duty. What did the
cost of a telephone call matter? Scotland Yard should be warned

that not all the county forces were as uncorrupt and trustworthy as—here she stumbled, but recovered—the Yard itself was known to be. ("Miss Seeton's very thick with that man Delphick, of course, Eric. Suppose he suppresses your message? You'd better talk to somebody else. Insist on it, won't you?")

And, thrusting the hesitant Miss Nuttel to one side, she dialled the number with fingers that shook only a little, then handed the receiver to Eric with a look of admiring encouragement that brooked no denial.

It was while Miss Seeton was out, shopping among other items for Bob Ranger's favourite gingerbread, that Chief Superintendent Delphick learned of the anonymous telephone call received at Scotland Yard and concerning their—well, his, he supposed, if she was anyone's—MissEss. He cursed to himself when he realised that it was far too late to stop rumours ever more wild proliferating once his sergeant, even in the unmarked car, arrived in Plummergen—which had to be the source of the anonymous message—to collect Miss Seeton and deliver her safely to London. He should never have rung her yesterday afternoon and asked her to come up to Town; he ought to have listened to the doubts expressed by Sergeant Ranger, who after all knew her far better, since marriage to Anne Knight had made him privy to more of Plummergen's secrets. Bob had dropped heavy hints that Miss Seeton, if she had to come to London, should come by train: but he, Delphick, The Oracle, had predicted mishaps (unspecified) and confusion (ditto, but inevitable where Miss Seeton was concerned) if she made the journey by British Rail, and had overridden his sergeant's warning.

He did his best to prevent mischief, of course. As soon as the Scotland Yard switchboard had relayed the gist of the anonymous message and he realised its import, he telephoned Plummergen 35 hoping to catch Miss Seeton and explain there was to be a change of plan. Useless to warn her of gossip, since she could never understand that anyone might find her affairs of consuming interest, and would dismiss Delphick's apprehensions as surely not applying to her, Superintendent, or rather Chief Superintendent, one did not always remember, one's age, he must understand, but really an unpardonable discourtesy and she apologised for it . . .

Delphick was so sure of her response that he'd rehearsed it through in his head as he dialled, and marshalled every argument at his disposal in readiness—only to hear nothing but the ringing tone at the other end. Miss Seeton was out: perhaps in the garden? The ringing tone rang on. She was not, then, weeding: he'd left ample time for her to reach the telephone. He deduced from the lack of reply that it couldn't be one of Martha's days working at Sweetbriars, or she would have answered in Miss Seeton's absence. He'd try again later, once she'd had time to come back from the shops, or wherever she'd gone; meanwhile he'd try to reach Bob Ranger on the car radio.

From Bob, too, there was no reply. Delphick consulted his watch: the lad was probably chatting with his in-laws at Dr. Knight's nursing home, making good his excuse for being in Plummergen in the first place before dropping in on Miss Seeton and, on such a lovely day, suggesting that she might care to go for a drive in the country.

Delphick cursed himself fluently. He really should have thought more about the village tom-toms, which beat louder and faster in Plummergen than in other places; and in view of the startling robbery yesterday, only a dozen miles or so from Miss Seeton's home, he should have guessed that somehow she'd be implicated by the tom-toms in whatever mayhem was now abroad. Plummergen, judging by that telephone call, was obviously convinced it was all her fault—he must ring Chris Brinton at Ashford to find out exactly what had happened—and no amount of dissembling would now be able to disguise the fact that Miss Seeton had been taken away by the police, a week foundational fact upon which the gossips would erect a towering edifice of speculation, rumour, and surmise.

But it was no use blaming himself; he'd chosen to bring Miss Seeton into the Sherry Gang case, and it was nothing but bad luck that at the same time the chance for her name to be linked with a totally unconnected crime wave should turn up. Probably she wouldn't even notice the trouble his actions had caused her: he and his conscience, however, would have to live with whatever consequences there might be. And so would the forked tongues of Plummergen . . .

"Chris? Delphick here. How are you? . . . Yes, longer than I'd realised, and yes again, I do want something—to pick your brains, as usual. I gather you've been having a jolly time of it in the sticks, highway robbery and any amount of fun and games—oh? . . . Hastings? Furneux? Not the chap they call the Fiery Furnace, by any chance?"

"That's him. Young Harry—a good copper, for a Sussex man," said Superintendent Brinton of the Kent Constabulary. "Never known anything like this on his patch before—well, few of us have. He's coped pretty well, I gather, though one thing that bothered him a bit this last time was coming up against a couple of friends of your Miss Seeton—Miss Nuttel and Mrs. Blaine. He couldn't make 'em out at all, and harboured deep suspicions of 'em till I put him straight."

"The Nuts?" exclaimed Delphick, much as Brinton had done the previous day. "Highway robbery? Never."

Brinton chose to sound doubtful. "Well, I wouldn't go quite that far in letting 'em off the hook. They're pals of your Miss Seeton, after all, and where she's concerned—what's up?" For Delphick had uttered a heartfelt groan.

"That's what the whole damned village is going to say about her, I know, but I didn't expect it of you, Chris. I thought you liked her."

"Did I say I didn't? Which doesn't mean I haven't got a healthy respect for the way she always manages to stir up a hornets' nest wherever she goes, and without even noticing, too. She's been quiet for a few months now; it's about time for her to start breaking out again. I'm not saying she's a Dick Turpin, of course I'm not. She'd think it was quite unacceptable to break the law. But you have to admit that if things are going to go wobbly, when she's anywhere near 'em they wobble a lot harder, and a lot sooner, than if she wasn't."

"The Nuts," protested Delphick, "aren't exactly near her—I don't believe they even like her. They certainly don't trust her—"

"They don't. Potter tells me they're forever hoping to catch her out on some illicit ploy or other, and they egg on the rest of the village to think the same. Half the schoolkids believe she's a witch, and their parents think she's a crook." Delphick spluttered, but Brinton carried on: "Never mind about it, Oracle, because you can be sure Miss Seeton doesn't. Even if she knew, which of course she doesn't. It really is water off a duck's back, with her."

"You seem to know a great deal more about Plummergen and its goings-on than I'd have expected, Chris. Could this be because you've been keeping an eye on Miss Seeton for me?"

Brinton blustered for a few moments before admitting, in an embarrassed tone, that with MissEss practically on his doorstep he felt a lot safer knowing what the old biddy was up to from the weekly personal reports PC Potter made to him in Ashford. "Not that she's under surveillance, Oracle—perish the thought—but I'd like to know when and where she's likely to erupt next. And if she has—if this latest little carry-on with shotguns and masks was anything to do with her, then it happened over the county border so it's not my pigeon, thank goodness. Not that I believe for one moment," he added, "that there's any possible connection with Miss Seeton at all. I was just winding you up. Privilege of an old friend who's light-headed at knowing somebody else, for once, has drawn the short straw."

"You may not believe it, Chris, but there are those who apparently do . . . " And Delphick told him about the anonymous call, and why he feared for Miss Seeton's reputation, and the reason he'd wanted to call her into the Sherry investigation. Brinton was thoughtful.

"So you want her to leave Plummergen under her own steam after all, and meet up with your young giant in Brettenden? Leave it to me, Oracle. I'll ring Potter and get him to pop down with a message for her to ring you for new instructions. Better still, I'll ask him to send his wife. Potter can be calling the nursing home to see if the doctor's son-in-law's still on the premises. Then *he* can ring you, too . . . "

"Thanks, Chris. I know I could do all this myself, but you've got the numbers to hand—and it won't seem quite so formal, this way. If the gossips should get hold of it, maybe they won't make such a meal of it . . . "

"Maybe," replied Brinton, sounding unconvinced. "That's the logical, sensible expectation, I grant you—but never forget it's Miss Seeton we're dealing with, Oracle. And for her, you need a whole new vocabulary . . . "

# chapter

# -7-

THE ELEVEN O'CLOCK news broadcast was over: and there had yet again been no mention of the Nuts in connection with the daring robbery on the Rye road. Cronies of Miss Nuttel and Mrs. Blaine now felt that they had done their duty in staying by their wirelesses for most of the morning, and that they should consider themselves free to utilise the services of an even more efficient propaganda machine, the Plummergen shopping circuit.

For more exotic, indeed even for some essential, items the Plummergen shopper will visit Brettenden, six miles to the northwest, but for most basic needs the village is well served. There are three shops in Plummergen, apart from the bakery (which recently became part of the Winesart empire, and no longer produces home-made bread) and the butcher, who still holds out against takeover by anyone: the only chains he is prepared to admit to his premises are those made of sausages.

The three main shops all sell, despite their official designations, groceries as well as their basic stock. From the grocer, the draper, and the post office may be bought produce that has been bottled, canned, jarred, or deep-frozen, as well as the fresh variety, with tobacco, confectionery, and off-licence sales also possible. The post office boasts a cold meats counter, a selection of books, and ironmongery and general hardware lines as well as stamps. It also has the largest floor-space of the three.

It was therefore in the post office, by some mysterious mass telepathy, that the gossips of Plummergen congregated shortly after eleven o'clock, just too late to observe Miss Seeton, Bob Ranger's gingerbread safely basketed beside her own favourite

chocolate biscuits, say goodbye to Mr. Stillman and hurry back
to Sweetbriars. Leaving, by her absence, the floor free for speculation even wilder than usual.

As the excitement grows when a royal personage is about to
appear, so the tension began to mount in the post office before the
Nuts arrived, as nearly everyone was confident that they would.
Not mentioned on the radio all morning—never a word on the
telly last night—there'd be something to say about that, mark the
speaker's words, because having been in the thick of things as
they had the Nuts wouldn't take kindly to being outsmarted by
a load of furriners with their pictures in the papers.

"Noses regular out of joint, I'd say," remarked Mrs. Flax in
satisfied tones. She, in common with a high percentage of the
Plummergen population, had entered the *Anyone's* competition
about famous royal mistresses: the first prize had been flashed
as a mystery tour, and there was laughter and mockery in certain
quarters when the Nuts, having announced their success to the
entire village, had learned the exact nature and destination of
their win. It served them right, thought Plummergen, for having
been so cocky about it all—and now this.

"Noses out of joint," said Mrs. Flax, "and it wouldn't surprise
me one bit if they didn't keep them noses inside for a day or two,
not liking to admit the truth of it." She lowered her voice so that
anyone outside on the pavement—the fine weather had encouraged Mr. Stillman to prop open the door of the post office to gain
the full benefit of the sun—would be unable to overhear. "For to
my mind, there's but one possible truth about this not being mentioned nowhere at all . . . " And she rolled her eyes meaningfully.

Mrs. Scillicough edged nearer, ostensibly to browse among
the tinned baby foods. Her triplets were a demanding little litter,
each insisting on something different, each, for every meal.
Plummergen, having taken bets before their birth as to the number
of babies she would produce, was now running a book on how
much weight the child-oppressed Mrs. Scillicough would lose—
and how quickly—in her all too frequent outings to Mr. Stillman's
grocery counter.

Now she sighed automatically, then picked up her day's quota
of tins with far less thought than usual. "So, what d'you reckon
the truth of it to be, then, Mrs. Flax?" asked Mrs. Scillicough,
handling her selection across the counter for Mr. Stillman to price.
"Secrets, you reckon?"

Everyone else stopped even pretending to shop, and drew

near with ears flapping and eyes agog. Mrs. Flax, savouring her moment as the focus of attention, breathed in deeply and swelled to twice her normal size. "Secrets," she said, "and beyond—dark plots and mischief, mark my words! Pretending and playacting, that's what, and it's not them highwaymen in their masks I mean—it's *them* who's the playactors, catch them ever admitting to it!"

"Them, who?" everyone wanted to know. Mrs. Flax nodded a sage head and pursed her lips.

"Them Nuts, is who I mean, making out they was on the coach and witnesses to it all. But, I ask you, if they was to have witnessed from the front seat the way they said, why no mention of 'em in the news and the papers?" She did not wait for anyone else to supply the scandalous answer she had worked out for herself. "Weren't there, were they? Just a lot of big talk and pretending. They didn't really win that competition how they said, so they never were on no coach, so they never saw no highway robbers—that's what *I* think!"

This was an idea which had occurred to nobody else, and for a moment or two the post office was quiet while everyone digested it. Mrs. Scillicough, her temper frayed by exhaustion, broke the silence first by remarking that she'd always wondered just what it was about the Nuts, but Mrs. Flax had made her start thinking . . .

At which there was a general chorus of realisation that yes, it was odd, wasn't it, and with all the stories they'd come up with over the years it wouldn't surprise anyone if it wasn't just one more Nutty story about winning the competition and being on the coach and witnessing the robbery—

"But what for would they do that?" a disaffected murmur was heard. The murmurer was rounded on at once.

"Make themselves look important, that's what," came the answer that was obvious, weren't it, because there was always them as thought better of theirselves than others.

This was true, everyone agreed; but further agreement was lost when somebody else wanted to know what they'd been doing instead, if it wasn't winning prize coach tours and spending the day with furriners, because they'd been seen yesterday morning hurrying to catch the Brettenden bus so's to be (the speaker had heard one of the Nuts explain) early for the coach and to get a good seat.

This was an obvious problem. The suggestion that they had skulked in various Brettenden shops all day in case anyone should spot them absent from their boasted excursion was vetoed loudly as being (a) unlikely—Plummergen regularly shops in Brettenden, and the risk of being encountered by a fellow villager would be too great for the Nuts to take; and (b) boring. Plummergen prefers its scandals colourful, not mundane; and promptly began now to invent more interesting destinations for the Nuts on that momentous Monday. Having to sneak away in such a hole-and-corner fashion must mean they'd been up to no good, so like enough they'd gone further afield to get up to it: London, the speaker would guess if asked, since weren't there the railway station close by and the trains running regular and fast?

"Plenty to get up to in London, that's rightly said . . . "

"These cities where nobody'll know your face . . . "

"Not like here where the shops know their regulars . . . "

"All them big department stores and such . . . "

It didn't take long before Mrs. Scillicough was seconding the suggestion of Mrs. Flax that the Nuts were in charge of a shoplifting circle which regularly descended upon Harrop's, Sellidge's, or Marker & Spence to deprive these prestigious emporia of their most expensive clothes: which were then—a happy thought from Emmy Putts, who served behind the grocery counter and, wearing a long blond wig, had been crowned as last year's Miss Plummergen—forcibly applied to their miserable victims in the white slave racket they ran in their spare time. Emmy's eyes held a suspicious hint of enjoyment as she proposed this theory, and a minority view held that she really ought to be ashamed of herself for speaking so, but on the whole it was felt that the true solution to the recent behavior of the Nuts had been found. Indeed, so plausible did the whole proposition sound that Mrs. Manuden, who had watched, entranced, the practised unfolding of the sheet of scandal, now ventured to exclaim in horror that she had no idea that her next-door neighbours were so shockingly unrespectable, and if she'd known before she and her Dennis come to spend the summer there, she wouldn't have taken the cottage for four months, low rent or not, and she'd be careful in future to drink none of the home-made wine or herb tea (if that's what it really was—she had her doubts) they'd offered her when she popped round once to borrow a cup of sugar.

Betsy Manuden smiled gratefully upon the entire company. She and Den had only been in Plummergen a few weeks. People said it took time to be accepted in a village, but people were wrong. Here she was, sharing the very hottest scandal with everyone as if she'd been born in the place, no trouble at all, and treating her like one of themselves. Oh, it was ever so interesting, living in the country . . .

The general air of satisfaction which now filled the post office was suddenly, shockingly, darkened by a shadow—two shadows, one angular and tall, one shorter and rotund, with a pronounced limp—that fell upon the post office floor. A horrified silence gripped the gossips as the Nuts appeared in the doorway and found every face staring at them, open-mouthed, wondering at their boldness in mixing with decent folk when by rights they ought not to show themselves.

But Miss Nuttel and Mrs. Blaine were far too big with news to pay any attention to the startled expressions which greeted them, and the uncomfortable wrigglings of scandal suppressed into hurried, tactful dumbness. Miss Nuttel moved towards the counter, remarking over her shoulder to Bunny that she'd forgotten to check how low their stock of seaweed biscuits was, and should she buy double just to be sure. "Can't be too careful, times like these," she said. "Been one robbery here in the past. Shouldn't like to have the place closed again and no supplies."

"You're so practical, Eric," praised Mrs. Blaine, while a muted shuffling indicated that Plummergen was sufficiently alert to wish to learn more. Doubts as to the probity of the Nuts would be suspended, at least until this new hinting at another sensation had been fully investigated. Everyone, without appearing to do so, drifted closer to Miss Nuttel and Mrs. Blaine, willing to risk the miasma of white slavery for the chance to pick up the titbit they were obviously about to let fall.

"Maybe make it three packets," reflected Miss Nuttel, just as Mr. Stillman was putting away the folding steps he kept behind the counter for those items seldom called for and stored on the topmost shelves.

"And a tin of soya chunks," chipped in Mrs. Blaine, as for the second time he prepared to stow the aluminium steps. Mr. Stillman sighed and waited. "And, Eric, shouldn't we perhaps try another box of those dried soya granules? Once we work out the correct recipe for the gravy to reconstitute them, they'll be so much cheaper than the tinned."

"Three packets," decided Eric, "just in case." Without a word, Mr. Stillman placed the items on the counter and waited for the next indication that the Nuts knew what they were talking about. As Miss Nuttel had said, he'd had one brush in the recent past with armed robbers—who, thanks to the efforts of Miss Seeton, had escaped with nothing but a cardboard box of anticlimax in the form of grated cheese with one postal order sticky-taped to its lid, and which in their flight they had dropped. If there was even the most remote chance that another gang was likely to carry out a hold-up, then Mr. Stillman wanted to know about it.

But with the Nuts, it was sometimes risky to press them for a direct answer. They would hedge, and back away, and use weasel words to keep you guessing, instead of coming right out with it. The best way of finding out was often to pretend you weren't really interested. Mr. Stillman began totting up the prices with the pencil he kept stuck behind his ear, and asked the Nuts nothing at all beyond: "Now, is that the lot, ladies?"

"I'm not sure. Eric, can you think of anything else?"

"Bit short on prunes, Bunny, unless you had time to pop to the shops yesterday and stock up."

Mrs. Blaine wasn't slow to seize her cue. "Oh, Eric, you know what a hurry we were in yesterday to catch the Brettenden bus for that coach trip. There certainly wasn't a moment to spare before, and as for afterwards—you remember what a state I was in, delayed shock, I'm sure it was, and the last thing on my mind would have been the shopping!" And Bunny did her best to tremble at the memory.

Erica Nuttel patted her on the shoulder before picking up the brown paper bag Mr. Stillman held out to her. "Best not to dwell on things, Bunny. Give you nightmares if you aren't careful."

Mrs. Blaine's eyes widened as she recalled the horrid sight of the shotguns and the masked men, and her gaze swept blankly over the now rapt audience. "Oh, Eric, you're such a strong person, you don't know what it means to be as highly-strung as me, and of course I've had nightmares, anyone else would expect to. I'm sure the police doctor ought to have given us tranquillisers, I know I never slept a wink last night with being so upset. My grandmother's beautiful gold ring with the cabochon ruby, wrenched from my finger by that dreadful man with the stocking over his head . . ."

This sounded authentic: this was worth listening to, and Plummergen was not slow to draw even closer. Miss Nuttel, turning to leave, stopped to stare at the book carousel and remarked: "Can't be sure it *was* a man, can we? Never spoke a single word, just collected everything in that duffle bag and left all the talking to the other one."

"Oh, Eric, surely you can't mean you think it could have been a woman!" breathed Mrs. Blaine, with an anxious glance over her shoulder. "How dreadful! Why, I shan't sleep easy in my bed until they've caught her!"

"Only guessing," said Eric, once more patting her friend in a comforting fashion, and taking no notice of the crowd now pressing close with straining ears. "Suspicious, though, not speaking. Might be in case we'd recognise the voice, sitting right at the front."

"Oh, Eric, then it was somebody we know—that's awful! But how many women of our acquaintance could be so—so very cold-blooded as that?"

Every woman there tried to look warmhearted as well as interested in what was being said, but the Nuts ignored them all. "Mention no names, Bunny—slander," said Erica Nuttel in a meaningful tone which accompanied a jerk of her head in the direction of Sweetbriars. "But odd, isn't it—the very next day, police coming all the way from Scotland Yard to question her!"

And on this glorious exit line, she headed for the door, giving the book carousel a brisk shove to send it whirling in sympathy with Plummergen thoughts. In the doorway, she stopped dead, so that Mrs. Blaine cannoned into her.

"Told you so," announced Miss Nuttel, quite blocking the view at which she pointed. Bunny Blaine squeezed past to stare. "Oh, Eric, you were right! It's the police car, and it's heading for London—and there's a passenger in the back, and it's a woman!"

"Oh, no." Eric shook her head and stood firm as everyone rushed to see what was happening. "Wrong word, if you ask me—not passenger. Prisoner."

And the Nuts hurried away back to Lilikot to savour the moment of triumph.

# chapter

## ~8~

MISS SEETON PATTED her hair into shape beneath her hat, then picked up her umbrella and smiled at Sergeant Ranger. "Such a beautiful day for a drive," she said, "and so kind of you to think of taking me." In her eyes there was the suspicion of a twinkle.

So unexpected of the chief superintendent to telephone and say that the little excursion to London with Bob, her—sometimes she found herself smiling at the thought—adopted nephew, might give rise to some comment, but one felt sure in this instance that he must be mistaken to feel any such anxiety, although of course one would not wish to tell him so, since this might seem ungrateful, when he evidently felt he was acting in one's best interests, and perhaps did not completely understand how one's private affairs, after all, were simply that, and no concern of anyone else, while one's professional relationship with the police was, again, simply that, and nothing for anyone to feel any need whatsoever to discuss. Curiosity could be distressing, one imagined, if ever for any reason applied to oneself, but one was fortunate in that one led a quiet life in which nothing that could be of possible interest to the more vulgar element in human nature—which, regrettably, one had to acknowledge existed—ever occurred.

Nevertheless, if Chief Superintendent Delphick thought it advisable for it not to be generally known that one was travelling to Town on police business (which was, one knew well, what Mr. Delphick understood far better than one who was merely a part-time IdentiKit artist), naturally one was happy to go along with whatever little pretence the chief superintendent deemed necessary. "A beautiful day," Miss Seeton repeated, wondering whether she ought to have waited until they were outside, so that more people could hear.

"I think you've forgotten something," said Bob, as she was heading for the door. Miss Seeton stopped.

In one hand she held her umbrella, over her arm she had hung her capacious handbag. "Oh dear, have I? Oh dear, yes indeed I have—my drawing materials!"

But Bob, who had bent to collect the case Miss Seeton had packed with her sketching block, crayons, charcoal, and pencils, among other items, straightened himself with the case dangling from one large hand, and shook his head. The look of gentle disapproval he directed at Miss Seeton made her feel guilty even before she had remembered.

She glanced once more at the umbrella in her hand and smiled vaguely as she recalled how—oh. Oh dear . . . Miss Seeton blushed. She gazed up at Bob with a worried frown creasing her brows. "Oh dear, the alarm, and so lucky you reminded me, although I sometimes do wonder if perhaps the chief constable might not have used me as a guinea pig for quite long enough now, and then it could be installed somewhere else where there is a real need for it, instead of in my little cottage where, after all, there is nothing worth stealing, and even when we had that outbreak of burglaries in the village it was other houses which were broken into, although—" her eyes twinkled once more— "the value of the items stolen was not, perhaps, as great as the owners would have wanted it to be, although perfectly natural, of course. That they would say it was—valuable, I mean. But I have nothing here of more than sentimental value, so . . . "

Bob was shaking his head at her once more. "That's not the point," he explained, leading her back to the main fusebox on the stairs and waiting while she hunted for the key. "It isn't the monetary value of what's taken that matters so much as the destruction of the, the victim's peace of mind." It was the best word he could find but it sounded—rather uncomfortable, thought Bob. He hurried on:

"Nobody likes the idea of strangers prowling about their homes and picking over their possessions—"

"Oh, I know!" Miss Seeton's eyes flashed, and she stood halfway up the stairs, the keys in her hand, looking like an avenging angel with power over heaven and hell. But angels, reflected Bob, seldom wear respectable tweeds, sensible lace shoes and grey stockings. Avenging, however, Miss Seeton certainly did appear.

"So very wicked," she said, "preying on those poor old people like, like vultures—taking cruel advantage of them and running the grave risk of destroying their faith in human nature, so very wrong, and if my poor efforts can assist in any way I shall, of course, be pleased to be able to help, though I fear the stolen items may very well be gone beyond recall by this time. Photography," said Miss Seeton, as she turned the key in the lock, "could be the answer, although I suppose it's far too late now."

Was she suggesting the victims should have taken snapshots of the chummies who'd turned them over? *Before* they turned them over? Bob tried to envisage the scene. "Hold it—the head a bit more this way, and do smile a little, you look so serious—now, steady! Thank you—and how many copies would you like?" No, even for one of Miss Seeton's suggestions it was farfetched.

"Beforehand, I mean." Miss Seeton gave the alarm box an absentminded pat as she turned to make her way back down the stairs. "I believe it is recommended for insurance purposes, always assuming one has a good camera and knows how to work the apparatus without blurring." She gestured as if in demonstration, and dropped the keys, which tumbled to the foot of the stairs with a crisp rattling sound. "Oh, bother—how silly of me. No, don't trouble . . . " But Bob was down on his knees already. Miss Seeton descended the remainder of the stairs to join him.

"The resulting picture, that is to say, and focus is important, too, though I understand there are modern cameras which focus without having to be set on a dial, yet rather expensive, I feel sure, for most old people, and one can't help wondering—oh, thank you!" She gripped the keys firmly as once more she headed for the door. Bob followed, dusting creases from the knees of his trousers, and watched as Miss Seeton picked up her bag and her brolly and turned, for the second time, to leave.

"Why the government," continued Miss Seeton, as finally she closed the door of Sweetbriars on an empty, but well-protected home, "can't provide some form of portable studio to visit old people and take a photographic record of their belongings for future reference." She regarded Bob thoughtfully. "An impertinence to suggest it, perhaps, but could the police not organise . . . ?"

"You know, in principle that's a pretty good idea," said Bob, "though not really what the police feel they should be doing. It's our job, unfortunately, to collar the villains after they've done the stealing, though of course we're happy to advise members of the public on crime prevention."

"And what a wicked crime," Miss Seeton said, as the car headed down The Street away from Sweetbriars. "Exploiting a lonely
old person's sense of loneliness and tricking them into absorbing
drugs—how callous that is! For it may well be," said Miss Seeton,
her voice indignant, "that these poor old people are already taking
some form of medication with which the sedatives will disagree.
It might make them seriously ill!" And her eyes shone with disapproval.

Bob said nothing; Delphick had decided she was not to know
of the death of Regimental Sergeant Major Brent unless it was
absolutely necessary. "Let her think she's simply coming to draw
a portrait or two of the female chummies who actually go into the
house. We might try taking her along to Brent's place if there's
time—though we needn't go into details about what happened—
just to see if she can pick up any atmosphere. I can never make
up my mind whether she's psychic or not . . . "

"Such a very boastful, public way of committing robbery, don't
you think?" continued Miss Seeton, leaning forward to speak more
directly into Bob's ear. He must be so bothered about this case:
normally he put her to sit beside him in the front of the car . . . but,
since he had settled her so carefully in the back, she must not disturb him by saying anything. "Swaggering," she went on, "indeed,
one might say defiant, like pirates in the olden days flaunting the
Jolly Roger and daring law-abiding ships to catch them if they
could. Which, being without guns, as far as I recollect from my
reading, of course they could not do, and were rather being chased
and caught themselves. And walking the plank, such a flamboyant gesture, and quite unnecessary, if the pirates had such sharp
swords, or do I mean cutlasses—or maybe," mused Miss Seeton,
seeing sharp metallic curves in her mind's eye, "I mean scimi-
tars . . . "

Bob was still considering her suggestion of pre-robbery photography, and as he drove was daydreaming with that part of his
concentration he could spare. Suppose each town council bought
one camera per a certain head of population, and trained up a town
clerk—he was hazy as to what a town clerk normally did, but
supposed it wasn't vital—to use the thing, and set up a darkroom,
to be paid for from the rates. And then somebody would have
to work out a rota, one street a week, say, and there'd have to
be a strongroom with a good lock for storing the negatives and
duplicates because otherwise all the chummies would have to do
would be burgle the town hall and find out where they could find

the most suitable things to steal . . .

"They'd be sure to find out," he said. Miss Seeton leaned forward again. "Indeed they would, but not until they had hoisted the skull and crossbones, I suppose," she said, "although my knowledge of that period of history is somewhat vague, Long John Silver and the _Hispaniola_, such a graceful, romantic name—but then ships always are, aren't they? Which is why they're always 'she' instead of it, except, I believe, for submarines, or is that boats? Anyway, it would hardly be before then, without sharp eyesight to read the name on the prow, or is it the bow, of the ship. Would it?"

Bob suddenly came to his full senses and realised that he had no idea what she was talking about. "You could well be right," he hedged, and then, before she had time to reply: "Good lord! I'm so sorry, Aunt Em, to have stuck you in the back like that—I wasn't thinking straight." He glanced in the driving mirror, flipped on his indicator, and slowed down into the side of the road.

"Come and sit next to me," he invited, mentally kicking himself for not having noticed before. "Why didn't you let me know? I was busy wondering if your idea would work," he explained, as Miss Seeton moved around into the front seat. She regarded him questioningly.

"About the pirates?" she asked, and he uttered a harsh laugh as the car pulled away again.

"Pirates is one word for them, yes. But I think you had a better feel for it when you called them vultures. Picking their way through old folks' belongings, and using such a nasty trick, too. Promise me," he said hastily, "that you're not going to let anybody strange help you home with your shopping, or—well, no, you wouldn't need helping to cross the road, would you?"

"Indeed I would not," returned Miss Seeton proudly, with thoughts of _Yoga and Younger Every Day_ very much in her mind and a glow of satisfaction as she considered her knees.

"Good. I don't like to say so, but there are times when you—when anyone—can be too trusting . . . "

"We're trusting to you, Miss Seeton," said Chief Superintendent Delphick, "to give us a little more of a line on this crowd than we've managed to get so far. The old folk are upset, bewildered. We try to gentle them along, send a woman police officer to talk to them and help them remember what they can of how the villains looked, but of course they don't remember much. One or two of your sketches . . . " With a smile, he indicated the flat case which Sergeant Ranger had set beside Miss Seeton's chair.

Miss Seeton looked slightly anxious as she replied, "Of course, I will certainly do my best to help, for as I explained to . . ." She hesitated. Did one acknowledge one's adopted aunthood when discussing what was, after all, a professional police matter with one's nephew's professional superior? Perhaps, she reflected, one did not. "To the dear sergeant here," she supplied brightly, and Bob blushed as Delphick favoured him with a quick look.

"You see," said Miss Seeton, "of course I am entirely used to life classes, and to still life, and portraits and abstracts, but . . . but I am not entirely sure of my ability to produce what I believe you want, which must be a portrait of the, the criminal—" she frowned—"drawn entirely from a description, of someone I have not seen—and I do so prefer to draw only what is there, or has been, but of course I was not there to see it, or them . . . " She coughed delicately. "I rather fear," said Miss Seeton, "that it may not result in the quality of picture for which you hope. And for identification purposes, it may be of no use—although naturally, I deplore such wicked, callous behaviour, such lack of respect for a person's privacy and dignity. I shall be glad to do all I can to assist you, but I should not wish you to be too disappointed . . . "

She gazed at Delphick with a worried look in her eyes, to which he was quick to respond. "I understand exactly," he said. "I feel the same way, too—about the callousness of it all. And I want to catch them, and, so far, all we know about them is that they're just an ordinary bunch of people, two women, one man, could be anyone. You have a real gift for drawing those little sketches that give us the impression of who we're after, not an exact likeness. We don't need a routine portrait, just the atmosphere, the feeling. Remember," he smiled at her, "how you and I and Sergeant Ranger—" with a wink—"first met? You sketched me the Covent Garden killer and we knew at once who he was. Even the sergeant," nodding in Bob's direction, "who isn't what you'd call artistic, recognised him."

"But," said Miss Seeton, "I had seen him, you see, and these poor people will have to describe these others to me, which is bound to distress them, when I have not. Seen them—the others, I mean."

Delphick decided to be a little stern with her, before she worked herself up into a state about not producing the goods for him, and sent her emanations or whatever they were completely skew-whiff. Because it was the emanations which he wanted to make use of, not Miss Seeton's routine skills in portraiture: he wanted one of her flashes of inspiration to inspire him when he looked at the sketches she eventually produced.

"Scotland Yard knows what it's doing, Miss Seeton," said the chief superintendent firmly. "You've no need whatsoever to concern yourself with anything except chatting to this Mrs. Birchanger and drawing what her statement suggests to you. Don't worry about accurate likenesses. You're not a camera, you're an artist. And that's what we pay you for."

Miss Seeton bowed her head in acknowledgement, and in a little embarrassment that Mr. Delphick should think she might be, well, forgetful of her duty. The generous retainer paid to her could never allow her to be that . . . but from the twinkle in his eye she could tell he was not really scolding her, merely reminding her there was work to be done, and that by her wish to be conscientious and explain she was guilty of taking up police time. Miss Seeton blushed.

"Very well," she said, rising to her feet. "When you are ready to leave, Chief Superintendent, then so am I!"

# chapter

## ~9~

DELPHICK HAD TAKEN great pains to study each file on all the earlier Sherry Gang cases, and his in-tray had mysteriously cloned itself a twin, overflowing as dramatically as its brother. His out-tray had as mysteriously vanished: there was no room for it on the chief superintendent's desk. Bob Ranger's desk, however, in a yet more mysterious fashion boasted two out-trays and one dangerously full in-tray, which loomed over his telephone and always seemed to be in the way. This, said Delphick, was a fair division of labour; he did not ask what the sergeant's opinion was.

"I think I've found just the one we're looking for," he informed Bob with relief, after reading through a dozen or more accounts that were distressingly familiar. Uniformed police officers first on the scene all reported the old folk dizzy, confused, and unable to help; detectives, arriving when in theory the victims should have calmed down and the drug was out of their systems, reported no great breakthrough. By the time they were sufficiently calm, their recollections were hazy, to say the least; and interviews of shop assistants or others who ought to have witnessed the skilful pickup of the marks were also unhelpful. "Didn't really notice her . . . nothing special to look at . . . just like anyone else, I suppose . . . "

Which was what the hardened policeman expected from the all-observant and cooperative public, and what the Sherry Gang had evidently bargained for. Their very ordinariness made them invisible, like Chesterton's postman; and they had guessed, as well, that their victims would remember little and be able to communicate less.

57

In every case but one, they had guessed correctly. But Mrs. Birchanger was different. "With a vengeance," Delphick told Bob, grinning. "And I use the word advisedly." For it might have been the Sherry Gang's big mistake when they met Elsie Birchanger outside the supermarket and offered to help her home with her heavy bag of groceries.

Elsie was voluble and vindictive. "Like to get me hands on the bleeders, I would," she informed the constable who took her statement. "Never in all me born days did I dream of such a thing, and what Mr. Birchanger would say if he'd been spared, I wouldn't care to repeat." She primmed her lips and looked wise. Her gaze drifted meaningfully towards a large photograph in a plastic frame on the sideboard: a man with a Crippen moustache, who looked scarcely capable of thinking, let alone uttering, unrepeatable thoughts. Elsie scowled at the doubtful expression on the young constable's face. "Oh, a regular devil he could be, could Birchanger, when he'd the drink in him. And stand for any nonsense? Not him! If he'd known what them bleeders was up to with their *Do let me help you with that heavy shopping bag, dear,* and coming right into the house offering me a glass of sherry, I can't tell you what he'd have said to them. Unless," she reflected in some honesty, "he was sober. Which he weren't, to speak of, much. And the sherry, that wouldn't have been enough to stop him, drugs or not. But there it is . . ." And she produced an artistic sigh. "He weren't here to protect me, his better half, all them years married and when the time come when he mighter been of some use at last, well, it were too late."

The young constable longed to ask what she was talking about, but decided it was better left unquestioned. Elsie Birchanger, he thought, would not be an easy woman to be married to: he wondered what the late Mr. Birchanger's death certificate gave as the cause. If suicide appeared in the printed box it would come as no surprise.

*Angry rather than upset,* he wrote across the top of the interview form; and it was upon this that Delphick pounced. "She doesn't sound like the weeping and wailing sort, Bob—she'll be able to come up with something, I feel it in my bones. Although what she'll make of Miss Seeton—and what on earth Miss Seeton will make of her . . ."

He had telephoned Elsie to make his unusual request. He was from Scotland Yard, the big time, was he, well, it was no more than she thought her due, given that she paid her taxes with the best and hadn't Mr. Birchanger done the same all those years, with never a murmur, so she was glad to see that at last it was paying off and she'd be getting a decent return for all that money, one of the high-ups coming to sort out what the local coppers couldn't cope with, only they were too proud to say so and what reason they'd got to be so full of themselves she really couldn't say, seeing as it wasn't the first time this had happened, was it, not by a long chalk, yet the police no nearer catching the bleeders as had done it as they'd been the first time, were they?

"I'm afraid we're not, Mrs. Birchanger," Delphick agreed cheerfully. "Which is why we're asking you for your help."

Elsie was intrigued. "An artist? To draw what I tell her? But I looked at all them photographs for you—well, for them other coppers, anyhow. And not a flicker of a likeness did I see, search as I might. You wouldn't be wasting my time, would you?"

"I hope not, Mrs. Birchanger. It's *because* you couldn't spot a likeness in any of the photos that we'd like to bring the artist along to talk to you, so that she can as we might say develop whatever you can tell her into a more realistic portrait. Miss Seeton is very skilful. With luck, you may be able to help us a great deal."

Elsie pondered. It was a flattering thought that there was at last to be someone hanging on her every word as she recounted her recent experience: the local paper hadn't been nearly interested enough, saying she wasn't the first—this had rankled until she felt she had a genuine grievance, as Delphick had heard—and so only worth a paragraph or two on an inside page, and no photo. Perhaps this artist might agree to do a proper picture of Elsie Birchanger, as well as likenesses of them thieving bitches. Look nice, that would, over the mantelpiece where her prized silver teapot used to stand . . . Wait. Teapot—now, might that mean . . . ?

"What time would you be thinking of bringing her along?" she asked in a wary tone. "I'm not making cups of tea or fixing to cook a meal, not with *my* knees, I'm not!"

"At whatever time would be most convenient to you," said Delphick quickly, in his most reassuring voice, although at the other end of the telephone his eyes danced. "And if you would care to join us for a quick bite of something, either before or after the interview, I'm sure Miss Seeton and I would be glad of your company."

Mollified—evidently the copper didn't expect her to pay out good money on feeding him and this artist—Elsie was about to grumble out her acceptance of the proposal when memory flashed bold headlines before her mind's eye. "Miss Seeton, did I hear you say?" she demanded. "Her what gets in the papers as the Battling Brolly? Coming here with a bloke from Scotland Yard to talk to me?"

And as Delphick admitted that it was the very same Miss Seeton, Elsie resolved that all the neighbours should learn of her approaching apotheosis. She, too, would be written and read about in *Anyone's*! She would be the envy of everybody—and it wouldn't cost her a penny. Almost as good, reflected Mrs. Birchanger with pleasure, as being on the telly . . .

The reality of Miss Seeton startled Elsie Birchanger as much as it always startled those who had only read about her exploits, and had never met her. The photographs Elsie had seen (front page, large, smudgy black-and-white) looked, as they always did, like anybody except their subject. But certainly she'd got the idea, from what she'd read, that Miss Seeton ought to have been—well, bigger, somehow. Not a poor little shrimp of a thing in stockings as grey as her hair, and looking like a puff of strong wind would tumble her to the ground. Elsie pondered her own comfortable bulk, and felt pleased. *She* knew what proper feeding meant, which is more than this Miss Seeton evidently did, for all she was supposed to be so clever, though if she'd ever caught herself a man she'd have had a different tale to tell. The only way to keep a man, through his stomach, never mind what people said—and the cheek of that doctor, saying it was his heart as took poor Birchanger and she ought to've kept him to a diet. Even if he *did* slow down a bit towards the end, not that he'd ever been much use in a married way of speaking right from the disappointment of the honeymoon, at least he'd died happy, Elsie had seen to that. And kept the death certificate, with *Apoplectic fit resulting from over-eating* written clearly in the box marked "Cause," out of sight and out of mind.

Elsie had a good appetite, and Delphick watched in some awe as she chomped her way through a full three-course lunch in startling contrast to Miss Seeton, who declined a starter and asked for a half-portion entree. "So warm today," Miss Seeton murmured, resolving to have plain ice cream for her dessert. Bob Ranger sat wondering whether he or Elsie, who must have weighed almost as much as himself while lacking eighteen inches of his height, would make the longer column on the chief superintendent's subsequent expenses chit. His calculations as the meal continued so unnerved him that when the pudding arrived, he found himself declining it.

Delphick glanced quickly at his sergeant, and followed Bob's troubled gaze to Elsie's plate, on which the waitress had just installed a helping of jam rolypoly with custard. The sight of all 'those calories made Bob long to loosen his tie, while Miss Seeton turned slightly pale. But Elsie was delighted with her choice: filling, and free!

Back at her house, she took her time removing her bulk from the shining police car for the full benefit of all the curtain-twitchers. She'd half hoped that the local paper might after all have sent someone, but perhaps a photograph wouldn't be as swanky as she'd thought, with Miss Seeton the wispy little scrap she'd turned out to be, hardly worth the bother. But the chief superintendent seemed to think a lot of her, so Elsie wasn't going to carp—not unless they had the cheek to expect a cup of tea or anything, when they'd had coffee (three cups, she'd had) at the restaurant. And if that was how the police did themselves every day, Elsie was a bit surprised they needed a Miss Seeton or anyone else to help them. They ought to be healthy enough to catch any number of villains, eating as well as that.

But they weren't catching them, were they? Not the lot the papers were calling the Sherry Gang . . .

Now Miss Seeton came into her own. With his deferential positioning of her in a high-backed chair near the window, Delphick intimated that it was her turn to command. From her sketching case she withdrew her block and pencils, setting out all her impedimenta on the table beside her and looking at Elsie with a questioning smile. "Suppose," invited Miss Seeton, "you were to tell me exactly what happened when you first met these women, and how they came home with you. That is, if the memory does not distress you too much," though privately she thought Mrs. Birchanger looked remarkably undistressed, considering the ordeal she'd undergone, those dreadful people drugging her and then hunting high and low throughout the house for things to steal. One realised, of course, that the poor woman was putting a brave face on it and must be suffering under the surface, her nerves . . .

Miss Seeton gazed at Elsie Birchanger and had to admit she'd seldom seen anyone so unsuffering and nerveless. Mrs. Birchanger's chief emotion was clearly anger, which she had suppressed during that delicious—but so filling, she hoped Mr. Delphick didn't feel insulted that she hadn't eaten more, but dear Bob had obviously understood, she could tell—that delicious lunch, and so bad for the digestion, one would suppose, to restrain one's feelings for so long and in such a way. It would do Mrs. Birchanger good to talk about it to one she hoped might be considered a sympathetic listener. She smiled at Mrs. Birchanger and prepared to listen.

"At the greengrocer's, it was," began Elsie, folding her brawny arms across her chest and glowering at the recollection. "Been everywhere else, I had, got everything bar my spuds and some green veg, but there was only the one girl behind the counter instead of two, like usual, so it took me longer than I thought, and when I come out that bleeding bus was heading up the road away from the stop, wasn't it? So I knew I'd have to wait a good half-hour for the next, with my knees not being up to the walk and having a bus-pass anyway, shame not to make use of it when the council's given it me, that's what I always think."

Miss Seeton nodded, and made a brief note on her pad to remind herself, once the official part of the afternoon was over, to mention the invaluable help her own knees had found among the pages of *Yoga and Younger Every Day*. Perhaps Mrs. Birchanger could benefit as she had done? Although, it had to be said that more benefit might be obtained if she were to lose a little weight, though one's feeling was that personal remarks of such a nature were not only impertinent, but likely to meet with rejection of no matter what sensible suggestion might accompany them. She would simply give Mrs. Birchanger the title of the book, then leave the rest to her good sense.

Chief Superintendent Delphick leaned forward as he saw Miss Seeton with her pencil in her hand, scarcely looking at the sketching block. At times like these she produced her most valuable drawings—but not, he soon realised, now. He sat too far away to make out exactly what she was doing, but it seemed that she just jotted down a few words without much effort and nodded to Elsie to continue: which Elsie did.

"Half an hour to wait, and me with three bags of shopping, and not a soul I knew to ask a lift off. I was that cross! Specially when the woman as had been in front of me and so slow at choosing what she wanted, she'd got into a car parked on them double yellow lines with a disabled sticker on it, and her no more disabled than what I am, with my knees, and what do the council do about it? I'll tell you, nothing is what they do, and people parking all over the show just as they fancy, getting in everyone's way and upsetting the bus timetables. Because that's what she said, this other woman as come along with what I took to be her daughter, walking from the centre of town they were, and it was the bus *before* I'd seen, they said, running late, lots of traffic hold-ups there were, and no idea when the proper bus'd be along. And me having to stand there with my poor knees, and the sun scorching hot enough for July!"

She glared round at her interested audience. "Well now, I ask you—what would *you* have done, if you'd have been me? When they was offering me a lift to my very door!"

"I imagine," remarked Miss Seeton quietly, "that you were grateful to them for their kindness, and accepted the offer as anyone would, in similar circumstances." She did not notice Bob Ranger's look as she added, "I'm sure in my own case I would have accepted just as you did, because who will suspect anyone of doing a kindly act from such sinister motives?" She went slightly pink. "It seems so . . . such a shame to be so mistrustful—"

"Catch me trusting anyone like that again!" broke in Mrs. Birchanger. "I'd not trust 'em as far as I could throw the bleeders, if as far as that, believe you me. Helped me and me bags right into the house. Set them down over there in the hall," with a directional nod, "and even asked if I'd like 'em to unpack and put away for me! But I said no," she added grimly, "what with not caring for strangers poking and prying about the place . . . "

For the first time a flicker of emotion other than anger crossed Elsie's face, but it was soon gone. "The bleeders did all the poking and prying they wanted, didn't they? Got me asleep as quick as a wink. *You still look a little weary, dear. How about a pick-me-up from this bottle of sherry we just bought down the off-licence.* And away I went, after only one sip and no more than that passing my lips, which is the honest truth." Elsie looked fiercely at Miss Seeton. "And powerful stuff, it must have been. I could've been killed!"

It occurred to Delphick that anyone with such an eye for a bargain as Elsie Birchanger would be unlikely to have held herself to only one sip. She probably drained the glass and asked for a refill, though you'd never get her to admit it—which meant she could indeed have had a narrow escape. The fate of the late Regimental Sergeant Major Brent was in his mind as he looked from Miss Seeton—what was it she'd just scribbled on her sketching pad?—to Elsie Birchanger, and back again.

Miss Seeton was looking troubled. Such a pity that by their unpleasant behaviour these people had destroyed Mrs. Birchanger's faith in human nature, or perhaps only for a short while, but anything one could do to help improve matters one would, naturally, be pleased to perform, but—well, the chief superintendent would not wish to see her first sketch, of Mrs. Birchanger standing on her head in the classic yoga pose which one had found so very helpful, if a little difficult at first . . .

She brought herself back to the present with an effort, but Elsie's complaining did not sound very different from what she had been saying before one drifted off into that inconvenient daydream. Nevertheless, Miss Seeton had to be sure she had missed nothing of importance: the chief superintendent would expect it.

She cleared her throat. Mrs. Birchanger broke off, and stared at her. Was the funny little soul going to say something important at last, and get down to business?

"Perhaps," suggested Miss Seeton, with an anxious eye on Delphick, "we could try to draw the likenesses of these two ladies now. For instance, which—"

"Ladies, you call 'em?" Elsie uttered a sharp bark of scornful laughter. "Not them! Proper tramps, they were, and to call 'em bitches is insulting dogs, that's what."

"Well," persisted Miss Seeton, "perhaps we could try to draw their likenesses, anyway. Two women, I understand, and of course one would be so much less inclined to suspect two when they appeared to be mother and daughter, a perfectly normal little shopping expedition . . . suppose we begin with whichever it was who first spoke to you?"

Elsie admitted that it was the older one. Looked just like anyone else, she did, in an old-fashioned kind of way, not so many people nowadays being given to head scarves and hair curlers, but done her best to smarten herself up, she had, with lipstick and earrings and at least she weren't wearing slippers in the street, which was a habit Elsie couldn't abide, being so slovenly, which if she'd looked it there wasn't any way she'd have accepted a lift in the first place . . .

What did the woman actually look like? Elsie was vague at first: dark hair, what she could see of it, and her eyes were dark, too, but that could have been the makeup, clever ways some people had with it, though Elsie didn't hold with painting her face, herself, being pleased with what the Lord had given and ungrateful to act otherwise . . .

Elsie talked, and Miss Seeton listened, nodding encouragement and from time to time putting questions. Suddenly, before Mrs. Birchanger's busy tongue had stilled, there was a further sketch on the top sheet of Miss Seeton's block—

A female pirate chief, her cutlass in her hand, complete with black eyepatch and dangling earrings and a scarf tied over her head.

She stood, one foot resting on a wooden cask, on the deck of her pirate ship, indicated by a few swift lines from Miss Seeton's pencil. Behind her clustered her pirate crew, hastily drawn and shown mostly by shadows, though two of the figures were more distinct: one male, one female.

Two women, one man, a flamboyant group of pirates . . . or had Miss Seeton simply not felt like drawing the vultures?

# chapter
# ~10~

RUMOURS OF MISS Seeton's arrest in connection with the Dick Turpin robbery witnessed, and experienced, by the Nuts were flying around Plummergen with even more exaggeration than usual. The previous inhabitant of Sweetbriars, Old Mrs. Bannet, had never done one part of the many strange and suspicious things her god-daughter and heir—at least, that's who she said she was, but with that crooked solicitor who'd handled the estate you could never be sure, could you?—got involved in, far too often, and far too deep.

"Rubbish," retorted Martha Bloomer, when this argument was put to her. "She'd been visiting the old lady on and off for years before Mrs. Bannet died, and I ought to know if anyone did, doing for them both as I have for so long. Was it either of them's fault if the solicitor wasn't all he ought to have been?"

Mrs. Spice was not appeased. "You'll not try to deny, I hope, that there's been some odd goings-on since Miss Seeton came to live in the village. Witchcraft, for one—" Martha snorted in disgust—"not to mention the fight all along the Street with them motorbike riders, and the burglaries, and that poor little kiddie being killed, and the drugs—"

"And why should Miss Seeton be blamed for any of that?" demanded Martha, but Mrs. Spice, wilfully deaf, continued her glum recital.

"Then there was the robbery at the post office, say what you will, that business with the cheese was suspicious, never mind Mr. Stillman denying it, but there *she* was again—"

"Rubbish, and slander, too!" exploded Martha Bloomer, favouring Mrs. Spice with a very hard look. "I suppose next you'll be saying how Miss Seeton buried that poor soul in the bunker, and committed the murder as well!"

But even Mrs. Spice could not pin that particular crime—if crime it was, being so far only on Plummergen's suspect list—on Miss Seeton, much though she would have liked to. Old Mrs. Bannet may have lived in the village since the start of the century, but her young cousin (if cousin she was, Mrs. Bloomer doing for the family or not) had not begun to visit her until several years after the last war, when the bunker murder (if murder it was) had taken place, and Miss Seeton was an even younger woman. Had she at any relevant time paid a visit to her cousin Flora, Plummergen would have noticed (being always on the alert for German spies) and remembered—Plummergen does not readily forget.

The bunker referred to was in the garden of Old Mother Dawkin's cottage, as it was still known. Old Mother Dawkin had finally died earlier that spring—some insisted that it was from grief at the loss of Dozey, her smelly Peke; others that she had never fully recovered from her exertions on that momentous night when the entire village went to exorcise the disused church at Iverhurst. And her death had resulted in an interesting problem for Plummergen gossip . . .

The vicar's sister was pouring tea. Arthur should have been there: but he was late, which was nothing new. Molly Treeves was sometimes a little vexed with her brother, although generally she didn't bother: life was, after all, too short to waste it in nagging for changes in someone's nature which were simply an impossible dream. And he was happy pottering about Plummergen on his pastoral round; she hoped he would long remain so. Provided none of his parishioners guessed at what she, with her sibling's instinct, had guessed—that he had lost his faith—then long might his absentminded happiness continue.

There was a clattering at the door, and the Reverend Arthur Treeves appeared. He blinked at the teapot in his sister's hand. "Dear me. Is it so late? I had no idea. I have been talking with the new young couple in Mrs. Dawkin's cottage, such a pleasant pair—Clavering, was the name? Manuden, I think, perhaps." The Reverend Arthur frowned. "Or possibly Albury, I forget—but a pleasant young couple, indeed."

Molly sighed briefly as she handed her brother his cup, but there was little point in wishing he would pay more attention.

"Manuden," she said, jogging his wayward memory. "They came to church on Sunday and introduced themselves at the end of the service, don't you remember? Betsy and Dennis, they asked to be called."

A smile lit his face. "Yes, of course! And Dennis is a splendid young fellow—somewhat older than his wife, I might have said, if that would not be an impertinence, but they do seem remarkably happy together, and he is intent on building his bride a proper home, even if they are only to live among us for the few months of summer. I fear that Mrs. Dawkin did not have your gift for running a household," said the vicar, blinking fondly at his sister. "Mrs.—er, Betsy, spoke of cobwebs and dust in a manner that disturbed me greatly—to think that a parishioner of mine should have lived in such squalor during her latter years!"

"The Manudens come from London," remarked Molly drily.

Arthur blinked at her again. "Do they? Yes, I suppose they do—at least I believe Dennis said something of the sort. A breath of fresh air, he said, something about his wife having been ill and needing the country life to help her convalesce."

"She looks healthy enough to me, but that would explain why they're making such a fuss about a few cobwebs. People from the city don't understand people from the country, and they expect it to be all thatched roofs and roses round the door and chickens pecking happily in the yard—"

"He said nothing about keeping chickens," the Reverend Arthur murmured with a frown. "Indeed, under the terms of the lease, I'm not at all sure that chickens could be kept."

"Really, Arthur! I was simply trying to explain that in the city life everything is, well, more *sterilised*, if that is the correct word. Milk comes in bottles, not from cows, and eggs arrive with a lion stamped on them, neatly packed in cardboard trays."

Why was Molly now saying that the Claverings *were* going to keep chickens—and a cow, as well? "Surely there is not enough room in the garden for so much livestock," protested Arthur, trying to envisage the size of Mrs. Dawkin's little patch of land. Dozey had never complained about lack of space, but a Peke probably didn't require much room. A cow, on the other hand . . .

"Who said anything about livestock?" enquired Molly, and smiled grimly. "If the Manudens are planning to set up a small-holding, they'll have their work cut out. Remember who their neighbours are! Miss Nuttel and Mrs. Blaine wouldn't care for it at all, I'm sure. What sort—" she fixed Arthur with a stern eye—"of livestock did they say?"

The vicar rocked back in his chair, and a few drops of tea splashed into his saucer. "They didn't say," he said, "at least I don't think so. I thought *you* did. And surely it was *I* who said that the lease would not permit it?"

Molly decided to give it up as a bad job: just another of Arthur's misunderstandings. She would visit the Manudens herself as soon as she could find time, to learn exactly what they intended to do while they were in Plummergen. She knew she couldn't rely on her brother to tell her anything accurate: she'd been foolish to expect it of him.

But she was mistaken. Thirstily, the vicar finished his tea, spilling hardly any drops from the bottom of the cup on his clerical grey trousers. He dusted himself down with an air of satisfaction and reached for a digestive biscuit.

"Such good news," he said with a smile. "Mister, that is to say, Dennis, has had a very clever idea for the church roof. He tells me, and I believe him, that he is rather a handyman about the place."

"Good gracious, he can't be volunteering to repair that roof singlehanded—it's far too dangerous, apart from any other considerations. *Any* roof needs a professional builder—working so high up—and a church is even higher."

"High church?" Arthur looked shocked. Was Molly, after all these years, about to profess leanings towards incense, candles, and elaborate vestments? Was she—he blanched—expecting him to conduct services in Latin?

"Oh, Arthur," sighed his sister. "Tell me about Dennis Manuden instead. What is his clever idea?"

Celibacy, reflected the vicar, as he crunched a thoughtful biscuit, would of course to him be no particular hardship, but even so—

"Arthur! What—did—Dennis—Manuden—say?"

He was so startled by the sternness of her tone that he answered at once. "A way to raise some of the money," he said, choking slightly on a crumb. "He thought it a great pity that the lead had all been stolen, otherwise we could have sold it for the silver content and the cost of reroofing would have been negligible, he said." He blinked. "It makes sound sense, does it not?"

"Not particularly. If that lead hadn't been stolen in the first place, then the roof wouldn't need repairing. If all he had to say was as helpful as that, you needn't bother to tell me the rest."

"Oh, dear, not at all. He says we have somehow to raise the money, and asked whether the summer fete was likely to be a source of income."

"Income, yes. Enough income, no." Molly Treeves smiled grimly. "It would take a century of fetes to earn enough to pay for the roof, judging by previous efforts. Which means that we do need clever ideas, I agree, so for goodness' sake tell me what he said, Arthur." And Molly hoped that it would be worth hearing, after the trouble she'd had urging him to explain.

"I told you, didn't I, that he's by way of being a handy sort of person about the house—and garden?" Molly nodded, but said nothing. The Reverend Arthur was getting into his stride now; and with relaxation usually came some idea of what he was really trying to communicate. "And, while his wife, a dear little woman, is attending to the house—" the vicar beamed at this vision of domesticity—"her husband plans to tidy the garden."

"If he's offering to work as a jobbing gardener, around here he isn't likely to earn enough to keep him in leather gloves and whetstones, let alone to help pay for the roof. No doubt it's a kind thought," said Molly, "but certainly not as practical as I'd hoped."

She prepared to collect the tea things together. It was a shame to dampen her brother's enthusiasm, but if she left him to bubble for too long unchecked, he was all the more disappointed when realisation finally came. "Perhaps," she began, "the insurance, after all—"

"Oh dear, no." It was so unusual for him to interrupt her that Molly stared. This idea, whatever it was, really had caught his imagination. She'd better be ready with her full powers of dissuasion . . .

"No," repeated the Reverend Arthur, for once on certain ground. "Not gardening—that is, not outside what we might call his own garden, at least for these few months of summer—he will be gardening there, he assures me. Indeed, he has already begun, this very morning—by clearing away the mass of brambles which poor Mrs. Dawkin had allowed to grow at the far end . . . " At her little cry of exasperation, he stared.

"What is the matter, Molly? Why should he not tidy the garden? It seems an admirable scheme to me."

Anyone but Arthur would have realised at once. "Because if he tidies the brambles away," Molly Treeves said, slowly, as if to an irritating child, "he will uncover that bunker. And you know what everyone will say once they remember." Or maybe he didn't, being Arthur—being the vicar.

The vicar of Plummergen.

But Molly Treeves, the vicar's sister, knew very well what Plummergen would say if the air-raid bunker reappeared from its long hibernation beneath the brambles. The war may have ended a quarter of a century ago and more, but gossip in Plummergen never really forgets . . .

# chapter
# -11-

AND PLUMMERGEN HAD indeed not forgotten. It had always, deep down, harboured suspicions, but during the lifetime of Old Mother Dawkin it had not seemed politic to mention them, she having rather too uncomfortable a knowledge of certain more serious scandals than that which concerned her family. What she could have told about, well, about things better left unsaid, was too worrisome to risk the telling. She could have spilled the beans, right enough— and those beans would have jumped sky high.

But when it was safe at last, the whispers had begun. Even those who generally ignored Plummergen gossip could not help but hear them: the whispers were more like the blasts of tremendous brazen trumpets.

"I was in the post office this morning," remarked Lady Colveden, spooning vegetables from a dish with casual grace. She looked vaguely round to see what response her remark had elicited. "I said," she repeated, when no response appeared forthcoming, "that I was in the post office this morning."

"We heard you, Mother darling." Nigel grinned at her as she passed him the loaded plate. He looked at the newspaper opposite, behind which sat, he supposed, his father, though all that was visible of Major-General Sir George Colveden, Bart, KCB, DSO, JP, was a pair of hands, one on either side of the broadsheet. "At least," amended Nigel, "I did," and he lifted the bottom of the newspaper to slide his father's plate underneath. The newspaper rustled its thanks.

Nigel accepted his own plate with more audible thanks, and energetically began to attack his meal. Nigel was too hungry, the force of his attack made plain, to press Lady Colveden with questions: if she felt there was anything the male side of the family needed to know, she would have to come right out with it.

"You are a very provoking pair," said Lady Colveden, and over-peppered her vegetables in irritation. "Aren't you the least bit interested in what they're saying in the village? And now look what you've made me do!"

Through a mouthful of spluttering peas, her only son made his amusement plain. The newspaper wavered, and as the wife of its reader sneezed for the second time was lowered.

"Bless you, m'dear." Sir George caught his son's eye, and winked, then coughed, and directed his attention to his plate. "Tasty piece of lamb, this," he said. "Stillman's, I suppose? Well stocked, for a post office."

Meg Colveden completed the discreet blowing of her nose, and picked up her knife and fork, waving the knife in her husband's direction. "George, if I stabbed you, nobody would blame me. My defence would be utter provocation, and they'd let me off without a murmur. You know perfectly well I wouldn't have told you I went to the post office simply to buy the meat."

Nigel's first hunger pangs having abated, he was able to turn part of his attention to his exasperated parent. "You are clearly bursting with news, Mother, so why not just tell us without waiting to be asked? We busy farmers rely on the gossip to come to us, not us having to go after the gossip."

"Nigel's right," put in her husband, spearing a potato with his fork. "Haven't the time to hang around shops—you do it instead. And no need to stab me, either. Not worth a prison sentence for the sake of a few wild rumours."

"There are certainly rumours," agreed Lady Colveden, and looked fondly from husband to son. How alike they were! If they seriously thought she was hiding anything from them, it would upset them dreadfully: but, manlike, they had to make a pretence of not caring one way or the other. "Going back before we came to live in Plummergen, too," she went on.

"And you've only just heard them? Honestly, Mother, you should listen harder." Nigel shook his head. "I suppose it might have been really important once, before Julia or I were born—but twenty-five years is a long time. It can't matter very much now."

"That's where you're mistaken," said his mother. "Even after all these years—thirty, not twenty-five, it happened during the war—the whole village is buzzing with it."

"Plummergen's buzzing," grinned Nigel, "and you, Mother dear, are bursting, as I said before. So, come on—better late than never. What are they saying, and about what?"

"Old Mrs. Dawkin," she began. Sir George snorted.

"Woman's dead and buried, thank goodness. Don't care to speak ill of the dead, especially a woman, but evil-minded—sharper tongue than the rest of 'em put together."

"That's why nobody's said anything until now, George, when they think it's safe. They were always afraid that if they talked about the Dawkin scandal, Mrs. Dawkin would start talking about *them*. And by all accounts she knew an awful lot that people wouldn't care to have known."

Nigel frowned as he helped himself to further vegetables and passed the dish to his father. "And now you've found out what it was she knew? Well, it can't have been anything about me, because I wasn't born until years after the war, and it can't have been about Miss Seeton, which will certainly make a change. Sometimes I wonder what the tabbies used to talk about before she came to live here and things started happening."

"Of course it isn't about either of you, though I think it's ridiculous for them to keep on about poor Miss Seeton the way they do, and perhaps this will take their minds off her for a while. She'd be so upset if she heard some of the things they've dreamed up about her."

"You don't," remarked Nigel, "seem to be worried that I might be upset by whatever they dream up about me."

"You're young enough to look after yourself. Poor Miss Seeton retired several years ago, remember, even if she did take early retirement." Lady Colveden began collecting the empty plates. "Mind you, she's remarkably fit for her age, and since she took up bicycling she's even more—"

"Mother, please!" Nigel clattered the lid of the vegetable dish in frantic tattoo. "Don't drift away like that—and don't try to tell us the village is up in arms about Miss Seeton's bike, and that La Dawkin predicted the whole business over thirty years earlier. I won't believe it."

Lady Colveden tried to sound cross. "You'd be extremely silly to believe anything of the sort. How could Mrs. Dawkin predict anyone like Miss Seeton? She's, well, unique." She paused for a moment to reflect on this word's inadequacy. "No, what seems to have set them all by the ears is this business about the body in the bunker."

Sir George, who had picked up his newspaper some moments earlier, lowered it to enquire: "Somebody dead on the golf course? Anyone we know?"

"Really, George! Do listen. I'm trying to tell you the whole thing, and all you and Nigel do is egg each other on to confuse me. Don't you want to hear?" She began to carry the pile of plates through to the kitchen; Nigel followed, with the dishes on a tray. His father smoothed the sheets of newsprint into a tidy shape and deposited it to one side of the table, then hurried after his wife and son to assist in the transport of coffeepot and cups.

"So, no body in the bunker, then. Misunderstood," said Sir George, fiddling with the spoons. "But you *did* mention someone dead, didn't you? And nothing to do with Miss Seeton? Makes a change, of course."

"Just for that, George, you can carry the tray for me, and Nigel can unload it. Then I shall hit one or other of you with it for being so annoying." Lady Colveden preceded her family back into the dining room, then whisked round to catch father and son grinning at each other. With muted smiles, they took their places at the table, Sir George casting longing eyes at the newspaper, which his wife had calmly moved out of reach before pouring the coffee.

"Now, this body, Mother," prompted Nigel. "You know you can hardly wait to tell us all about it. *It* sounds wrong, somehow— a bit callous . . . a male body, or a female?"

"Susannah Dawkin," said Lady Colveden in triumph, and stirred half a spoonful of sugar into her cup.

"I've never heard of her," said Nigel, after a pause.

"Thought her name was something far more outlandish," volunteered his father. "Hepsibah, Theodosia—Susannah's a pretty normal handle for a woman like that."

"Her name was Delilah. Delilah Dawkin—I'm surprised anyone, even you, George, could have forgotten. Susannah was her son's wife's name, and when she died they called the baby after her. And *she's* the Susannah who is supposed to be buried in the air-raid bunker in the Dawkin garden—the bunker those new people, the Manudens, are going to raffle tickets for the winner to open. And of course everyone's remembered the scandal there was at the time."

Nigel grinned. "Raffle tickets? They'd be better off having a treasure hunt, with the body as the trophy. Much more interesting than a policeman's helmet—sorry, Mother," as Lady Colveden reached for the coffee tray. "Do continue, or shall I guess? The

Manudens in La Dawkin's old cottage are hoping to curry favour in the village by raffling the chance to unlock the air-raid bunker—goodness knows why it should be worth raffling, because unless there really is a body there it won't be very interesting, I'd have thought. And if they know that she *is* buried there, I can't think why they haven't done something about it before."

"Mrs. Dawkin's son Albert was rather queer in the head—he suffered from religious mania, and belonged to those odd Holdfast Brethren in Brettenden, from what I gather. He dug himself an enormous air-raid shelter at the bottom of his garden to guard against hellfire, or something, though he never actually used it—and don't snigger like that, Nigel, you know perfectly well what I mean. I mean not even use it as a shed, or for the children to play in on wet afternoons, or anything of the sort."

"But the Dawkin children, or child," suggested Nigel, "didn't live long enough to play in it, anyway? Is that what they're all saying?"

"Typical," snorted his father, clattering his coffee cup in its saucer. Silently, Meg Colveden handed the pot to her son, who gave Sir George a refill and took one himself.

"More or less," she agreed. "Of course, they couldn't ever be absolutely sure Susannah was dead in the first place. There was a tremendous row one night, the whole village heard Queer Albie, that's what they called him, thrashing his daughter when she came home wearing lipstick and nylons and earrings instead of the ghastly costume the Holdfasts still make the poor girls wear. You must have seen them—so ugly and impractical, I'm not surprised Susannah rebelled in the end. She wanted to join the Forces, but he wouldn't let her, not even to save his country." Sir George, the former major-general, snorted once more. "And he used to read the Bible at her for hours, and pray at the top of his voice, in a generally fanatical sort of way, and nobody was a bit surprised when she disappeared, really—they said she'd always talked about going to London, and after the thrashing she'd finally done it. Only nobody ever heard anything from her again. There were rumours she'd died in an air raid, but it seems Queer Albie wouldn't even talk about her to his mother, so nobody really knew. And then, of course, they started wondering whether it hadn't been a bit too much for her—the beating, I mean—and saying that Queer Albie had killed her by mistake, and buried her in the air-raid bunker."

"And they've been saying it ever since, I suppose," said Nigel. "Funny you haven't heard about it before."

"They did start muttering," replied his mother, as Nigel and his father began to look at their watches, "as soon as Delilah Dawkin died, but I could never quite make it out. I expect they didn't feel it was safe to say anything definite until she was well and truly buried. You know how superstitious they are. Look at the way half of them are convinced Miss Seeton's a witch. . ."

"But this time it's the latest newcomers who've stirred things up—the Manudens. Dennis Manuden has taken it on himself to uncover Albert Dawkin's air-raid shelter, and it's locked and bolted, and he's letting the vicar raffle tickets to see who'll win the chance to open the door—for the church roof—and of course they're taking bets on whether there will be a body lying on the floor, or just lots of bits and pieces left over from the war, souvenirs or whatever you care to call them."

"No use trying to live in the past," said her husband, the major-general, DSO. "England's finest hour and all that—history to be proud of, but have to look to the future."

"It will be *interestingly* historical," pointed out his wife, "helmets and gas masks and ration books. Mr. Jessyp is apparently all set to stake the claims of the school museum, if there does turn out to be anything there."

"Apart from a body," Nigel said. "No doubt there might be a ration book—Susannah's, because she wouldn't exactly need it anymore, would she? But I don't see the trustees of the school letting Mr. Jessyp, even if he *is* the headmaster, keep a body in the museum. The police will be keen to stake their claim to the body, if you ask me. Perhaps we should buy a ticket and send it to Superintendent Brinton at Ashford," he suggested, while his father, the Justice of the Peace, tried to recall what he could of coroners' inquests and delayed notification of a death. He frowned.

"All very unfortunate," he said, as his wife was about to warn Nigel to do nothing of the sort. "Rumours enough in this place at the best of times, but bodies in bunkers—bad show. Unhygienic, for one thing. Manuden may come to regret the whole idea very soon, in my opinion."

"The vicar seems enthusiastic about it," Lady Colveden said, "from what I hear. I don't suppose his sister is, though. She has too much common sense. I gather she tried hard to squash the first rumours when they started up again, about the time the Manudens moved in. Her hairstyle didn't help, of course."

Father and son gazed at her in surprise. "Hairstyle," said Sir George, blankly.

"Don't say the vicar's sister has—gasp—dyed her hair and become a painted woman," cried Nigel. "No wonder the gossips of Plummergen are in an uproar!"

Meg Colveden pushed back her chair and rose briskly to her feet. "I can't think what's wrong with you two today, making fun of everything I say. I thought you'd both be interested, and all you do is snigger. Molly Treeves would no more paint her face or dye her hair than—than—"

"Than Miss Seeton would," supplied Nigel, gurgling with mirth. "Or you, Mother dear. But are we to assume that Mrs. Manuden's done just that? I can't say I've noticed anyone outlandish in the village recently."

"She seems to be rather an old-fashioned little thing," said his mother, "from what I've seen, which isn't much. Hardly goes out at all, quiet, speaks only when she's spoken to, dresses quaintly—a definite Forties look, hairstyle—" she glared at Nigel—"included, so I can understand why all the rumours of Susannah's disappearance began. I wonder," she murmured, a thoughtful expression on her face, "if I oughtn't to call on her and welcome her to Plummergen? Just to see how they're settling into the cottage. It was really in rather a sorry state, or so I gather, though the husband is doing splendid work putting things to rights. But he's quite a few years older than she is, so perhaps it's his second marriage and he's taking care not to make the same mistakes as the first time around, not paying attention—" she frowned at her husband—"and never listening to her when she told him what needed doing about the house."

The expressions on the faces of Sir George and his son were identical as they stared at her. It was Nigel who at last managed to find words.

"When did you and Dad first come to live in Plummergen, Mother darling?"

She seemed surprised at this change of subject. "Just after your father came out of the army and we were married. Julia was born here the following year—let me see, 1947, that would have been. Over twenty-five years ago. It was our silver wedding last year, surely you remember that?"

"Of course I do. And—would you say they've been twenty-five happy years? You've fitted into village life without too much difficulty?"

"Don't be silly, Nigel, you know I would. And of course I have. We all have, haven't we? Fitted in, I mean. I'm sure I shouldn't feel comfortable living anywhere else but Plummergen, after so long."

And her undutiful son grinned at her. "Yes, Mother, we thought that's what you'd say. About fitting in with everyone in Plummergen so well . . . "

# chapter

# -12-

DEAD SUSANNAH DAWKIN'S possible discovery upon the bunker's raffled opening had displaced the Nuts' competition win as the major topic of Plummergen conversation. Indeed, Miss Nuttel and Mrs. Blaine might have felt almost aggrieved to be so supplanted, had it not been that the supplanting topic was a scandal of such high quality. They eagerly listened to every speculation from long-time inhabitants, and stirred (once they'd had time to think of something) several ideas of their own into the simmering brew.

But any grievance, however slight, felt by the Nuts was soon dismissed when the most recent Dick Turpin robbery made head-line news on national television. Eric and Bunny were delighted: shocked, but pleasantly so, and the excitement nearly made up for the loss of Bunny's beautiful ring. The leading part they had played—their major role as eye-witnesses—crowds of journalists would rush to interview them, and their photographs would appear in all the newspapers.

As has already been shown, this did not happen: and with what result has also been shown. The Nuts, in short, were sulking. Though they did their best to foment interest in the carriage of Miss Seeton to London by the police, their hearts were not in the business. They were suffering, they decided, from delayed shock, and would feel better with a change of scenery.

"Not Brettenden, Eric, I wouldn't care to be stared at," Mrs. Blaine said, as they sipped the tea brewed from freshly-pulled nettles which was supposed to be so good for the kidneys. Only the tips of the nettle shoots were used, picked by a Miss Nuttel protected by stout gardening gloves, as supplied by Mrs. Welsted at the draper's at a cost of (since decimlisation in February last year) fifty-two-and-a-half new pennies, formerly ten shillings and sixpence. Eric was a keen gardener—utterly organic vegetables, so much better tasting and without the carcinogenic risks of fertiliser . . .

"Could do with some broccoli seeds," mused Miss Nuttel, "and chervil, as well. New handle for the hoe too, perhaps. Buy everything in one place—that shop in Ashford."

"Oh, yes!" Bunny was delighted. "Nobody knows us there so we'll be able to relax. I'm sure a little outing to Ashford is just what we need. My ankle," she added bravely, "probably ought to be able to withstand the strain."

"Bus in forty minutes," Eric said, consulting her watch and for once ignoring Mrs. Blaine's plaintive tones. "String bags, not baskets—easier to carry on the bus."

"Oh, Eric, how sensible," breathed Bunny, forgetting her troublesome ankle, "then we won't have everybody wondering what we're doing. I do dislike the way the entire village seems to interest itself in the affairs of others. Too intrusive, isn't it?"

And Miss Nuttel pursed her lips, looking wise, as Norah Blaine sighed and shook a sorrowful head at the intrusiveness of Plummergen interest.

The Nuts made their escape from prying eyes to Ashford as privately as they professed to wish. They spent a few anxious minutes at Brettenden bus station waiting for their connection, but not a soul who knew them saw them; and they looked smugly about them as they were decanted at Ashford, congratulating each other on the wisdom of their choice.

After full consideration of the proposed outing, Bunny was heard to murmur of a hunt for pillowcases—quite worn through, their old ones, and there was a limit to the number of times she could sides-to-middle sheets, as well. While Eric busied herself at the hardware shop and selected seeds, and a hoe handle, and anything else her gardener's soul might crave, Mrs. Blaine would study the Manchester goods in the town's largest department store, and note down prices for comparison with the stalls on the market.

"Though perhaps," she said in a peevish tone, "we ought to have brought my little basket on wheels, after all. It's so much easier than carrying anything heavy in these silly string bags," shaking hers under Eric's startled nose. Miss Nuttel stared at her.

"Thought you agreed with me it was a good idea. Nobody

knowing what we planned or where we were going—hidden bags in our pockets. Basket on wheels takes up too much room and goes half fare on the bus, as well. Anyway, too late now."

"Yes, Eric, I know," pleaded Bunny, as her friend looked rather crossly upon her, "but I hadn't really had time to think properly about my ankle when we talked about it first, you did rather spring it on me, you know. And I don't see how I can be expected to carry heavy sheets and pillowcases by myself—"

"No need to. Choose what you want, then wait for me."

"But, Eric, you'll have your own shopping to carry. Oh, and I was so looking forward to this little jaunt, but maybe it's a judgement on us for not sticking to Brettenden shops, where they deliver."

"At a price," Erica Nuttel reminded her grimly. "Better value for money here, if you shop wisely, so no need to get in a stew, Bunny."

And she patted her friend briskly on the shoulder before nodding her farewells and heading for the seed and gardening supplies shop at the far end of the street. Mrs. Blaine, her string bag limp in her hand, gazed after her for a few brief moments and then made up her mind. She stuffed the bag into her pocket, and hobbled, sighing, along to the shop where she hoped to find sheets and pillowcases and—if Eric really was going to carry them all for her—maybe towels as well, if the price was right.

She didn't know just how long it would take Miss Nuttel to purchase her requirements, and therefore took care to be limping at all times as she moved from counter to counter, examining quality, price, and colour—very important, with the wrong vibrations the aura of sleep could be totally destroyed, even if the pillow that was encased happened to be stuffed with dried herbs. Not blue, for instance, and pink could only be acceptable in certain shades, closer to the peach end of the range, more natural, of course. Or green, apple-green—but the pink of apple-blossom, if they had it matching in sheeting, was always acceptable . . .

Mrs. Blaine was pottering along in contented calculation when a strange female voice accosted her.

"Are you having trouble walking, dear? You look rather tired, I must say. Does your foot hurt?"

Mrs. Blaine stopped limping and turned. "Why, yes, it *is* troubling me rather. I sprained it the other day, you see, and the swelling simply won't go down. I've tried footbaths and hot poultices—"

"You don't have to tell me!" The young woman shuddered artistically. "All you can do is grin and bear it. I know, only too well. And it's a real pain, isn't it, trying to do things on your own, carrying heavy parcels and trying not to put too much strain on it."

"Oh. Yes, it is." Mrs. Blaine resolved to limp even more once Eric had finally appeared: somebody, she was pleased to see, recognised the sacrifice and inconvenience she'd been put to, coming out like this without proper thought for how she was supposed to carry everything, and her ankle being a nuisance, no matter how Eric told her to stop thinking about it. How could you possibly forget, when you were suffering? "Oh yes, it's a real pain," she agreed.

"You're just about to start your shopping," the young woman said. "Do you want any help? I mean, this is heavy, awkward stuff in here. You could really do with a trolley or a wheel-basket, but if you like I could give you a hand." She shifted her own shopping bag, which bulged in an unusual way, to the other side, and smiled brightly. "I've finished all I came out for. I wouldn't mind helping you, if you had things you wanted and couldn't really manage on your own."

Mrs. Blaine was pleased and flustered. Here was someone who sympathised with an invalid's struggles from counter to counter, with the frustration of not being one hundred percent fit and able to cope, with the awkwardness of shopping for bulky parcels—but wouldn't Eric niggle a bit at her, if she hurried through her own shopping to find that Bunny was managing perfectly well on her own? Eric liked to spend long agreeable minutes choosing things for the garden: she'd be cross if she curtailed her pleasure for her friend's sake and then learned there'd really been no need to rush at all.

"Well, that's very kind of you . . . " began Mrs. Blaine, with a brave smile. The young woman smiled back at her in a very understanding way.

"Just doing my good deed for the day," she said briskly, "so don't you give it another thought. What were you thinking about buying? If we start with the larger things, then pile the others on top as we collect them, it'll be easier for me to carry to the car, you see—"

"The car? But—"

"Now, I told you not to worry about it," the young woman said in a smiling, scolding tone. "Naturally, I'll run you back home. What sort of neighbour would I be if I left you to struggle with your parcels when I've got my car parked just around the corner? And if you didn't think you could manage to walk that far, well, I could pick you up outside the main doors, and I'm sure just this once the traffic wardens would turn a blind eye to the double yellow lines. Not another word," she insisted, as Mrs. Blaine opened her mouth to protest, "about anything, all right? Let's just get on with the shopping. And if there's anywhere else you need to go after here, maybe we could fit that in, as well. I'm not in any particular hurry." And she leaned back against the counter in a grand gesture of exaggerated laziness, yawning and then grinning at a bewildered Mrs. Blaine. As she leaned backwards, her shopping bag knocked against the wood of the counter with a strange, clinking sound.

Bunny was beginning to feel that she was losing control. "It's very kind of you," she repeated, "but there's really no need for you to go to all that trouble. We came by bus, you see, and bought return tickets."

The young woman's expression suddenly changed. "You're not alone, then? With—" her swift glance darted to Mrs. Blaine's left hand—"your husband, are you?"

With Humphrey? Norah Blaine shuddered at the thought of spending any time, voluntarily, in the company of her long-divorced spouse. "With a friend," she said, wishing, not for the first time, that her plumpness did not prevent the removal of her wedding ring. More than once, she and Eric had tried soap, and cold water, and brute force; but on the third finger of Bunny's left hand that golden band remained. A visit to a jeweller would of course result in a charge for cutting the ring, and why should she pay to be freed from her shackles? "My friend Eric," she enlarged, "who's shopping for garden supplies down the road, and ought to be here any minute. I'd like you to meet—"

"Well," interrupted the young woman briskly, "it sounds as if you don't really need my help, doesn't it? Eric can give you a hand with the shopping, and then I can get on with my bits and pieces. I'm a little pushed for time after all, I've just realised. Nice to have met you, though—and I enjoyed our chat. Bye, now!"

And, with a smile which looked somehow slightly forced, her bulky shopping bag still clanking at her side, the young woman waved and hurried away.

Mrs. Blaine blinked after her, then shrugged, primmed her lips, and muttered to herself about how strange some people were. She turned to inspect a further display of sheeting, and decided that perhaps she might try apple green . . .

"Talking to yourself, Bunny?" Erica Nuttel, that tall, thin woman, appeared beside her friend carrying a long, thin parcel wrapped in brown paper. "Still making up your mind? Better not decide finally," she said, with a stern eye fixed on a hovering sales assistant, "until we've checked out the market. Almost bound to be cheaper there."

The assistant, who resented having been called back from her coffee break before she'd finished exchanging gossip and newspapers with her cronies, tossed her head, and flounced back to the far end of the counter. But she kept a watchful eye on the Nuts as they talked, in case they were potential shoplifters. Not easy to slip a cellophane-wrapped parcel of sheets into your bag or under your clothes, but some of these old girls were dead cunning, and it wouldn't do her any harm to collar a pair, not with the bonus scheme coming into operation next week . . .

Mrs. Blaine protested to Eric that she'd been standing on her bad ankle far too long, and would appreciate the chance for a nice sit-down somewhere. "Maybe we could try a cup of tea," she suggested, with a quick look at Miss Nuttel to see how that dedicated vegetarian felt about the idea. "I mean, it would only be just this once, and we needn't use sugar if there's no honey— just this once," and she did her best to look exhausted, leaning lopsidedly against the counter to rest in an unconscious echo of the pose adopted by the young woman who had been so willing to offer her a lift home until she learned that Bunny was not by herself.

Erica Nuttel hesitated. The seed shop had certainly had a slightly dusty atmosphere, and it was a long time since breakfast—and in their hurry to catch the bus, they hadn't thought about making sandwiches or packing a flask—and the next bus back was over an hour away, and in any case Bunny still had shopping to do, it seemed.

"If that's what you really want, Bunny," she said, in the tone of a grudging martyr. "Principles all very well, but needs must, I suppose. Coffee shop on the top floor here, isn't there?"

"And an escalator," beamed Bunny, almost forgetting to limp in her relief that Eric wasn't going to be sticky over her proposal. She must have had a good time and found all the things she wanted. "We'll have our tea black, won't we, unless they have goat's milk, which I doubt," and she went trotting after her friend without sparing another thought for the good Samaritan who had so abruptly vanished from her life. The sales assistant watched them disappear: she had still been having her coffee in the canteen upstairs when the young woman had been talking to Mrs. Blaine, so there had been no witnesses of the brief encounter at all.

"No witnesses at all, barring the poor woman herself, and she's too upset to remember anything," said Superintendent Chris Brinton wrathfully, his grip on the telephone receiver so tight that Detective Constable Foxon, sitting on the far side of the desk, could almost hear the plastic cracking. "I heard on the grapevine, Oracle, that you'd hauled MissEss up to the Yard to do some of her fancy little doodles, at a guess. Did she come up with anything useful?"

In London, Chief Superintendent Delphick sat silent, his free hand absently drawing a pirate chief, complete with the earrings and eyepatch Miss Seeton had portrayed, on the fresh sheet of paper in his blotter. He realised what he was doing, and scowled at the scrawl before saying:

"Sorry, Chris, but I'm not sure we can help you all that much—oh, yes," as Brinton tried to expostulate, "she came and talked to one of our witnesses and drew a sketch or two, but you know what she's like. The first attempt, the fast cartoon type I'd been pinning my hopes on, turned out to be a reflection of the conversation she and Bob Ranger had in the car when he was driving her up to Town—and the second was just a routine drawing, anyone could have done it. You know how IdentiKit pictures are all supposed to look exactly like David Frost? Well, this was a woman, and Miss Seeton got even her looking like David Frost. The run-of-the-mill rubbish she must have taught in that Hampstead school before she retired. Maybe we'd recognise the woman if we stood her right beside it, but I'm not hopeful."

"Oh . . . " Then in his turn Brinton was silent. "Well, I suppose it was a long shot, but—dammit, Oracle, you've chased them out of London and they seem to have ended up on my patch. I need all the help I can get! Couldn't you send me a copy of what she produced—just in case it makes some kind of sense to me even though everyone knows you're the one who understands her best?"

Delphick attempted to demur, but Brinton overrode him. "How many did they rob in your area before that old chap was killed? They're getting careless about the dosage. I don't want another death in any case, but certainly not when it's partly the Yard's fault if one occurs." Delphick protested more vehemently at this, pointing out that the Sherry Gang never seemed to strike in the same area more than once or, if they'd had a particularly good haul, twice:

"Which makes them almost random, Chris, and you know as well as I do they're the hardest kind to catch. And it may also mean they'll only do perhaps one more before they leave the Ashford area and move elsewhere, if that's any comfort."

But it was black comfort. No policeman cares for crime, and cares for it even less when the victims are the very old or the very young, or the otherwise vulnerable. This latest victim, though not even as old as Mrs. Blaine, had been in a wheelchair. The drugs she took, medically prescribed to make her life at least bearable, had reacted with what was dissolved in the sherry and resulted in her having to give her disjointed witness statement from a hospital bed. "This one could have died, as well," said Brinton, in a controlled voice. "I want them caught, Oracle, every bit as much as you do, and I'm not going to turn up my nose at any help you or anyone else can give me . . .

"Even," he concluded, with a sigh, "Miss Seeton."

# chapter

# ~13~

IT WAS ONE of Martha Bloomer's two days a week spent "doing for" Miss Seeton, and she was being as busy as ever: but something, Miss Seeton decided after a while, seemed to be wrong. There was less cheerful clatter and tuneless song—Martha was tone deaf, though Miss Seeton would never have dreamed of passing comment on her inability to hold a note, as this would have been a personal remark and ungrateful, as well. Martha and Stan had made her so welcome, and looked after her so well, and now that it seemed poor Martha might be in need of looking after herself, Miss Seeton's duty was clear.

"Is everything all right?" she enquired, as Mrs. Bloomer emerged from the kitchen with a feather duster in one hand, and her apron crooked. "You seem a little anxious, Martha."

Martha ran the back of a sturdy hand across her brow and smiled. "Oh, it's nothing, just that I didn't sleep too good last night, tossing and turning for hours, I was, and Stan, too. Means there's bad weather to come, that's the usual way of it, and I can't abide thunder. Makes the top of my head feel like it's about to explode."

"Oh, my dear, then you shouldn't be here bothering with my nonsense, if you aren't well—"

"Nonsense it is," interrupted Martha, "just a bit of a headache—no, not even so much as that, just a funny sort of feeling, a build-up to the storm. When it finally breaks I'll be fine again, just you see." She glanced through the window. "Clouds building up, and it's getting darker. We shall have rain before long, and that'll please Stan. What with all the sunshine we've been having he's none too happy about the state of the garden."

Miss Seeton nodded. "He spoke to me the other day about a second water-butt, and I confess it had completely slipped my mind, but will you tell him, please, that of course he is to do whatever he thinks best." Greenfinger, who pointed the gardening way so very clearly, waxed eloquent on the dire results of inadequate watering at critical times, and Miss Seeton had no intention of ignoring either of her mentors. "And anything else he might need, Martha—and you too, of course," said Miss Seeton. She turned slightly pink with the embarrassment of discussing money, which she always felt had no place in polite conversation. "Tell me of your requirements, Martha dear, and I will, that is to say, after what is needed has been bought—er, selected, then payment, I mean a cheque, rather than the bother of cash . . . "

As Miss Seeton flustered to a halt, Martha took pity on her, turning away to wield the feather duster against which no cobweb would dare to dangle. "Don't you worry," Martha told Miss Seeton brightly, forgetting her incipient headache in her amusement, "about a thing. Stan and I will manage fine, and let you know all you need to know."

"Dear Martha," said Miss Seeton in gratitude, and behind her eyelids felt a little prickle of tears. How emotional of her—the approaching storm, no doubt, so unsettling, as dear Martha had already found, although what she owed to Martha and Stan she could never be too thankful for, and it would seem callous to attempt to deny the emotion. Miss Seeton blew her nose briskly on the neat linen handkerchief she kept in her pocket, and, with a final fond look at Martha's busily dusting back view, trotted upstairs.

As she was uncurling from her favourite Cow-Face Posture—yoga, so relaxing, she had entirely managed to forget that storm which was still, it seemed, looming—she heard the voice of Martha from downstairs.

"All right with you if I hoover now, is it? Whatever the black stuff was you spilled on the carpet, you didn't manage to get it up properly. A brush is no good for the likes of that. You need a good go with the vacuum to shift it, short of taking the carpet outside to beat it."

Miss Seeton was now at the top of the stairs, looking pink once more. "Oh dear, yes, I did my very best, but the charcoal seemed to crumble even more than when I trod on it, and so spreading, too, but I thought, as it was in a corner behind the sofa, nobody would notice . . . "

"I've my reputation to keep up," Martha informed her, a laugh in her voice. "I'd never be able to look my other ladies in the face again if I knew there was that great patch of black—charcoal, did you say it was?—in your sitting room for anyone to see if they went round the back of the sofa. And now you've finished tying yourself in knots I can get the hoover out to see what can be done."

Miss Seeton, feeling guilty, came back downstairs and crept into the kitchen as Martha was rummaging in the understairs cupboard for the vacuum cleaner. A temperamental piece of equipment, it functioned best of all for Martha, if in a grudging way: but for Miss Seeton it never seemed willing to beat, or to sweep, or to clean. The electric kettle, however, was something she could easily cope with.

Above the steady roar of the vacuum cleaner there seemed little point in calling to tell Martha that she was making a cup of tea. Miss Seeton, whose voice had in its time been sent ringing across an entire classroom, shrank from applying a similar number of decibels within the confines of her own home. She switched on the kitchen light—really, that storm was going to be rather spectacular when it finally broke, maybe the atmospheric effects would be worth trying to capture on canvas—and, having checked that the kettle was full, plugged it in. Miss Seeton remembered enough of the war—although not a householder, she had taken her fair share of responsibility—not to rely upon the continuation of the water supply. Last thing at night one should always top up the kettle, so that there would in the morning be at least the makings of a cup of tea.

Having plugged in the kettle, she switched it on.

There was a sudden flash which hardly had time to dazzle before it was followed by a tremendous bang, immediately overhead. From the blackened sky came a downpour of rain; from the blackened socket came a whiff of burning; and from Martha in the sitting room came a startled scream.

"Sparks! Oh my word, running up and down the flex—oh my word, what's happened?"

Miss Seeton shook her head to try to clear the ringing from her ears and the blobs from before her eyes—rather an interesting abstract pattern, and one that might serve as a basis for the storm painting she hoped to achieve, but now there was no time to think of art when Martha seemed to be in trouble, and maybe it was partly one's carelessness that was to blame . . .

"I only switched on the kettle," began Miss Seeton, "and I suppose it must have been a fuse, although I confess I had no idea the results would be so dramatic—oh, dear!"

As she spoke, she came into the sitting room, to find Martha on the hearthrug, breathing deeply and pointing with a finger that shook at the vacuum cleaner on the other side of the room. Her frozen stance suggested to Miss Seeton's skilled eye a pose adopted after a momentous leap—as far away as possible, she realised, as she followed that pointing finger, from the vacuum cleaner.

Which was emitting a series of ominous crackles as the sparks which had startled Martha continued to run up and down the flex. "Oh, dear," said Miss Seeton again, feeling foolish and inadequate. "Did I do that, too? I never feel entirely happy with electricity, though of course—"

"We've been struck by lightning," interrupted Martha, who had been roused from her trance by Miss Seeton's daft willingness to accept the blame for everything. "Nobody's fault at all—and your insurance ought to cover it. But I was a bit surprised, I admit, and what are we going to do about those sparks? We can't have the whole place burning down round our ears, but I don't fancy touching it, yet it's got to be switched off somehow, and unplugged."

Into Miss Seeton's mind, relieved that none of this had been her fault, came a long-forgotten memory of Mrs. Thorley, who taught science at the little school in Hampstead where Miss Seeton had spent so many years. Mrs. Thorley's physics party-piece, so the girls would excitedly inform her (their art lesson being time-tabled immediately after the physics class), was, every year on the introduction of "electricity" to the course, to wire herself somehow into the mains with suitable cable while standing on an overturned plastic washing-up bowl, there to stand for some minutes while a breathless class timed her with a stopwatch.

And at the end of a given period, Mrs. Thorley would leap from her insulating bowl to the floor, her feet giving off a burst of sparks and crackles, in otherwise perfect safety. But the bowl, Miss Seeton recalled, had to be perfectly dry; and hers, she knew, was full of soaking pans.

"It must not be touched directly," she said, remembering other snippets of information as annually disseminated by an enthusiastic class. Indeed, so enthusiastic were they that Miss Seeton always encouraged them to paint abstracts of the thrills they had just witnessed, in shocking blue and vivid green and slashing scarlet, in order to calm themselves down in time for the next lesson.

"It must not be touched, but it has to be disconnected from the mains. Now, I wonder . . . "

The vacuum cleaner was still fizzing as she came hurrying back from the hall armed with her second-best umbrella, the one with the wooden handle. "Martha," instructed Miss Seeton, "you must not attempt to touch me if I become, I believe the term is *live*, or you will run grave risks. While I am attempting to deal with this, please go into the kitchen and empty the washing-up bowl and bring it to me, but it must be absolutely dry . . . "

And, without looking to see whether a startled Martha was following her instructions, Miss Seeton proceeded to creep up on the fizzing vacuum cleaner in the manner of a big-game hunter stalking a tiger, holding her umbrella before her like an unwieldy rifle.

The tiger continued to snarl at Miss Seeton's approach, her rifle poised to knock it over; then she hesitated, and reversed her grip, so that it was the curved handle that was now free. With a brief prayer and a deft tweak, Miss Seeton seized the fizzing flex with her umbrella and jerked the plug out of the socket, just as Martha came to her senses and was about to go into the kitchen.

"Oh, well done, Miss Emily!" she applauded, and Miss Seeton, breathless, flushed with triumph, bent cautiously over the now silent vacuum cleaner and prodded it, without sparks or shocks or other signs of distress. It was dead.

And so, as the electrician from Brettenden informed her, was the kettle, though the rest of the house, including the ring-main, had fortunately survived the thunderclap. "Not worth the bother of repairing, these aren't," he said, with a frown and a shake of the head. "Reckon you had a lucky escape there. What did you say you used?"

"My umbrella," said Miss Seeton, thankful that Martha was not here to see the expression on his face. Evidently she had somehow misunderstood the exact nature of the feat performed by Mrs. Thorley, and Mr. Spellbrook had delivered a stern lecture.

He had also delivered an electric kettle. "Brought it along on spec," he told her, as Miss Seeton was delightedly boiling water for tea and biscuits. "You don't have to take it if you don't want it—we've got others in stock—but this is as good a model as you'll find, though I says it as shouldn't. Your cleaner, now, that's another matter. Best come into the shop and take a look round yourself—more choice, and you might want to try a cylinder instead of an upright, or one of them fancy round ones . . . "

Miss Seeton explained that she must consult Mrs. Bloomer on the subject, and would drop into the Brettenden shop once a decision had been made, either with Martha or, if she was otherwise engaged, without her, but with a note of what exactly was required. She and Mr. Spellbrook parted company on the best of terms, once he had repeated his warnings of the inherent dangers of electricity, and Miss Seeton tied a knot in her handkerchief to remind her to speak to Martha.

The powers that be had reduced the Brettenden bus to a once-a-week service, but Plummergen is not so easily thwarted. Crabbe's garage, where Old Mr. Crabbe was reluctantly handing over the reins to his grandson, Very Young Crabbe (whose father, Young Crabbe, had died during the war), after a year of listening to the grumbles of the village had come up with a solution. Twice a week, on days not covered by the official bus, a charabanc decorated in the Crabbe livery of dark red and olive green would chunter its steady way the six miles to Brettenden, wait there throughout the day, then turn round and chunter back. Very Young Crabbe's oldest son (distinguished by his Christian name of Jack) drove the bus, and whiled away his waiting hours in the compilation of cryptic crossword puzzles, which he submitted, with regular success, to one of the more literary periodicals.

It was an arrangement that pleased everyone in Plummergen except Old Crabbe, who would have liked to drive the bus himself. His grandson had vetoed this on the grounds of his insistence that the safest place to drive was as far from the edge of the road as possible: the centre white line, he said, was much easier to see, as well. Very Young Crabbe hid the spare set of keys from his grandfather, and on days when the charabanc service ran took care to lure the old gentleman to the workshop at the back of the garage, so that the sight of all that red-and-green glory setting out for Brettenden should not disturb him.

In the little notebook which she always carried in her handbag, Miss Seeton had carefully inscribed Martha's first and second choices; she made sure her chequebook and gold pen were also there, and, picking up her umbrella—today's weather forecast had promised a repeat of the recent thunder and heavy rain, perhaps she should take a lightweight mackintosh, as well—made for the front door. She cast a guilty look back up the stairs in the direction of the control box for the burglar alarm: the bolt of lightning, she had found on the next occasion when she had left the house, had somehow killed that system as well as the kettle and the vacuum cleaner. Miss Seeton could not help feeling slightly glad, almost as if one had wished misfortune upon the whole apparatus, ungrateful though this might appear, and really it was so much less troublesome to be without it, although she must mention its demise to that kind Mr. Spellbrook who had been so knowledgeable about her kettle, and perhaps he could be persuaded to take a look at it . . . some time. Meanwhile, one could revel in the freedom from worry, and the comfort of being able to leave one's house in the normal manner, without the tedious checking and re-checking that the alarm system had required . . .

Miss Seeton was surprised, on her arrival at Crabbe's Garage, not to see the familiar red-and-green charabanc in its usual place. She consulted her wristwatch: she must be early, for there was the bus, still parked on the forecourt—but why was there a tree lying across it?

"Struck by lightning," Jack Crabbe told her gloomily, when he popped out of the petrol booth to find her prodding with her umbrella at the branches which scraped against the dented flanks of the red-and-green conveyance, and sorrowfully clicking her tongue.

"The tree, I mean," he went on, "and just look at them scratches on the paint, not to mention the other damage, and it may be insured but it's not the same, is it?"

"Indeed it is not," she assured him. "So forlorn, those broken windows, aren't they? Like eyes that have been suddenly struck blind, and the rain on the upholstery, as well. So distressing for you. Does this mean—I hardly like to mention it, but—will there be no service to Brettenden now until market day?"

He grinned at her. "Crabbe's won't let you down, Miss Seeton. No need to wait till Friday to go to town. We know how much the village depends on us, so Dad's hired another bus, from Omney's, for every day till we've got ours fixed, and a driver with it, for I'm not insured to drive the Omney bus, regulations, see. With luck it shouldn't be for long, though. I hope not, I enjoy our little jaunts." He looked as regretful as a man can who sees his chance of compiling a cryptic crossword snatched from him for at least one day, and probably more. He glanced over her shoulder. "Here's Omney's now, so you'd best get going if you want a decent seat, and the driver knows to wait for just as long as I always do, so no need to hurry your shopping. Have fun!"

And Jack Crabbe, whistling bravely to hide his disappointment, returned to his solitary gloom in the petrol booth.

Miss Seeton was not the first to enter the Omney bus, for she paused to study its colour scheme of dark blue and deep orange, and to compare this with the familiar Crabbe's livery. Such a great pity, but how very public-spirited of the old gentleman, or whichever Mr. Crabbe it had been who thought of it, to propose hiring another coach, for indeed it would have been an inconvenience to have to wait until Friday, as dear Martha had strong views about dusty carpets and there was still the stick of charcoal she'd trodden underfoot to be cleared up, so careless to have dropped it, but when one's sketching equipment is being transferred from one bag to another, these accidents will happen . . .

Miss Seeton recognised most of her fellow travellers as she climbed up into the bus, and nodded a greeting to those nearest. The Nuts were in the front seat, and could hardly meet her gaze as she passed them with a courteous inclination of the head. She moved down the aisle to choose a seat on the other side of the bus, and the Nuts began to mutter.

"Did you see, Eric? The effrontery of it, trying to act as if nothing was the matter! And why do you suppose," Mrs. Blaine hissed, "she wants to go into Brettenden today?"

"Following us," suggested Miss Nuttel, after a thoughtful pause. "Star witnesses. Knows we're on to her."

"Oh, Eric, you're right of course," thrilled Mrs. Blaine, her black-currant eyes glittering with excitement. "We must be very careful the whole time. Think how easy it would be for her to arrange some sort of accident to be rid of us." As the engine of the bus began to turn, she raised her voice as she glanced back over her shoulder. "She could easily push us under a car, or something . . . "

Even for Miss Nuttel, this was too much to accept. "Not both of us at once," she objected. "But true enough—have to take care. Best be very careful while we're shopping—eyes skinned all the time, Bunny. All the time . . . "

"Or, better still," suggested Bunny, "we could keep an eye on her *before* she tries anything, couldn't we? There's nothing we desperately need to buy today that wouldn't wait for another time. It would be much more sensible to watch what Miss Seeton does and where she goes, wouldn't it? Then we'll have real evidence to give Scotland Yard, next time!"

And so it was with their hearts full of sleuthial zeal, and their intentions of shopping abandoned, that, once the Omney bus had arrived in Brettenden, the Nuts were the last people to leave. Miss

Seeton bowed again as she passed the front seat where they waited in anticipation . . .

And, as she walked towards the Brettenden shops, wondering whether it would rain, she had no idea that she was being followed . . .

# chapter

## -14-

WITH HER UMBRELLA and handbag over one arm, and her light-weight mackintosh packed neatly into a sturdy carrier held in the other hand, Miss Seeton set out to enjoy her day's shopping. It would be most sensible, of course, to consult the electrician first, since one had no idea how long these matters might take, although Martha had given very detailed information, but there might by some chance be a shortage of both the models she recommended, and then one would have to ask for advice as to what was nearest Martha's choice, and perhaps there would be several to choose from, which would be confusing when one knew that there were differences in the model numbers and to one's unpractised eye they tended to look more or less the same . . .

"Look!" gulped Mrs. Blaine, and grabbed at Miss Nuttel's bony elbow. "She's checking something in that notebook—a contact address, I'm sure it must be!"

"Fence," suggested Miss Nuttel. "Usually a jeweller, or a pawn-broker. Strange, being a chain store." For Miss Seeton had drifted to a halt outside the plate glass of the local branch of Marker & Spence, and was studying its display of electrical goods.

"Oh, Eric! Do you suppose this is entirely safe?" And Bunny peered doubtfully over her shoulder, as if the streets of Brettenden might suddenly erupt into gang warfare with themselves in the middle of it all. "They must be desperate people she's dealing with—you don't go waving shotguns all over the place if you're not planning to use them, do you?"

"Nobody in sight," Miss Nuttel reassured her, after some anxious moments of frantic scanning. "Anyway, seems to have

changed her mind," for Miss Seeton, shaking her head slowly
at the bewildering selection of vacuum cleaners, and hoping that
Martha's preferences would both be in stock, was once more
walking in the direction of the electrician's.

She was utterly oblivious to the stalking advance of the Nuts
down Brettenden High Street behind her. It was fortunate for their
tracking skills that the number of shoppers, even though it was not
a market day, sufficed to mask the peculiarities of their progress:
they kept stopping, with a series of startled little gasps and grabs
at each other, to leap into nearby shop doorways, or they would
realise their retreat had given Miss Seeton several yards' distance,
and would break into a curious gait midway between a scuttle
and a trot in order to catch her up. "Must be drunk," observed
one old gentleman, who was handing out teetotal tracts to unwary
passersby. He was a Holdfast Brother, and wondered whether he
should try to redeem the souls of Miss Nuttel and Mrs. Blaine
before it was too late: but while he was still making up his mind,
they had skittered out of sight behind a group of chattering people
all armed with large carrier bags and holdalls.

"Spellbrook: Electrician" was located in a side road off the far
end of the main street. Miss Seeton, following the instructions Mr.
Spellbrook had given her on the back of an envelope—("Look,
Eric, she's checking her contact address again!")—arrived there
just as the first few drops of rain were thinking about falling from
an overcast sky. How thankful she was that she had thought to
bring her mackintosh with her, and of course her umbrella as
well . . .

Miss Seeton hitched the umbrella more comfortably over her
arm after groping in her handbag for the notebook with Martha's
list—("Eric, she's holding it in *such* a strange way! Do you suppose it could be a shotgun in disguise?")—and pushed open the
door of Spellbrook's. In triumph that they had succeeded in tracking her to her lair, the Nuts proceeded to keep observation on Miss
Seeton by lurking together in the doorway opposite, which was
the entrance to a flower shop.

"Suppose," breathed Bunny, "she escapes through the back
door? We'd lose sight of her then!"

"Better not separate," opined Eric, after some thought. "Divide
and conquer, risky business. Stay on watch here and be ready to
pursue if we spot her making a break for it. That service alley—
we'd notice."

Mrs Blaine was full of admiration for this scheme, and so thankful that Eric didn't expect her to stay in this shop doorway by herself while covering the rear exit singlehandedly. Or perhaps Miss Seeton would come out of the front, after all, and leave Bunny to face her alone . . . Mrs. Blaine shivered, and wished she hadn't thought of mentioning the other way out of the suspect shop. Suppose Eric changed her mind, and went there, and left her!

"Eric," she began, "promise me you won't try to be brave. You said yourself we'd have to face this together. There isn't any point in being a heroine if—"

"Oy," broke in a voice from behind her, "and just what d'you think you're doing, then? I bin watching you two—squashed in here like pips in an orange, neither buying nor planning to buy, it seems to me, and don't try to hand me that sheltering from the rain excuse, when it hadn't barely begun when you first started blocking my doorway. So, now," and the speaker, an enormous red-faced man, folded his arms and glared at the startled Nuts, "what are you going to do about it, is what I want to know."

"We *were* sheltering from the rain," began Mrs. Blaine in a peevish voice, indicating the puddles beyond the pavement which danced and rippled with falling drops. "We could tell that a storm was on the way, so—"

"So, if you've no plans to buy, you can be on *your* way, and be quick about it," said the red-faced man, a veritable mountain of menace. Miss Nuttel gulped; Mrs. Blaine uttered a quavering squeak. The mountain ignored them. "Blocking my door and scaring my customers," he said grimly. "Like to have the law on the pair of you, but if you was to purchase a few choice items of the florist's art, I dare say I could be persuaded to overlook the matter."

"B-b-bl-black-black—" began Mrs. Blaine, unable to complete the protest when the mountain turned his furious red gaze upon her.

"Black flowers, you was wanting, was it?" he enquired, a note of wrathful amusement in his voice. "For a funeral, I suppose. Well, perhaps—"

"Oh! No!" Cries of sheer terror erupted from the Nuts, and they darted from the flower shop doorway and fled along the street as fast as their trembling legs would allow. It was not until they had turned the corner out of the side road that they controlled themselves to a halt and stood in the shelter of a flapping canvas awning which protected the windows of a clockmaker and jeweller, breathing hot, shuddering breaths.

"Obviously the gang's look-out," opined Miss Nuttel at last, peering round the corner of the awning in search of pursuit. "Just our bad luck to have raised the alarm—"

"He threatened us, Eric! *Planning your own funeral, are you?* And the way he laughed—he was gloating! Positively gloating, and trying to threaten us into keeping quiet about what we know!"

"Blackmail," Miss Nuttel corrected her, remembering what Bunny had so bravely begun to say. *She'd* stood up to that bully, all right—no doubting Bunny's courage! But as for herself, she was ashamed—bolting down the road in quite the opposite direction from—

"Bunny," cried Miss Nuttel, "Miss Seeton! Forgot about keeping watch—making a break for it this minute!" But she was strangely reluctant to lead the way back into the little side street that had seemed so empty of other shoppers—so far from any help, if the worst came to the worst.

Mrs. Blaine wrung her plump hands and lamented, "They've made such careful plans, we hardly stand a chance against them. Oh, Eric, what are we to do? To have come so close to solving the mystery, and then—that awful man, I shall have nightmares about him tonight, I know . . . "

"If," said Miss Nuttel darkly, "they let us survive till tonight. Star witnesses, remember?"

And Bunny, shivering, remembered.

Miss Seeton, smiling, remembered, without having to consult the list in her notebook, which of the vacuum cleaners would best suit dear Martha. She double-checked her choice, just to make sure, but the sales assistant—that nice Mr. Spellbrook's wife, apparently—was so friendly and helpful, and they had a most enjoyable chat about all manner of things before Miss Seeton duly enquired about a delivery charge, was delighted to find that there would be none if she was willing to wait until next week when the van would be in Plummergen anyway, and happily signed her cheque. "And don't forget your umbrella, Miss Seeton," Mrs. Spellbrook called after her. "Just look outside—it's going to pelt down any minute, wouldn't you say?"

"So it is," said Miss Seeton, "and how fortunate that I packed my lightweight raincoat. I had an idea we had not seen the last of the stormy weather. And I sincerely hope there will be no more lightning, so unpleasant when one is in the open air away from shelter, though of course there are more trees in Plummergen High

Street than there are here in Brettenden, aren't there? Lightning, you see . . . "

"Your umbrella handle," said Mrs. Spellbrook, studying it with interest. "It's metal, isn't it, but it looks like . . . well, this sounds silly, but—gold." She reached out and touched it gently. "Surely it can't be—a gold umbrella?"

Miss Seeton blushed. "My very best umbrella—a memento from a most courteous gentleman of a little adventure in which he kindly allowed me to play a small part. Hollow, of course, or the cost would have been . . . " She shook her head. "I think," she said, deftly turning the subject, "I shall be extremely glad of it today," and she pointed down the shop towards the windows, against which the rain had now begun to lash. "It is fortunate that there were a few other shops I intended to visit, some art supplies and perhaps a cup of coffee or a light luncheon somewhere, but—"

"You can't go out in this," protested Mrs. Spellbrook, in a voice that wasn't sure whether to be amused or horrified. "You'll catch your death!"

"Death and danger, Bunny," said Miss Nuttel bravely. "A risk we have to run—our duty as citizens." She glanced at the clocks in the window. "Ought to be on our way back," in a voice she tried to make resolute. "Mustn't skulk here all day, not if we're trying to find out the truth."

"Oh, Eric, you're too brave!" Yet it did fleetingly come into Mrs. Blaine's mind that the drips from the now-sodden canvas awning, which leaked surprisingly badly for such a high-class shop, might have something to do with the sudden decision of Miss Nuttel to go once more in search of Miss Seeton, criminal mastermind.

"Too brave," repeated Mrs. Blaine, dismissing her unworthy thoughts and gazing proudly at her friend. "When should—"

"Look out!" gasped Miss Nuttel, grabbing her by the arm and shaking her in her shock. "Almost on top of us—didn't spot her in disguise!"

"Disguise?" Mrs. Blaine's beady eyes peered round the side-flap of the awning. "Oh, Eric, how lucky she's on the other side of the road! But she must have guessed we were following her. She deliberately found that mackintosh from somewhere, and look how high she's turned the collar up! I knew we'd catch her out in the end, and how clever of you to spot her through the disguise!"

"Just happened to see her first," muttered Miss Nuttel, feeling that she'd somehow atoned for her previous cowardice in the face of the flower shop foe. "Dare say you'd have recognised her as well, Bunny."

Mrs. Blaine looked pleased, then suggested quickly that they should set off once more in pursuit of Miss Seeton now that she had left her lair and was apparently on the prowl again. She did not want to give Eric the chance to propose a return visit to that unnerving back street where the ferocious florist lurked. "Don't forget," she pointed out, "she may have turned her collar up to stop us seeing it was her—but it will make it harder for *her* to see us, as well!" And so it was agreed that they should continue to track Miss Seeton through the Brettenden streets rather than attempt to find out what she might have been doing in Spellbrook's, which was obviously a front for something sinister and when they had positive proof Eric would telephone Scotland Yard again.

The remainder of their day was uneventful, fortunately for the Nuts: their nerves were still rather shaky after the shock of being shouted at by the enormous red-faced man, and Mrs. Blaine's ankle had started to ache, so that they could not go as fast after Miss Seeton as they would have liked. But Miss Seeton was in no particular hurry: she visited the art supplies' shop, and filled her carrier with a gratifying selection of items such as blocks, brushes, and a packet of the new range of colour crayons with which she hoped to capture some of the violent mystery of the thunderclap. She enjoyed a cup of coffee and a chelsea bun at a very pleasant little teashop; she window-shopped her way back down the High Street, and only when it began to rain hard again did she decide to abandon her day out and hurry, instead of simply walking at a steady pace, towards the bus station.

"Running away," said Miss Nuttel, wriggling damp toes in leaking leather shoes. "Do stop moaning, Bunny. Caught her at last, haven't we!" And, as fast as they could, the Nuts hurried after their quarry.

With her umbrella up and her bulky bag, Miss Seeton had a difficult time of it against the wind and the rain, every now and then pausing to catch her breath and check that she was heading in the right direction. The points of her up-turned collar jabbed wetly into her cheek, and her umbrella spokes twanged melodiously as the wind dashed the raindrops against them. With relief, in the distance, she could make out the welcome black and orange livery of the Omney coach: she put her head down and her brolly up, and hurried, holdall banging against her breathless side, towards it. Before she had time to catch her breath, the driver opened the door and beckoned her in; a chorus of voices called congratulations at her having struggled through the storm.

The Nuts came panting up behind her, disappointed that the promise of their day had resulted in nothing better than a soaking, and climbed the steps with relief. They were a little peeved to observe that their favourite front seats had been taken—and taken by strangers, too. They hoped they would not have to sit next to Miss Seeton: the bus was remarkably full . . . surely, fuller than when they had set out from Plummergen?

And why were so many of these faces—why were *all* of these faces unfamiliar? Who were they? What had they done with the villagers? The Nuts stood, staring . . .

And with a jerk and a judder, the engine began to turn. "Sit down, missus," roared the driver. "You don't want to go to France with a broken leg, do you?"

Without waiting for a reply, he put the bus into gear, tootled on the horn, and above Miss Nuttel's stricken cry of "France? Never!" gunned the engine and set off out of the bus station.

"There's been some mistake," bleated Mrs. Blaine, while Miss Nuttel gasped in the seat beside her. A voice from the seat in front said:

"You and your friend just made it, didn't you? Doesn't look as if she's left much room in her holdall for the duty free, though—and it's much cheaper to get it in France. But I suppose you all know your own business best."

"*France?*" repeated Mrs. Blaine in horror. "Why, we haven't even got our passports with us!"

"Oh, you don't need 'em," said their new acquaintance cheerfully. "All you need's money and a holdall—or two," he added. "Quick trip from Lydd Airport, round the shops, a club in the evening, back home next day. Lovely!"

"Oh, dear," moaned Mrs. Blaine, while Miss Nuttel gasped again. "France—oh, no! Whatever will happen next?"

# chapter

# ~15~

THE JERKS AND judders of the engine had sent the Nuts stumbling almost the full length of the bus before they managed to find somewhere to sit; Miss Seeton, travelling alone, had been luckier. An empty aisle seat barely halfway down the bus had welcomed her, and with a smile and murmured greeting to her window neighbour she prepared to settle her damp self in comfort.

Her umbrella—loosely furled and, though briskly shaken outside, still dripping—she hooked over the seat arm to drip tidily on the floor: such a rich purple shade of plush, she hoped it would not be spoiled. The seat cover, that was to say, not the floor. People must, after all, have walked on it with wet feet before—the floor, that was, although if there had been a rack at the entrance one would naturally have placed it there, out of the way. Her umbrella, that was to say. Not that there had been, or otherwise the holdall, so awkward, could have been placed in it instead of pressing against one's stockings with such an unpleasantly damp sensation . . .

"Oh, bother," muttered Miss Seeton, peering down at her holdall and brushing raindrops off her legs. So preoccupied was she with her discomfort that she did not notice the Nuts as they staggered past her; nor did she, the first time of asking, hear her neighbour as he enquired:

"Would you like me to put that up on the rack for you?" And, as there came no reply from the little grey-haired lady at his side, he asked again, speaking slowly and clearly for the benefit of one who was obviously deaf.

"Excuse me," he said. "Your bag—would you like me to put

it out of the way for you?" And he pointed emphatically first at the holdall, then up at the rack.

Miss Seeton wondered why the poor young man had to speak with such gestures, and such a very mobile mouth: some form of speech impediment, one supposed, and no doubt it was not kind, although inevitable, that one should for a moment have a mental picture of a goldfish with human features. A smile flickered in Miss Seeton's eyes, but faded as she reproached herself for lack of sympathy towards one less fortunate than she knew herself to be. "You—are—very—kind," Miss Seeton mouthed back, enunciating clearly. "Thank—you."

The young man grinned the fatuous grin of the self-conscious do-gooder and wordlessly held out his hand for the holdall: no point in trying to talk properly to the poor old biddy, it was clear she must be as deaf as a post, and he was blowed if he was going to practise sign language all the way to France. Although, come to think of it, sign language might be a handy way of getting through to the Frogs, if the ones he met didn't speak English. He wondered if the old girl could say "As many ciggies as I'm allowed on the Duty Free, please," and whether they'd understand her.

"Blimey," he muttered, as he hoisted Miss Seeton's bag to the sagging string rack above. "Brought everything bar the kitchen sink, I should say! She'll never cart this lot round with her the whole time," and he resolved, after all, to lose Miss Seeton at the first opportunity. He had no wish to end up carrying her purchases as well as his own.

Miss Seeton had caught the words *kitchen sink*, and made haste to explain: such haste that she failed to hear the cry of distressed horror emanating from the rear of the coach as the Nuts learned of their mistake. "Oh dear, no," said Miss Seeton. "Not a kitchen sink, a vacuum cleaner. They are to deliver it," she added with pride, "next week. Martha will be so pleased."

So she wasn't as deaf as he'd thought. Lucky he hadn't said something stronger than that about the weight of her bag. "Good for Martha," he said, with a grin, speaking in his normal voice. "Your daughter, is she?"

Miss Seeton blushed. "A close family friend, so very kind and helpful," she corrected him gently. "And you, too, have been so kind, putting my holdall away for me. They always seem so high, don't they?" She gazed up at the rack; thus missing the horrified rush of the Nuts back down the aisle of the bus towards the driver, and the way Mrs. Blaine slipped on the spread of water from the tip of the dripping umbrella, and bumped against the seat on the other side of the aisle. Miss Nuttel, ignoring her stricken friend, went hurrying on to bid the driver stop, stop at once, because there had been a dreadful mistake.

"Who says so?" enquired the driver, as Mrs. Blaine, rubbing her bruised hip, blundered up to stand at Eric's side and add her protesting bleat to those barked commands. The bus lurched with unnecessary force around a corner, and both the Nuts clutched at each other for support. "What do you mean, mistake?" The driver grinned, and spoke in a calmer tone. "What are you talking about? One at a time, girls, please," he added, as they both began to explain in unison.

Miss Seeton had by now settled herself in reasonable comfort, and was smiling out of the window at the passing and familiar scenery of what, in Brettenden, was known as the Plummergen Road. By the time it reached her much-loved home it was the Brettenden Road; and when it left Plummergen, it was heading for Lydd, and the airport.

"So no need to panic, girls," the driver was saying, as the bus approached the Gibbet Oak bend. "There's some might call it an unofficial stop, but who's to care? Once we get near your house just give us a shout and I'll stop the bus and you can hop out home and no questions asked, okay? That is, if you're sure you don't want to come with this lot to France," with a jerk of his head to indicate the passengers behind him. "You don't? Oh well, back to your seats, then, and next stop Plummergen!"

But the Nuts, and Miss Seeton, were not the only ones to be mistaken that day. Even as the driver concluded his kind reassurance that the Plummergen contingent had no cause for concern, he found himself making an unscheduled stop much sooner than even he had anticipated. The bus had passed the Gibbet Oak bend and was heading along the straighter stretch of the Brettenden-Plummergen Road, picking up speed now that they were out in the country. The road was empty of other vehicles, and the driver whistled to himself . . .

Until a saloon car suddenly pulled out of a field just in front of the coach and stopped. Dead. Blocking the way ahead . . . just as the way back was blocked by a small dark car which had apparently been hiding in another gateway, its outline half-hidden by vegetation grown summer high.

The driver braked and swore. The passengers were flung forward in their seats, and there came cries of outrage and alarm.

There was a clatter as Miss Seeton's umbrella jerked from the arm of her seat and fell to the floor, although she was too busy catching her breath to notice it.

The saloon car completed a deft manoeuvre to block the coach completely while now facing an easy escape route . . .

And out of the saloon stepped two figures, dressed in the style favoured by motorcyclists: jeans, and leathers, and helmets . . . although normal bikers surely did not wear black masks across their faces.

Or carry shotguns.

The driver knew what was happening: the Dick Turpins had been talked about on television and radio and in the papers for long enough for him to be fairly confident that, if he did as the gesticulating figure outside was clearly ordering him to do and opened the door of the coach, no great harm would come to him. Or to his passengers—if they, too, did just as they were told.

The robbery began by following the same pattern as all the others. Shotgun aimed at the bus driver's head, the taller of the two masked and helmeted figures easily menaced the passengers into opening handbags and wallets, into stripping off necklaces, watches, and rings; into unpinning brooches, unclipping earrings, emptying purses and trouser pockets, as the smaller masked figure walked slowly down the aisle, carrying a wide-mouthed and greedy duffle bag into which the booty was sadly placed by its former owners.

Halfway down the aisle, the figure stumbled, and at once the pattern changed. The shotgun aimed at the driver's head wavered as a finger grew tight upon the trigger. "Forget it—or he gets it," said the man behind the shotgun. Everyone forgot it.

"Oh dear," said Miss Seeton, apologetically, as the smaller Turpin figure rubbed a bruised and bejeaned knee. As the umbrella had fallen, it had twisted, bouncing off the back of the seat in front to end up with its handle under Miss Seeton's startled feet, and its elegant ferruled point pointing out into the aisle, a rounded, rolling trap for the unwary. The Turpineer had been too intent upon collecting the swag to think of looking for obstacles along the way. Miss Seeton, responding with the automatic courtesy of the gentlewoman, might have gone on to apologise in more detail, only the glaring grey eyes above the mask subdued her into speechlessness. Silently, she withdrew from her handbag her gold fountain pen, and passed it over with a sigh, meanwhile shuffling her feet to drag the offending umbrella back from the aisle out of harm's way.

The collector of the swag pointedly rubbed again at the battered knee, then jangled the contents of the duffle bag viciously and slapped Miss Seeton's wrist with a sharp blow. She winced with surprise, and her helpful neighbour uttered a shocked word of protest. The Turpins, so far, had never shown violence towards their victims: it was something else out of the pattern . . .

And in his turn he quailed at the expression in those grey eyes, as Miss Seeton murmured blankly: "Oh, yes, I had quite forgotten. My watch, of course," and dutifully unbuckled the strap. Her thoughts seemed to have turned elsewhere, and she barely looked at the angry face of the Turpin as the leather-clad figure leaned across her to collect the belongings of her neighbour. Once she had yielded up her watch, her empty hands began to dance and fidget together on her lap, and her gaze drifted upwards to the luggage rack in which her bag of drawing materials was stowed . . .

The Turpins never troubled with items in luggage racks: too easy for a victim to tumble a bag accidentally and cause a diversion. The smaller figure passed on its way down the aisle collecting only what the unfortunate passengers had kept by them—the passengers who all sat stunned and silent as they were robbed.

At the far end of the coach cowered the Nuts, so stunned and silent that they might have been statues. Mrs. Blaine was so terrified that she could not have worked herself into a fit of hysterics to save her life; Miss Nuttel, as the Turpin swag-bag was presented for her donation, rolled up her eyes, turned greyish green, and fainted. And as Eric collapsed across her friend, Mrs. Blaine, in her anguish, found speech.

"Twice in one week!" she cried, her voice shaking with emotion. "It's too much—poor Eric! Twice, two times, do you hear me? We've nothing left for you. Everything's gone and you've already got it!" And she burst into tears, her plump cheeks creased with woe. "Eric, oh, Eric! Look what you've done to her. You should be ashamed of yourself!"

Careless of the risk she might be running, Mrs. Blaine glared at the masked Turpin figure in front of her; and, to her astonishment, the eyes above the mask dropped, for one moment, almost as if in shame. But not for long. A leather glove shot out and seized Bunny's left wrist: which proved to be watchless. Eric's sleeve had dragged up her arm as she fell, and her lack of a timepiece was evident. Neither of the Nuts was wearing any visible jewellery: but they both had handbags, and Mrs. Blaine was forced to empty both Eric's and her own, for the second time in a week as, voiceless now after her brief spurt of bravado, she found herself quite unable to point out.

A car horn sounded at the rear of the bus, and the man with the shotgun called out a warning to his companion, who snatched the purses Mrs. Blaine's trembling hand held out and turned to rush back down the aisle. Not a passenger stirred as the masked and helmeted figure hurried towards the door of the coach, although Miss Seeton's gaze, which had been for a time abstracted, followed the two Turpins as they made their escape with great concentration; and once again on her lap her hands danced and fidgeted their bewilderment . . .

# chapter

# -16-

BETWEEN ASHFORD, IN Kent, and Scotland Yard in London, the telephone wires were frantic.

"This," lamented Superintendent Brinton, "is a judgement on me for looking forward to saying *I told you so* to young Harry Furneux over at Hastings. I tried to do him a good turn by warning him to be prepared, but it was pretty clear he didn't believe me. Well, who would, if they haven't been exposed to the Miss Seeton phenomenon before. You have to get acclimatised to it. You have to learn to operate on an altogether different plane, because she's in a league of her own, that's what she is. And now this has happened—and I can't cope with her, Oracle, I simply can't. Do you know," he snarled, "when I woke up this morning, I had a fine head of dark brown hair—well, all right," as Delphick cleared his throat with force, "dark brown with a few distinguished highlights, if you insist—but I swear to you, there's more highlights than colour now. I've turned snow white, and it's your loopy lady friend who's to blame."

"You're not suggesting, surely, that Miss Seeton was in league with the Turpin crowd." The voice of Chief Superintendent Delphick did not even trouble to sound incredulous: he understood perfectly well how his old friend needed to let off steam. Maybe he could lighten the mood by making the suffering superintendent laugh. "You told me that when young Furneux told *you* what the Nuts told *him,* you bit his head off. You said it was ridiculous."

A hollow groan was all that greeted this. Delphick, who was partly speaking for the fascinated benefit of Sergeant Ranger, tried again. "Suppose you take a deep breath, Chris—take two, if it'll

110

help—and tell me again exactly what happened." He sounded more official now, more impersonal, a detective taking a statement. "Why," he wanted first of all to know, "was Miss Seeton on that bus, anyway?"

"Her umbrella," muttered Brinton, still not entirely believing it himself.

"Did you say—?" Delphick broke off to answer his own question with a sigh. "Her umbrella—yes, that figures."

"She'd put it up, because it was raining so hard—quite a storm we had down here, everyone in a hurry to get in the warm and dry, and Miss Seeton with the collar of her raincoat turned up, too. So she wasn't seeing so well, with the wind driving the rain right in her face, and her brolly sheltering her *and* blocking her view, of course—and the coach wasn't the usual Plummergen shuttle. They'd hired another because theirs was out of action, so naturally Miss Seeton didn't recognise it."

"Naturally," said Delphick, with a sigh, "she wouldn't, armed with her umbrella and all set to stir up trouble . . . But didn't the, let's call them regular passengers notice that they didn't know her when she got on? Why didn't somebody tell her she'd made a mistake?"

Brinton sighed. "It could only happen to her, couldn't it. Nobody told her, because nobody knew—because they were as much strangers to each other, by and large, as she was to them. One of those charter coaches doing a private cross-Channel trip, buy your ticket at the travel agent's and have a lovely twenty-four hours stocking up with duty free. So they'd got their holdalls ready, hadn't they, and so had Miss Seeton—full of artist's clobber she'd bought in Brettenden, but of course they weren't to know that. So when she comes blundering along with her brolly in the rain, and her carrier bag at the ready, naturally they think she's one of them. A whole gaggle of 'em had been plundering the Brettenden shops earlier that day, anyway, stocking up on bits and bobs to take with 'em—sandwiches, paper hankies, extra nappies for the baby, pills for Great-Aunt Ethel who gets travel sick, you can imagine the last-minute sort of thing—and your Miss Seeton simply tagged along in the crowd, and everyone said *Glad you could make it okay* and practically patted her on the back before they set off. For France," he concluded, in an incredulous tone, "instead of Plummergen."

Delphick smiled as he imagined the scene. How typical of Miss Seeton—and how embarrassed she must have been once her error had been pointed out to her. But she wasn't, it seemed, the only one . . . "And the Nuts simply tagged along behind Miss Seeton, did they?" he enquired, trying to suppress the laughter in his voice. Bob Ranger's eyes widened as he listened.

"They did," said Brinton, simmering sulphur in his tone as he thought of Erica Nuttel and Norah Blaine. Inspector Furneux believed he'd had a bad time of it with them, did he? Well, just let him try telling Superintendent Chris Brinton, gone grey overnight, and asking for sympathy, and then he'd know what needing sympathy was really all about. "The pair of them—nutty as fruitcakes, they are, and how I've put up with their nonsense for as long as I have before ringing you, don't ask me."

Delphick was startled. "You mean the Nuts—I do beg their pardons, Miss Nuttel and Mrs. Blaine—they *suggested* that you ought to telephone me? Why?"

The laughter had left his voice, which sounded almost as grim now as Brinton's. With a noticeable degree of control, the superintendent replied:

"Not exactly, no, they didn't. In fact—don't take this the wrong way, Oracle, I'm only reporting what they said—but they sort of suggested that you were in league with her for a share of the profits, and that's why nobody has caught these Turpins yet."

There was a pause. "Not the first time," said Delphick mildly, "that someone's made a similar suggestion, though not recently, I hope. And I also hope you aren't going to take it seriously— even if this whole series of robberies does seem to be succeeding remarkably well."

"Remarkably," echoed Brinton. "As I told Harry when we first spoke about it, this damned Dick Turpinning is here to stay for a bit, because it works, doesn't it? Chummy and his friends have found themselves a nice little formula that isn't messy or slow or particularly dangerous. And they'll try again, I feel it in my bones. It's quick, and effective, and I wish to goodness they'd stayed over in Sussex, instead of coming into my patch. Dick Turpins I suppose I can just about cope with, but when you add Miss Seeton . . . !"

As words failed his suffering friend, Delphick enquired: "What's she done to upset you, Chris, and make you telephone me? I refuse to believe that *she* has suggested I'm in league with anyone."

Bob Ranger's eyes were out on stalks as he listened to this part of the conversation. "Sir," he began to protest, at the very idea of his and Anne's Aunt Em accusing anybody of anything, especially the policeman from Scotland Yard who was, in a manner of speaking, her boss. Or who at least was responsible for her having been attached to the force as the IdentiKit artist she remained convinced that she was. "Sir, there must be—"

Delphick waved him to silence, but favoured him with a brief grin as he did so. Bob subsided, mollified. Oracular humour, he supposed he'd better put it down to, that talking of Miss Seeton suggesting a conspiracy. If it had been anyone else but Aunt Em, he'd have seen the funny side of it himself—but she was different.

"She *had* to be different," gloomed Brinton at last, when he'd finally brought himself to explain. "Everyone on that coach agreed on what they'd seen—even your precious Nuts—except Miss Seeton, of course. It's my own fault—I should never have tried to out-Oracle *you*, Chief Superintendent Delphick, by asking her if she could do one of her little sketches to give me an idea of what went on. I mean," said the superintendent in a near-pleading voice, "she'd been and bought herself a fine new lot of sketching stuff only that morning, hadn't she? Fate, it seemed like to me, so I asked her to oblige . . . "

As he trailed off into a despairing choke, Delphick said in some surprise: "Chris, d'you mean she wouldn't do you a drawing? That's not like her at all," and he waved Bob to silence once more. "She's most conscientious, and she knows this is police business, and we pay her, so—"

"Oh, she drew me a very clear sketch, thank you, quick as winking and hardly looking at the paper." Brinton drew in his breath deeply, which gave Delphick time to say:

"When she draws like that, you'd best take notice of it, Chris. The slow, routine stuff hasn't got the Seeton touch, but the quick cartoons—they're what we want." Then he paused, recalling the pirate sketch Miss Seeton had produced when helping with the Sherry Gang killing; and how there had been, as far as he could tell, nothing useful in it at all. Maybe she was losing her touch— maybe she was growing old. It happened, after all, even to the best . . .

"Tell me what the drawing looked like," he invited, with a quick glance at Sergeant Ranger. "Just because she saw, or rather interpreted, something a different way from everybody else doesn't mean there might not be a purpose of some sort behind it, if we could just understand it. A matter of interpretation by ourselves, if you like."

Brinton groaned. "I knew it," he said. "Anyone who has to

deal with Miss Seeton needs an interpreter because she's talking a different language—*and* they need a whole new vocabulary just to think about her. Or," he added, "in this case, a history book. Because that's what the drawing was, Oracle—not modern times at all, but obviously a war-time scene. The chummies wore helmets, you see—motorbike gear—and she translated it into your typical air-raid tin helmet, on your typical ARP warden's head. Oh yes, we got the lot," he said, above Delphick's startled interjection. "Ruined buildings, searchlights, sandbags—and very cleverly done, even I can see that. It looked as if she only did a couple of quick squiggles, and bingo! There it was. But about as much use," he concluded, "as one of those tin helmets would have been if a doodlebug'd scored a direct hit."

Delphick was silent. Old people, he knew, as they grew older developed a tendency to dwell more and more on their past life, rather than on the present and uncertain future. He had no idea of Miss Seeton's exact age, but when they'd first met she had still been teaching, and thinking about an early retirement. Surely—he did a brief mental calculation, then frowned and double-checked it on his blotter—the mid-sixties was rather young to start living in the past—and (with thoughts of that female pirate very much in his mind) how far into the past was she likely to regress? Had all her adventures proved too much for Miss Seeton, and was their cumulative effect now to render her . . .

"She's *not* senile," he said firmly. Bob Ranger goggled, then looked likely to explode. Delphick scowled at him and returned to the telephone. "Chris, I don't know what she's playing at, but there's bound to be a good reason for these, well, historical drawings she's doing now. I told you about the Sherry Gang pirate she sketched for me, didn't I? And I thought at the time she was simply recreating from memory the conversation she and my sergeant—yes, the young giant who invited you to his wedding," as Brinton said something, and Bob grinned a sheepish grin. "Miss Seeton and the sergeant, you see, had been talking about the Sherry lot being like vultures and pirates on the way up to Town, and I was daft enough then to suppose she'd just reproduced the talk. But I'm sure, now, there's got to be more to it than that."

"If you say so," said Brinton with a sigh. "The Oracle has spoken, and who am I to argue? What do you suggest I do with this damned air-raid then—frame it and stare at it until inspiration strikes? I prefer a method of policing that's slightly more efficient, thanks."

"Carry on detecting, by all means," Delphick said, "and don't worry too much about Miss Seeton's sketch. When the time's right, everything will fall into place, and you'll be kicking yourself for not acting on such an obvious clue much earlier, after she's handed it to you on a plate. Just as I'm hoping will happen with the pirate—eventually. But Miss Seeton would be the last person to expect us to neglect the ordinary police routine while we wait for inspiration to strike—so, while we're waiting, what's the routine news?"

Brinton told him. The Turpin robbery had been just like all the others, and details of those were well-known to the general public, let alone to the police. "All we've got to go on—what I hoped would help—is Miss Seeton, Oracle, and her doodles. I wish I'd listened to myself," he almost moaned, "when I warned Harry Furneux there was worse to come. I wish I hadn't been so relieved it hadn't happened to me because, like I said, this is a judgement on me . . ."

"Surely it's not as bad as that. Oh!" For Delphick had remembered the other case in which his Ashford colleague had an interest: the Sherry Gang, and their wheelchair victim. "Er, yes, I was just wondering," he began. "How's that poor young woman in hospital?" If she were on the mend and able to give a clear statement, that could be at least something to lighten the gloom.

"No better," Brinton told him. "And did you know the driver in the Hastings incident had a heart attack? The sawbones said it was brought on by stress. He's still on the danger list. These Turpins could be facing a manslaughter charge if he dies, never mind the Sherry killers. Tell me, Oracle—why do the chummies all seem to prefer my patch to yours? What's got into everybody?" And then, before Delphick had a chance to reply, he answered his own impassioned question.

"It's because *she's* here," he said. "She doesn't have to do anything—she just opens that umbrella of hers, and everything goes wobbly. I'm tearing my hair out by the handful, let me tell you, and I'm sure there's worse to come—which is why I'm ringing you, Oracle. You seem to be able to cope with her—and your Sherry lot have turned up here—so how would you like to do me a big favour? Come along to Kent and join in the fun, can't you? Bring your tame giant, and see if between the pair of you you can cope with Miss Seeton . . . because I don't believe," groaned Brinton, "that I'm up to it . . ."

# chapter
## -17-

THOUGH THE MAJORITY of those now converging carelessly upon the post office had done most of their shopping in Brettenden, in the interests of scandal-mongering, it is always possible for Plummergen gossips to find that their shelves are bare of some absolute essential which must be purchased at once.

The storm might have blown over to leave skies of summer blue, but Mrs. Flax insisted that she planned hot bread-and-cheese pudding for her supper, and would thank Mr. Stillman to serve her with a pound and a half of strong cheddar, two of onions, and to mind as they weren't shooting because the green bits did no good to anybody's innards, and she'd got troubles enough already. "Fairly soaked through this morning, I was," she grumbled. "And then having to wait around with wet feet in case them Nuts decided to come back on the bus with the rest of us, lucky if I don't end up with galloping pewmonia."

"And it's no time for *me* to fall sick, neither," sighed Mrs. Scillicough, brooding on her triplets. "I'll take one of your biggest tins of mustard powder for a footbath, Mr. Stillman, and the last time I go on that bus if there's to be no regular timetable kept to."

The field was now open. Mrs. Spice, in urgent need of a fresh lemon and a pot of honey, and then she'd be along to the George and Dragon's off-licence to buy the makings of a hot toddy, added her own complaint about the selfish tardiness of the Nuts. "Never known such a thing to happen, not once before, I haven't," said Mrs. Spice. "Mind you, there's no telling, is there, with some people."

"Only to be expected from newcomers, not used to our way of doing things and only thinking of theirselves, that's the truth of the matter. Never fitted in properly, have they?" And Mrs. Scillicough looked round, pleased with herself, then caught the warning eye of Mrs. Spice. Oh, dear, what had she said . . . oh. That little Mrs. Manuden, young Betsy as lived in Old Mother Dawkin's place next to the Nuts, she'd come in and was listening, turned pink, she had. Mrs. Scillicough turned slightly pink herself. But if young Betsy'd had so little sleep as the mother of triplets, maybe *she'd* be less watchful with her tongue and not sure of what, much of the time, she was saying. Mrs. Scillicough tossed her head and slapped down on the counter enough money for ten tins of mustard powder.

Mrs. Spice took pity on her friend. "Nobody," she said, "could be expected to go fitting in when they're up to such mischief as them Nuts seem to be. For what reason could they have for missing the bus back? Up to no good, I'll be bound, and in such dreadful weather you'll not convince me it was window-shopping they was about, not never you won't."

"They'll be in London by now, about their evil business, *luring* people," breathed Emmy Putts from behind the grocery counter. "Slipping drugs in cups of tea, and the poor girls waking up in rooms with mirrors and red velvet curtains and, well, *double beds*," and she shuddered with delicious horror. There was a general murmur of agreement, which was broken by a sharp word from Mrs. Stillman.

"Don't talk so silly, Emmeline. A young girl like you oughtn't to know about things like that, never mind speaking of them in such a fashion, so you get on with your work and put these nonsensical matters right out of your head. What your mother would think, if she could hear you talking this way, I couldn't say," said Mrs. Stillman, as her husband gave her an approving nod. Emmy flounced and turned red, and was heard to mutter rebelliously, though nobody could quite make out her words.

In the ensuing slight awkwardness, Mrs. Manuden decided to ignore any aspersions that might have been cast upon her status, and to introduce a fresh topic of conversation just like any real villager. "My Den," she said proudly, "is doing ever so well with the garden, you know. Looks a proper treat now. He's got rid of nearly all those nasty brambles in the far corner, and you can see almost to the door of the air-raid shelter." She looked round, delighted with the effect of her words. There was much shuffling of feet, and nobody could meet her eyes: a casual observer might have supposed everyone to have been struck dumb with embarrassed gratitude. "And won't the vicar be pleased when Den's sold all his raffle tickets," she added brightly, "and there'll be that much more money for the church roof."

Plummergen might have been expected to rejoice at the notion that its collective head would no longer run the risk of repeated soakings in wet weather, but Betsy's remarks met with continued uncomfortable silence. Betsy's smile wavered as she advanced on Mr. Stillman behind his counter. Here was someone she could talk to. "You'll put some tickets out for sale when Den's had them printed, won't you, Mr. Stillman?" she enquired prettily. With her old-fashioned costume and style of dressing her hair, she could even have pouted and got away with it, but Betsy was shrewd enough to calculate exactly how far she could go. "The vicar's going to mention it in his church newsletter," she said in conclusion, since nobody else was saying anything. "Ever so glad we'll be, Den and me, to do something for the village when you've all been so nice and friendly . . . "

Plummergen does not possess a conscience, as such, but from time to time it can feel uncomfortable, as it did now. It hurried to be nice and friendly to little Mrs. Manuden, since it could hardly gossip about her as it wished to do when she was there in person. "Well, it's very kind of you and your husband, dear," said Mrs. Henderson, "to think of us like this. I'm sure I'll be buying a ticket, maybe two."

"I'll certainly be stocking them," said Mr. Stillman, "as the vicar's in agreement—raffles being along the lines of gambling, you see, which some folk don't approve of. But he seems happy enough with the idea, and anyway it'd be a shame to waste my window display, so tell your husband, Mrs. Manuden, to bring along as many books as he likes. And now what was it," he asked her, "that you wanted?"

For Mr. Stillman knew that by serving this interloper—despite her greatest efforts, that was all Betsy Manuden could ever be— he would help to speed her on her way; at which time the conversation, and the concurrent commercial transactions, could thankfully resume. Mr. Stillman did not approve of gossip, but was realistic enough to understand that it was the lifeblood of the villagers, whose custom was his own livelihood.

Village instinct was in his favour. "And when you've finished serving Mrs. Manuden," said Mrs. Skinner, quickly moving to form the start of a queue at Betsy's rear, "I'll have a pound of jacket potatoes and a half of butter, thank you. Quite fancy something hot for my supper."

Mrs. Henderson added her voice to the requests and her person to the queue. She would like a bar of soap, please. Mrs. Spice remarked on her need for some dried fruit and a packet of icing sugar before lining up behind Mrs. Henderson, whose support for Mrs. Skinner was felt to be something of a miracle. The two ladies had barely spoken one civil word to each other since a little dispute over whose turn it was to arrange the flowers in church; but in the general interests of the village, old scores are, if not forgotten, at least put into abeyance for the duration. Betsy Manuden found herself being edged out of the way, and out of the shop, by a splendid example of crowd co-operation.

Once she had departed, with her shopping in her bag and a crooked smile on her face, everyone felt free to indulge in the wildest speculation, although there was a certain amount of confusion as to which of the two items of greatest interest should be talked through first: the disappearance of the Nuts on some presumably unimaginable private ploy, or the possibility of Susannah Dawkin's body being discovered in the air-raid bunker and a posthumous charge of murder being directed against Queer Albie.

After much discussion and confused argument, victory was claimed by Mrs. Flax, who had the loudest voice. She pointed out with regret that, since Albie was long dead, and there were (with his mother's recent death) no other interested parties, there'd be little sense in raising a cry of murder, as what could they do about it even if they knew for sure? "There'd be some business in it for me, I make no doubt," she said, reminding everyone of her function as Plummergen's layer-out of the dead, "but's not to say I'd welcome finding the poor girl's corpus, although glad to see her put to rest in a proper place at last. But them Nuts, now, they're fine and alive this very day, and up to mischief, what's more, to make no bones about it . . . " which was accepted as a valid argument. Everyone began to prepare themselves for some enjoyable imaginings, and indeed Mrs. Henderson had opened her mouth to speak, when Mrs. Flax capped her triumph by adding, in sinister tones:

"Not that they were the only ones as never come back on the bus with the rest of us. Didn't nobody notice but me?" She beamed round at the suddenly enthralled little group and savoured her moment of glory. And then:

"Neither did Miss Seeton never come back," piped up Mrs. Scillicough, who was feeling crotchety at the thought of returning to the demands of the triplets, and consequently cared not a jot about hurting the feelings of one who, a school of thought insisted, as the local wise woman had powers beyond ordinary folk. Mrs. Scillicough had recently consulted Mother Flax about the behaviour of the triplets, but all the herbal potions and nostrums the fat old fraud had come up with hadn't done not a pennyworth of good. So much, thought Mrs. Scillicough, for trying to keep her sweet all these years—it was all pretence, and there wasn't nothing she could do about nothing, for all her fine talk, so no need to act scared of her, and: "Miss Seeton never come back on the bus," she insisted, with a weary hand shoving the hair back from her face.

"No more she did," agreed Mrs. Spice. "I was that wet about the feet and looking forward to being home in the dry, I never noticed before, but you're right." A general murmur of assent rose from everyone else, overvoiced by Mrs. Flax, who saw her advantage being snatched from her.

She stared round with a burning gaze at the audience she was in danger of losing, and uttered the thrilling words: "So, why d'you reckon she never come back? Supposing she wasn't never to come back no more? Those Nuts, they've not bin exactly what you'd call friends to Miss Seeton. They've got it in right and proper for her, and you'll never tell *me* as they'll have gone off somewhere the three of 'em together being sociable. But we all know," she said slowly, nodding a sage head, "how it is when people set to quarrelling, so we do. Queer Albie Dawkin quarrelled with Susannah, and look what happened to her—"

"You said he didn't kill her," objected Mrs. Scillicough, above the scandalised gasps of the others. The burning eyes of Mrs. Flax began to spit fire. Such rebellion, especially from one she'd thought her ally, would have to be quelled if she was not to lose her position as Plummergen's fount of all wisdom. It had its advantages to be respected, *feared,* as was her intent, in a rural community. There were placatory presents left on her doorstep overnight; people stopped to pass the time of day and were always polite; hers was always one of the most comfortable seats in the village hall for any public function. Now here was Mrs. Scillicough, the ingrate, twisting her words and making her look foolish.

"I never said no such thing," said Mrs. Flax firmly, "for what I *did* say was how the poor girl's body might be lying there this very minute in that bunker, and none the wiser, but there's no chance of seeing him as killed her brought to justice. But," she said, projecting her voice to the most distant corners of the post office, "if them Nuts have done away with Miss Seeton, and hidden *her* body, and escaped the law, well . . . "

This was one of the choicest speculations Plummergen had enjoyed for years. The air was fizzing with ideas, politely suppressed until Mrs. Flax had finished.

"They've had a full day's start, and no police'll catch neither hide nor hair of them!" concluded Mrs. Flax grimly, and fixe Mrs. Potter, wife to Plummergen's village bobby and a fascinated, if silent, observer of recent proceedings, with a knowing look. "Two against one," said Mrs. Flax, "and she no longer in her prime—wouldn't have stood a chance, Miss Seeton wouldn't, mark my words!"

Her words had been duly marked, and Mabel Potter (though she believed them no more than, in its scandal-loving heart, Plummergen as a whole did) reported them to her husband; who thought it his duty to report them to Superintendent Brinton in Ashford, though it was not his usual day for ringing in. With the result that when, chauffeured from London by Bob Ranger, Chief Superintendent Delphick made a special effort and arrived at the police station early that evening instead of the next day, to render his old friend whatever assistance he could, he was met by a man whose hair, Delphick would have been almost prepared to swear, really had turned several shades whiter than it had previously been.

"I don't know how much more I can take," Brinton greeted his colleague with a groan. "I've just had Potter on the phone from your favourite Kentish village, Oracle, and you'll never guess what they're saying now."

"I couldn't begin to," said Delphick, "so tell me. From the look on your face, Miss Seeton must come into it."

"She's been murdered," said Brinton. The two Scotland Yarders jumped and exclaimed, but the superintendent hurried to set them straight.

"No, no, nothing like that—she was fine when I popped her into a Panda car a couple of hours ago and sent her home. But she hadn't reached home before Potter'd rung to warn me that the whole damn village seems to have worked it out that Miss Seeton's been bumped off by Miss Nuttel and Mrs. Blaine, because she somehow found out that they're running a white slave ring—don't shout at me like that, I'm just telling you what he said. And, wait for it—her body has been hidden by a henchman of the Nuts. In— now, this may interest you—in an air-raid bunker at the bottom of somebody's garden."

# chapter
# ~18~

AFTER MABEL POTTER had left the post office, and even while her spouse was telephoning to his superior in Ashford, those members of the Plummergen gossip circuit who remained in Mr. Stillman's emporium were thrilled when a car drew up outside Lilikot.

"A police car!"

"A Panda car," amended more knowledgeable citizens, with glee, and there came a concerted rush to the door. Somebody more practical than the rest closed the door, so that the Nuts, if they should happen to glance across the road, might not observe too many interested faces peering at them from the other side of the glass. Several tins and packets were swiftly removed from Mr. Stillman's careful window display to give a direct visual line across to The Nut House; and Mrs. Scillicough scored mightily by sneaking round to the back of the grocery counter and appropriating Mr. Stillman's set of aluminium steps, which she mounted in triumph in order to see over the top of Plummergen's collective head. Everyone held their breath and waited.

The uniformed driver climbed out of the Panda to open its rear door, through which, tottering, emerged first Miss Nuttel and then Mrs. Blaine, so shaken by all she'd undergone she barely remembered to limp. The young policeman said something which nobody inside the post office could hear, to which Miss Nuttel made some equally inaudible reply. There was a spirited discussion on the wisdom of re-opening the door of the post office, but before a decision could be made the Nuts had said goodbye to their— chauffeur? warder?—and, leaning one upon the other, lurched up

Lilikot's front path, groped inside handbags and pockets for their keys, and vanished within.

Everyone's breath was expelled, then quickly drawn back in for the purposes of speech. It was a race to see who would volunteer the first opinion. Mrs. Scillicough, who'd had by far the best view of events, won.

"They've not got enough evidence yet to hold 'em, the police haven't, so they're letting them bide while they investigate further. That's what it must be."

"They'll be keeping watch to see if'n when they contacts that Dennis Manuden about hiding the corpus," Mrs. Skinner decided. "He'll not be opening up that bunker with raffle tickets, mark my words. We'll have her in here again, *We've changed our minds, such a pity*, that's what she'll say, and nothing to be done about it, for the police don't seem to be bothered to do their jobs proper. They should've kept them in Ashford till they admitted everything, so they should, not let them come home as if nothing was the matter."

This was felt to be true, but a waste of effort, since Mrs. Potter was no longer around to hear the slur on her husband and his colleagues. Mrs. Henderson, who had not forgiven the flowers for the church but was willing to forget, in the interests of scandal, jumped in at once.

"The police'll be watching the house for evidence, like Mrs. Scillicough said, and they'll get it, see if I'm not right. Then they'll open up that bunker and find . . . " She shuddered expressively. "Oh, I don't like to think about it—not that I remember Susannah so well, her being so much older'n me, but she'll be just a skellington by now, which won't be so bad. But poor Miss Seeton—somebody known to all of us . . . "

"That little Mrs. Manuden has a look of Susannah," said one who'd been at school with Queer Albie's daughter until her father had decided that Holdfast Brethren should attend nothing but Sunday education. "Them clothes, and her hair, just like living through the war again to see her, it is."

"And a lot of them war-time things were made better than this modern rubbish," volunteered Mrs. Skinner. "Supposing, when they opens up that bunker, the bones are wearing one of Susannah's own dresses!"

Mrs. Henderson couldn't resist the chance. "Well, whose else would the poor girl have been wearing?" she demanded, to a chorus of agreement. "And there'll be her teeth," she added vaguely. "Tell a lot from the teeth, so they can."

"They won't need teeth for Miss Seeton," scoffed Mrs. Skinner. "Hardly cold, her corpus won't be, and what with her clothes and her umbrella, won't be hard to know who it is when they've found her. And then," indicating the quiet plate glass of Lilikot, "we'll see things start to happen!"

This was doubtless true, but what happened at that particular juncture was that Mr. Stillman cleared his throat. Loudly, in a meaningful fashion. And, now that the police car had departed, people remembered the ostensible purpose for their being in the post office, and began to make their reluctant way back to the counter, stepping over the tins and bottles that nobody had bothered to replace in the window. Mr. Stillman said nothing, but his eye was eloquent, and it was considered prudent to humor him by starting to buy things again. Only Mrs. Flax, for some reason feeling her nose to have been put out of joint, did not join the drift to the counter, preferring to linger by the door, peering into the street.

Suddenly, with a startled and indignant yelp, she drew back, but not in time to prevent herself being caught by the door as a new customer, breathless, excited, came rushing in. Mrs. Flax was about to remonstrate mightily with such impertinence when she recognised the light of excitement in the newcomer's eye.

It was Mrs. Putts, Emmy's mother, home from her job in the Brettenden biscuit factory. "You'll never guess," she cried, ostensibly to her daughter, but with a watchful eye on the rest of the audience she'd felt sure would be there. "Another Dick Turpin robbery, that's what there's been, seen it on the news on telly— and right near here, this time! A coach full of trippers going to France, it was, and driving from Brettenden to Lydd, and held up near the Gibbet Oak—and on the telly, it said that *some local residents were believed to have been involved!*"

Then there was uproar. All talk of Susannah Dawkin's long-ago disappearance was forgotten in favour of this new, enthralling possibility. It was clear that by *local residents* the telly must mean the Nuts: why else should they have been brought back by a police car? They'd missed the chartered Omney bus which was supposed to bring them back, but if they'd had a good, legal reason for missing it they could easily have taken a taxi the six miles from Brettenden to Lilikot. They must have been on that other bus, and this wasn't the first occasion they'd been Turpinned, was it?

"Which is suspicious enough, if you ask me, without them doing away with poor Miss Seeton, too," opined Mrs. Skinner. "Look at what she's always doing to help Scotland Yard, and how thick she is with the police! And them Nuts, twice is too much of a coincidence. They're obviously in league with the Turpin lot and they've realised Miss Seeton was on to them somehow, so they lured the poor soul on that bus—"

But development of this promising line of speculation was suddenly halted when Mrs. Flax, still brooding by the door and rubbing her bruises, came out with an announcement that stopped everything dead. "There's another police car coming down The Street—but," in a puzzled tone, "it's going past The Nut House . . . "

Everyone turned and rushed back to the door (which the ample bulk of Mrs. Flax blocked almost entirely) and windows, desperate for a view. Mr. Stillman raised his brows, sighed, folded his arms, and prepared to wait once more.

"It's gone right past," said Mrs. Spice, very puzzled. "I made sure as they'd be coming back to ask those Nuts a deal more questions, but . . . "

Anxious and inquisitive necks were desperately craned, but there is a limit to the elasticity of human bodies and the field of view from a flat-fronted window. The police car had driven past: the door must be opened, and somebody must stand outside on the pavement in order to report back on where that car had gone, who might be in it, and what he or she or they might be doing.

Mrs. Putts, who'd been the focus of all attention, was a little miffed now to be ignored in favour of Mrs. Henderson, Plummergen's choice. Mrs. Henderson stood nearest the door, after Mrs. Flax (tacitly admitted to be too large for a lookout) and was therefore best placed for a quick exit from the post office to the pavement, where she was instructed by an excited chorus to hide as much of herself as possible behind one of the trees which lined The Street, and watch what was going on, and where.

It is hard to be unobtrusive behind a tree and to appear as if one has a valid reason for being there, but for the sake of Plummergen Mrs. Henderson was willing to try. Behind the tree she lurked, looking as casual as she could, peering down The Street and reporting back, after a few moments:

"They've stopped outside Sweetbriars!"

The babble from inside the post office was earsplitting. Everyone crowded even closer to the open doorway to catch every golden word.

"There's a policeman getting out—in a uniform . . . "

"Going to check for bloodstains," came the suggestion from someone who was instantly shushed. Miss Seeton, after all, had disappeared from Brettenden, not Plummergen—that is, so they thought. But supposing she'd come back under her own steam, unnoticed, and violence had occurred in her own home, after all? However, there was no time to enlarge on this theme, for Mrs. Henderson was hissing:

"*It's Miss Seeton!*" Gasps of amazement from those who were near the door and could hear; cries of frustration from those at the back, who demanded to be told what was happening. Mrs. Henderson's words were relayed as she spoke them.

"Getting out of the back of the car . . . now the copper's seeing her up the path . . . now she's opening the front door, and he's coming back to the car . . . she's gone inside and shut the door, and the copper's driving away!"

Furtive glances were cast across The Street towards the windows of Lilikot. Had the Nuts been somehow maligned by the village? Could there be an explanation?

There could; and Mrs. Flax, savouring her moment of triumph, produced it. "That weren't never Miss Seeton," she said, so firmly that they knew it must be true. "Who's in Sweetbriars this minute's no more Miss Seeton than what I am. She's an imposter, a policewoman pretending to be Miss Seeton, that's who she is!"

"Whyfore would anyone pretend to be Miss Seeton?" asked Mrs. Scillicough, while the others digested this and found it acceptable, if puzzling. Mrs. Scillicough was prepared to be argumentative. "Seems downright daft to me—"

"Because the police has to negotiate," crowed Mrs. Flax, "and while they're doing it there's nobody supposed to find out what's happened, that's whyfore! Nobody knows the truth of the matter barring them Nuts, natural enough, seeing as they was the ones as set up Miss Seeton for their gang to nobble—and worse than nobbled, she's been. She's been," Mrs. Flax said with certainty, "kidnapped!"

Which was the perfect note on which to end the session, for Mr. Stillman was clearing his throat and looking very pointedly at his watch. Those with less brazen natures did indeed head for the counter for the third time, and make a pretence of buying, but most people hurried out of the post office to watch the police car disappearing down The Street over the Royal Military Canal towards the Ashford road. The door of Sweetbriars remained shut fast; the imposter stayed out of sight.

But not out of mind. Suppers that night throughout the village were as rife with speculation as any Plummergen meal had ever been . . .

And when *that Scotland Yard copper and his sergeant as married Dr. Knight's girl Anne* arrived to book rooms in the George and Dragon, then crossed The Street to call on Sweetbriars, everyone knew why they were there.

To help the imposter of Miss Seeton play her part with as much accuracy as possible, of course.

# chapter
# ~19~

As Chief Superintendent Delphick and Sergeant Ranger walked up Miss Seeton's path to the front door of Sweetbriars, they sensed the collective gaze of curious Plummergen burning into their backs. It was as much as they could do not to turn round and wave the watchers away: they knew it would be an empty gesture, for there would be nobody in sight. The village knew better than to be caught out so easily.

"They'll have heard about the Turpinning by now," said Delphick, "and no doubt believe we're here to arrest Miss Seeton for whatever part she's supposed to have played this time. A great pity Miss Nuttel and Mrs. Blaine had to be on the same bus—their tongues won't have stopped wagging for a minute, I'll wager."

"Everyone's tongues wag in this place, sir," Bob Ranger, husband to the doctor's daughter and budding expert in local customs, reminded him. "Well, nearly everyone's." He could hardly envisage Doctor and Mrs. Knight, or the Colvedens, or, of course, Miss Emily Seeton, as being over-oscillatory in their vocal habits: but Plummergen as a whole . . .

Delphick reached the front door, and his brisk rapping broke into Bob's train of thought. He rearranged the frown with which he'd brooded briefly on Plummergen's thirst for gossip, and turned it into a smile with which to greet Miss Seeton, his (off-duty) and Anne's Aunt Em.

"Mr. Delphick—and dear Sergeant Ranger, good evening." Miss Seeton was there, smiling in welcome, looking delighted to see them. "It would be foolish of me to pretend," she continued, leading the way through the hall and into the sitting room, "that

129

I had not anticipated the likelihood of some visitation from the police. This afternoon's little adventure, you see, and Mr. Brinton so disappointed, I could tell, although he is far too much of a gentleman to say so. But I do regret that I was unable to assist him then beyond a most unhelpful statement: it was so very quick, and rather a shock. But I never believed," Miss Seeton smiled again, "that it might be both of you."

Delphick disentangled her true meaning and smiled back. "Normally, you'd be right: the hold-up took place within the Kent County area and wouldn't as such be Scotland Yard's responsibility, but we were on our way here in any case. There's been another Sherry incident, locally, and Superintendent Brinton suggested it might be a good idea for us to pool our information."

Miss Seeton went pink. "My sketches, I suppose? Such a disappointment, when one naturally wished to do one's duty, and a golden opportunity, I would have thought. Having been an eyewitness, I mean. To the robbery, that is, not this sad sherry business—so cruel, the pretence of help, and most people would be grateful, I know, and never dream of coming to any harm—such a very plausible excuse, and they must be very good actors." Bob Ranger stirred, but had no time to say anything before she continued: "Somehow one is less inclined to harbour suspicions against a woman, don't you agree? And with such a very normal appearance, too, it seems. No masks," said Miss Seeton, "or shotguns. Only, as I said, it was all over so quickly. And one cannot help but feel guilty—the retainer," and she blushed. A lady does not discuss money; but when on police business, Miss Seeton was a professional, not a gentlewoman, and must try to adopt a more professional attitude. "So undeserved, when the call to action finally came—I was wondering," and she blushed again, "whether a deduction ought not to be made, for failing to assist one's colleagues in the manner they would be entitled to expect. A penalty clause," she said earnestly. "It would seem the correct thing to do. Dereliction of duty, you see."

Delphick knew and understood Miss Seeton's conscience, and, hiding a smile, shook his head firmly. "There's no need to worry about it, you know. As you say, it was very quickly over, and it would hardly be fair to expect even the trained eye of an artist like yourself to recognise people with stocking masks over their faces and motorbike helmets on their heads. But we were certainly interested," he went on quickly, over her half-voiced protest, "in the sketch you produced—in both of them, in fact, which is why we're here now." He opened the cardboard file he'd been holding in one hand. "May I?"

He moved to the low table and set the two sketches side by side, then switched on the standard lamp. "Does anything strike you, Miss Seeton? Take your time."

Miss Seeton came to stand beside him, and gazed at the evidence of her talents in some bewilderment. The sketches that she drew so speedily, so instinctively—the cartoon-type drawings for which she was so highly valued by Scotland Yard—often did not linger in her memory very long after she had drawn them. Not that one was ashamed—perhaps a little embarrassed would be an acceptable word—of one's work, such as it was, and certainly it should not be thought of as serious art, of which one might more justifiably feel a modest sense of pride. But sketches, after all, were only the scribblings of one's subconscious, and as such undisciplined. The great masters of art might be able to transform their scribblings into great masterpieces, but one's little efforts served rather as reminders that one's talent, too, was small. Far better, in Miss Seeton's view, to draw only what one saw, which was there as a reference point, and not to attempt to draw from inside one's own head what could not be seen, and which therefore could be no reference point at all, and must show a sad lack of self-discipline.

Miss Seeton would have been amazed—shyly proud, but amazed—to be told that Chief Superintendent Delphick waged perpetual guerrilla warfare with his ultimate superior, Sir Hubert Everleigh, Assistant Commissioner (Crime), over those same undisciplined scribblings. Sir Heavily always tried to pull rank and acquire Miss Seeton's sketches for his private collection, for he had a connoisseur's eye as well as the instincts of a shrewd financial investor. Delphick regarded the sketches as evidence, and thus police property, and said that Sir Heavily could have photocopies, if he wanted, but the originals should remain filed in a safe place. A place which he had so far insubordinately refused to identify . . .

He'd have to ask Chris Brinton, of course, what he would be doing with the air-raid sketch once the Turpin crowd had been caught and popped behind bars—always assuming that they were. Delphick acknowledged that the few clues they'd so far acquired didn't seem likely to lead to early arrests, but this business with the sketches made him more hopeful. And maybe the Ashford superintendent would be so relieved when it was all over that he'd relinquish the sketch without a murmur, glad to do without even more reminders—if indeed he needed any—of Miss Emily Dorothea Seeton.

Who was studying her handiwork now with interest, and a dawning awareness in her eye. "Why, how very strange, and what a coincidence," she remarked at last. "Different, yet somehow the same—do you suppose they might be? The same, I mean—two women, and one man . . ."

The female pirate, with her eye-patch and earrings and her scarf tied across her head, swaggered at the head of her motley band of ruffians with her cutlass held high, a symbol of leadership. One booted leg was bent, and rested on what looked like a cask of grog, or rum. Her form was lightly, but plainly, sketched: no doubt of her femininity, nor that of one of her followers who was more obvious, although in the background, than most of the others, whose presence was indicated by cross-hatchings speedily executed, their angles altering to indicate form without detail. But the second pirate, as shapely as the first, was more clearly sketched. She was younger than her leader, although Delphick could not say how he knew this for sure; in one hand she seemed to be holding a bottle, while the other grasped the hand of a man, who in his free hand brandished, like his chief, a cutlass. The chief was the focus of attention, her followers a more shadowy, uncertain group hovering on the deck of the pirate ship, well to the rear.

"I should have looked much more closely at this," said Delphick, as Miss Seeton did so herself. "It never struck me until Chris Brinton showed me the other . . ."

The other was the air-raid scene that must have been a familiar sight to anyone who endured the war in any of England's cities. A bombed and battered building reared up against a sky crossed by the beams of searchlights; there was the unmistakable shape of an aeroplane caught in the beams, and an impending sense of guns about to open fire and bring it down. People in the street scurried for the nearby shelter, drawn there by a figure, presumably an air-raid warden, wearing a tin helmet and seeming to blow a whistle. The entrance to the shelter was sinister, a looming mouth, shadowed by the same cross-hatchings that had portrayed the pirate crew; the warden, beneath the stiffness of uniform, had a curved, female shape, as had one of the two people who were at the front of the group rushing to the shelter. The other members of the group, save one, were indicated by that curiously angled cross-hatching;

and the one who was not was shown clearly enough to be identified as a man . . .

"How very curious," remarked Miss Seeton. "Of course, I remember the war, fire-watching on rooftops and the doodlebugs, so unnerving. Once they fell silent all one could do was hope that they would drop in the street, rather than on people's houses, although under the stairs was supposed to be the safest place if one did not go to one of the shelters provided. The street shelters, that is, although there were some people who were fortunate enough to have their own, in the house. Morrison, I believe, large tables made of metal and with iron curtains to keep out the debris, although now an iron curtain has connotations even more ominous, doesn't it? And there were other shelters for gardens, if one was fortunate enough to possess one—Anderson, and such a great deal of digging, as well."

Miss Seeton drew in her breath sharply. "Oh dear, such a foolish habit, this dwelling on the past, and nothing at all to do with our present problem. I cannot imagine what must have possessed me, to draw such very old-fashioned subjects, but I am right, am I not, Chief Superintendent?" She regarded Delphick with a bright and knowledgeable eye. "You, too, believe that these little scribbles of mine show there to be some connection between those scoundrels—" she went pink—"who prey on the unwary and elderly, and the ruffians who waylaid the omnibus this afternoon?"

And Delphick, still looking at the two sketches, said, "Yes, Miss Seeton, I do, though I don't know yet what it can be— unless the same gang is responsible for both types of crime. And that's certainly a possibility. We'll have to check this out, but in my recollection there's never been a Sherry Gang incident at the same time as a Turpin robbery. The Turpins began to operate in this area after the Sherry lot had done a dozen or more in London, and before they started up again in Kent. Maybe they fancied varying their style a little, and are making up their minds which they prefer. Maybe they'll grow even greedier and carry on with both. Unfortunately, for now, we can only wait and see . . . "

He gathered up the sketches and replaced them in their folder. "I suppose," he remarked, "there wouldn't by any chance be a third drawing to add to these two, would there? Something you might have dashed off when you arrived home—just jotting down your impressions of what happened to you this afternoon?" He looked at Miss Seeton as a hopeful dog will watch a cupboard in which there might be a bone. Miss Seeton fidgeted under his gaze, and dropped her own.

"I'm so sorry," she said. "I suppose I should have made an effort—but it was all such a shock, so unexpected to be involved, with the embarrassment of having caught the wrong coach, as well. Everyone was very kind, but after Superintendent Brinton seemed so disappointed, I confess I felt a little guilty, and wanted to forget the entire unfortunate episode. I feared, you see," she said, with a sheepish smile, "that I had let my colleagues—" she blushed—"down, in such a serious matter. I, well, I came straight into the cottage and made myself a nice cup of tea."

She looked up with an even more guilty look on her face. "Oh dear, I forgot to offer you any refreshment, Chief Superintendent! Would you or Sergeant Ranger care for tea, or perhaps a cup of coffee? It is rather late in the evening for me, but if you wish . . . "

Bob looked wistfully at Delphick, but the latter shook his head with a smile. "Thank you, but we must be getting back to the George and Dragon. We're making an early start tomorrow, visiting the scenes of the other Turpin incidents and comparing statements from the Sherry victims with Superintendent Brinton at Ashford. I know we have your statement here," and he tapped the folder, "but I'd be grateful if, once we've gone, you'd try to compose another. Don't hurry over it, you've got all evening, but if there's anything you feel you want to add, please do so. We'll drop by some time tomorrow, if that's convenient, to pick up whatever you manage to produce."

Having said their farewells, Delphick and Bob thoughtfully crossed The Street back to the George and Dragon. "D'you reckon she'll come up with the goods, sir?" asked Bob, who'd felt sorry for the anxious look on Aunt Em's face yet powerless to remove it. Her conscience was in overdrive—luckily the Oracle had tried to direct it into something more productive, whether it was worth the effort or not. But MissEss was one of Scotland Yard's most valuable assets, and if they could stop her fretting herself into a tizzy, in which state she might perhaps lose her talent altogether, it would be a good day's work. A couple of her intuitive sketches would help her feel she was once more pulling her weight—and might just possibly hand another clue to those waiting for it.

"It's always worth a try," said Delphick. "I can't help wondering, though, how much that second drawing—the one of the air-raid—has been influenced by the talk there's been, according to

Superintendent Brinton via PC Potter, about the body which may be in the bunker in some old woman who's just died's garden."

"Mother Dawkin," said Bob, adopted son of Plummergen.

"The tendrils of scandal stretch far and wide," remarked the chief superintendent. "I suppose you also know the full story of the raffle tickets and the time capsule effect, in aid of the church roof?" Bob nodded. Though Anne might no longer live in the village, Dr. and Mrs. Knight still ran the local private nursing home, and, while not hounding the newlyweds with perpetual parental contact, exchanged letters and telephone calls from time to time. Anne relayed such items as she thought would interest or amuse him, and a fresh instalment had been submitted the previous evening.

"Then no doubt," said Delphick, "you're able to show me, Sergeant, which cottage is, or was, the home of Old Mother Dawkin, deceased. I'm curious to see it—not that I expect a guided tour of the bunker," he added, as Bob hesitated. "But even Miss Seeton, and we know she never listens to gossip, hasn't been able to remain impervious to all the excitement there's been, which means the rest of 'em must be fermenting like nobody's business. And somehow it seems to be catching."

Bob still hesitated. Delphick favoured him with a grin. "Local knowledge not as detailed as you'd like, Bob? You've no need to worry about impressing me—it's not important. If I really want to goggle, we can always ask someone."

"It's not that, sir. I think I know where the cottage is—but, well, it's the neighbours I'm bothered about. If we go along just to look . . . "

Delphick's austere features registered controlled and disapproving surprise. "You, Sergeant Ranger, worried about what the neighbours will say? I can hardly believe it."

Bob dropped his voice to a cautious murmur. "Next door to Lilikot, sir, if you insist," he said, grimly leading the way with vast and rapid strides further up The Street past the George and Dragon. Delphick waited a few moments, then enquired, in a tone that was not too breathless:

"Lilikot? That name sounds familiar. I wonder why . . . "

"It's the plate-glass place with the curtains already on the twitch, sir—see?" Bob indicated the curtains with an abrupt movement of his head. "Lilikot—otherwise known as The Nut House," he said, turning to examine the contents of Mr. Stillman's newly-arranged post office windows. Delphick, after a quick look across the road, joined him. They stared together at the tins, bottles, packets, and—

"Good heavens. A ration book—and that cardboard box looks suspiciously like a gas mask to me." The chief superintendent chuckled. "Nostalgia isn't what it used to be, I know, but they're evidently doing their best—that poster," he nodded towards the glass door, blocked not by a blind but by handwritten advice to *Get your Bunker Raffle tickets here and support the Church Roofing Fund. Your chance to go back in time.* "It almost makes me feel like buying a book or two myself, for the honour of wielding the chisel or turning the key or whatever they're planning to do."

"Sir, really," protested Bob. He didn't think Delphick meant it, but with the Oracle you could never be sure. Miss Seeton's sketch seemed to emphasise the war-time influence, and it could be just coincidence, but . . . "That bunker, sir. Suppose the gang's making use of it somehow, say for hiding the swag until they're ready to fence it. Plenty of room in air-raid shelters, so my parents tell me . . . "

"Why make all this kerfuffle about the grand prize of opening the bunker on the Manudens' last day here? Why draw attention to the very place you'd suppose they'd want to keep quiet about?"

It was a valid objection. Bob brooded a while, paying far more attention to the window display than even Mr. Stillman would think it deserved, before he came up with what was the obvious solution. "Double bluff, sir. By focussing our—everybody's—attention on the day they say they plan to leave, and the raffle to be drawn that day by Lady Colveden, they'll make pretty sure we'll take it for granted they've nothing to hide—as we have, haven't we? Sir," he added hastily. Delphick said nothing. Bob went on, after a pause: "It was their bad luck not knowing the rumours about Susannah's disappearance, and not realising how everyone would get worked up about whether her body might be in there. And then, by all accounts the girl is rather old-fashioned in appearance, Forties hairstyle and makeup, which Anne tells me isn't the most popular style nowadays, not even to be different and do your own thing. She or her husband, if that's what he is, could have worked out that to emphasise the war-time connection would make everyone join in the bunker raffle fun without stopping to think there might be a good reason behind it. I thought. Sir," he added, as Delphick still said nothing. Bob shuffled his feet and felt uncomfortable.

"Let's go and ask them," suggested the chief superintendent.

"I won't say I hadn't wondered about it myself, but I agree you may have a point there, Sergeant Ranger. It's not too late to pay a call, even for Plummergen, is it?" And he led the way across the road to Old Mother Dawkin's cottage.

# chapter

# -20-

IN FADED WHITE letters not repainted since Albert Dawkin's death, the front gate announced to the policemen that they were about to visit Ararat Cottage. Albert's mother might have lacked his biblical enthusiasm, but, truer than her son to the Plummergen heritage, lacked also any desire either to remove the nameplate or to alter it. Like the rest of the village, she saw no need, since Plummergen does not bother with modern niceties such as street numbers: it remembers its past too well. When it travels abroad and sends postcards home, it directs them to the old addresses and expects the postal services to have absorbed such nomenclature as "Mrs. Spice's first house" (where she dwelt briefly as a bride over thirty years previously, until the demands of a growing family forced her to move) or "the new tied cottage" (erected by farmer Mulcker's grandfather, just before World War One began).

When Bert the red-haired cockney postman had joined the GPO, longer-serving colleagues handed him a list and told him to memorise it lest half his letters might never leave the bag; or, worse, might be delivered to the wrong house. No doubt, in time, the letters would reach their correct destinations, but during their misplaced hours would be virtually certain to undergo every indignity of thwarted curiosity to which Plummergen might choose to submit them. There are people in the village, Bert was warned, who steam a mean kettle, past mistresses at holding envelopes up to strong artificial light; Plummergen is not given to minding its own business in preference to that of anyone else.

"Eric, do come quick!" One of the most notable steamers was peering out of the windows of Lilikot. "It's those two

138

policemen—the ones who are under That Woman's influence—
and they're going into Mrs. Dawkin's old place! What do you
suppose they can want with the Manudens?"

As Norah Blaine twitched an inquisitive curtain, Erica Nuttel
hastened to join her. "Been at Old Mrs. Bannet's," she reminded
Bunny, leaning on her shoulder to peer at the two official figures
as they trod heavily up the gravel path towards the front door.
"Questioning them, too, I suppose." She leaned still harder as
Delphick and Ranger moved out of easy sight, and Mrs. Blaine
squeaked a protest as her nose was pushed against the glass.
"Sorry," muttered Miss Nuttel in an absent voice. Bunny tossed
her head, and grumbled a little, but was ignored while Eric
pondered.

"Newcomers," she announced at last. "Probably in league with
the Seeton woman. She'll have made a statement. Need to check
it out before arresting anyone, of course."

And with a further squeak, this time of excitement, Mrs. Blaine
agreed that Eric was so right; and resolved to remain by the
window watching for any further developments.

"See those curtains twitching, sir?" Bob enquired of the chief
superintendent, once they'd moved out of range.

"Yes, Sergeant Ranger, I did—my eyesight isn't too far gone
just yet, thank you." Delphick favoured Bob with an austere smile.
"Lilikot—that's the Nuts, I take it, longing to pin something on us,
or Miss Seeton. They must know we've been to see her this evening.
Let's try not to give them anything further to gossip about. No
police brutality, Bob, no third degree when the Manudens answer
the door, or we shall never hear the end of it."

But, though they knocked at the door of Ararat Cottage three
times, leaving sufficient space between each knocking for anyone,
no matter how occupied, to interrupt themselves and answer, there
came no reply. "It's a lovely evening," said Bob rather wistfully,
looking at the sunset and thinking of Anne. "Maybe they've gone
somewhere for a drink." He brightened. "Should I slip round the
back and check things out? If this bunker's already been cleared
for action, then I might be able to—"

"Good heavens, no. Have you had a touch of the sun? We don't
want our friendly neighbourhood snoops reporting us for trespass,
thank you, Sergeant Ranger, adopted son of Plummergen though
you may be. I doubt if even the influence of your respected father-
in-law would prevent serious charges being laid at our door if we
take one step beyond this one." Delphick knocked once more,

half-heartedly, then turned, and led the way back down the path, while the curtains of Lilikot twitched behind him.

Next morning, they were enjoying the George and Dragon's traditional English breakfast when Doris, the head waitress, came bustling over to interrupt the discussion with Maureen, her junior colleague, as to the merits of a second pot of coffee. Doris was clearly full of news, and addressed Chief Superintendent Delphick in a breathless voice.

"You're wanted on the telephone, sir. Superintendent Brinton, from Ashford—that'll be about the Sherry business yesterday, I reckon."

Delphick paused in the act of rising from his chair, and favoured Doris with a curious look. "Yesterday? Sherry?" Bob Ranger blinked, but said nothing. Doris smirked with all Plummergen's traditional pity for the ignorance of foreigners concerning the efficiency of its grapevine.

"Bert told me all about it when he brought today's post. Another Sherry case, he said, Brettenden again, just like the local paper wrote, help some poor soul home with their shopping and then force poisoned drink down their innocent throats." Doris drew in a deep breath of scandalised enjoyment. "Wicked, I call it, and a crying shame, with Scotland Yard almost on the very spot and powerless to help, we could all be murdered in our beds next and nothing done about it."

"No such luck," murmured Delphick, just too low for her to be sure what he'd said, and before she could beg pardon and ask for a repeat, he was gone to the telephone. Maureen was dismissed, with regrets that the second pot of coffee must go unordered, by Bob, who nodded thanks to Doris for having brought the message, and addressed himself to eating the last piece of toast before hurrying after his superior.

He arrived in time to hear Delphick uttering farewells and promises that he would be with Superintendent Brinton just as soon as possible, "Though we'll call on Miss Seeton first, I think. I want to see if she's managed to come up with anything now she's had time to brood."

They were in a hurry, and as they strode across The Street to Sweetbriars their hurry was apparent to everyone. Behind windows, as eyes followed their progress, mental shopping-lists were being put together. No sooner had the door of Old Mrs. Bannet's opened to admit the two policemen than Plummergen collected purses and shopping baskets, and made haste to the post office, eager to comment on this latest episode. The substitute Miss Seeton was entertaining her bosses again—something must be happening, and Plummergen wanted to know, or to speculate in company, what that something might be.

Miss Seeton had only just finished her yoga exercises and was feeling the healthy glow of physical well-being coupled with mental refreshment which the book-jacket had promised her, when Delphick rapped politely on the door. Really, the unfortunate events of yesterday—the wrong bus, so very embarrassing, and those people with helmets and guns, rather dangerous—were put entirely into perspective now. One was confident that they could be banished from one's memory as the unimportant matters that they were, mere interruptions to the ordered way of life one was thankful to resume. With a delighted smile, she welcomed the two detectives into the house, and offered them tea, or coffee, and perhaps a slice of gingerbread, if they had time. Then she caught the look in Delphick's eye, and wondered if this was rather a business call and should she just listen while the chief superintendent explained?

"We're hopeful that you've managed to produce another of your sketches," Delphick told her. "You did, didn't you? Last night, after we'd gone? I'd like to see it."

Miss Seeton stifled a little sigh: she'd so hoped that it was over and done with, though of course one understood that one had a duty to perform, but it had all been slightly disturbing and one would prefer to be allowed to forget it. She led the way through to the sitting room, and withdrew her portfolio from behind the sofa, hoping that Mr. Delphick would not notice the smudge of crushed charcoal which, even with a dustpan and stiff brush, poor Martha had been still unable to remove. What a pity the vacuum cleaner had broken! But Mr. Spellbrook had said he expected his van to be delivering in the area soon, and so, though it worried poor Martha not to have Sweetbriars looking spotless, it should be only a few days more until once more it did.

Miss Seeton undid her portfolio, then turned to Delphick and said hesitantly: "I'm not at all sure—that is, I hope you will not be disappointed as Mr. Brinton was. But I fear I was unable to—nothing *different*, you see, it seems that the two—somehow, I'm afraid, instead of being separate I seem to have—I don't understand why, but I've muddled both cases together and they will mean nothing now. I am so very sorry. Perhaps it would be best—"

But before she could close the portfolio, Delphick held out his hand and said, firmly, "I'd still like to look at what you've drawn, please. Artists aren't often the best judges of their own work, remember, or the best interpreters either. That's why I'm here . . . "

The pirate chief still brandished her cutlass, and her earrings dangled bravely, but instead of her headscarf she now sported a tin helmet, which somehow gave a much clearer view of her face; and the barrel of spirits was gone from beneath her booted foot. It appeared to have been commandeered by the crew, the foremost of whom also wore tin helmets instead of scarves, who were clustered about the foot of the mast. Evidently they had just hoisted the skull and crossbones, which fluttered defiantly over a searchlight on the deck beneath, and in celebration of this bold act had broached the barrel; their hands, emerging from the hatched and cross-hatched shadows, held glasses and, a few clearly more greedy than their fellows, bottles. The searchlight's beam pierced the darkling sky to throw the figure of the pirate chief into stark relief, and the skull on the flag above her head grinned a wide, evil grin above the white crossed bones.

Delphick drew in his breath, and shook his head slowly as he studied Miss Seeton's sketch. For once, he found it hard to say anything, and so at first said nothing at all. Miss Seeton looked quickly and apologetically at Bob, who was staring over his chief's shoulder. She'd tried to tell them—she'd really done her best, but all it seemed she'd achieved was to combine the two cases, the unpleasant Sherry Gang and those unexpected Dick Turpins, as the newspapers called them, and she was sure the chief superintendent must have expected something rather more, well, helpful, from her—in much the same way as poor Superintendent Brinton, who had been so disappointed but too polite to say so.

"Interesting," Delphick said at last, "but puzzling—no two-women-plus-one-man this time. Is that because there's no further need to point out the coincidence, or . . . ?"

"I'm afraid I don't know," said Miss Seeton at last, Bob still staring and saying nothing. Aunt Em's—Miss Seeton's—MissEss's drawings had never made much particular sense to him, barring that sketch she'd done of him in football kit running along behind herself as the Red Queen. Anne laughed every time she looked at it where it was framed and hanging in pride of place in their little sitting room, and said it looked exactly like him. But the Oracle usually understood what her instinct was trying to make clear, and it wasn't like him not to have even a suggestion of what was going on. But he seemed pleased, anyway . . .

"Thank you very much, Miss Seeton," Delphick said, as the pirate sketch joined its fellows in his folder. "I'll be letting Chris Brinton take a look at it, and maybe with the other two one of us will work out what it's all about."

"Oh, dear." Miss Seeton cast another anxious look at Bob. "I haven't been of any help after all, have I? I was so afraid that might be the case. And with these unpleasant people still at large, how worried you must be. I'm sorry."

"Three heads are better than two, Miss Seeton, so don't worry about a thing," Delphick told her. "I have a feeling that once Chris Brinton sees the three at once, he's going to tell us it means something to him—or there's always the outside chance, I know," with a grimace at the silent Bob at his shoulder, "that I myself might make sense of it, though my sergeant, I can tell, has his doubts." As Bob was starting to splutter, Delphick spoke on over his protests. "He's pretending to deny it, of course, but I know how his mind—such as it is—works, you see. I'd better remove it, and him, and myself, from your presence, and carry on to Ashford for an honest day's work."

The Oracle might well have been stumped by that picture, Bob thought as the farewells were being spoken, but if he had it didn't seem to bother him too much. Maybe he'd seen more in it than he was letting on. In which case, why the pretence? Miss Seeton was far too conscientious to chatter about police business or to let valuable information slip in careless talk. But when Delphick flannelled, there was often some good reason for it . . .

"May I ask, sir, what Mr. Brinton had to say?" enquired Bob as soon as they were in the car en route to Ashford. "I know it was another Sherry case, but—"

"Ah, Doris, of course. Well, Doris was wrong, for once: the grapevine occasionally is, you know." Delphick coughed. "Mr. Brinton was very agitated, Sergeant Ranger. There were *two* Sherry incidents yesterday, both of which have only just come to light. No deaths, fortunately, though one isn't too good and has gone to hospital. Her Home Help found her, and I hope we haven't got another RSM Brent on our hands. We'll be keeping in close touch with the quacks. The other old girl's more resilient, but even so it's as nasty a case as ever. Both old people nodded off in their chairs in the afternoon, it seems, and when they woke up popped themselves to bed without wondering what had happened.

Apparently they both have a tendency to these little lapses, so it didn't surprise them."

"Not very nice, sir," said Bob. "They always manage to pick people who live on their own, don't they, sir? Careful questioning of the likely victims before they decide to go ahead, I suppose. If I could only get my hands on them—"

"You'd pop them in a cell before they could say *sleeping tablets*," Delphick interrupted him. The sergeant was starting to sound as if he took this as a personal matter: he was probably envisaging each victim as somebody he knew, which wasn't altogether wise. No sense in becoming a crusader and getting too involved. You had to remain calm and detached and clear-headed enough to follow up clues. Delphick didn't want Bob up on a charge of assaulting a suspect, whether or not he sympathised with the action.

"Mind you, sir, if they ever had a go at Miss Seeton, do you suppose they'd get away with it? She'd probably set her umbrella on them and tie 'em up with ribbon for us to arrest all nice and tidy. Something seems to look after her," Bob said, sounding as if he was trying to convince himself.

Delphick frowned. Better take the lad's mind off it all by asking: "And, talking of Miss Seeton, any more constructive thoughts on all this, Sergeant Ranger? Perhaps taking into account the statements she's made for us?"

"You know I can never make sense of those pictures of hers the way you can, sir. The only thought that comes to mind is that it must be costing them a fortune in sherry—and a waste of good liquor, too. That is, if they're still leaving the full bottle behind?"

"Carefully wiped," agreed Delphick with a nod. "Defiant— flamboyant—blatant, these people. No wonder she keeps seeing 'em as pirates, Bob. But what, I wonder," mused the chief superintendent, "is the World War Two connec—damn!"

"Sir?" It wasn't like the Oracle to start cursing when, so far as Bob could see, nothing had happened.

"It's too late now—I don't want to waste time turning back. But in all the excitement I forgot about dropping in on the Manudens again, to see if we could have a guided tour of their air-raid shelter. Perhaps this evening, when we've finished our business for the day. But now I want to get on to Ashford as soon as possible. Maybe this time, with what we got from Miss Seeton, we might just manage to crack the Sherry Gang case, even if the Dick Turpins are still something of an unknown quantity . . . "

"The only thing we know about 'em," Superintendent Brinton grumbled, "is that they must have a pretty good knowledge of local highways and byways. Look at how they manage to disappear so fast once they've committed the robberies. Unless they're taking themselves off in a helicopter, they're scuttling back to their lair along the sort of minor roads that even the Ordnance Survey hasn't got properly mapped. Which to my mind means they've got to be locals. My lads are pretty quick at blocking roads once the alarm's been raised, and so," grudgingly, "are the Sussex lot, who've had their fair share of the fun, as well."

"Do you mean Harry Furneux and his crew?" said Delphick with a grin. "I don't know so much about Fiery Furnace. I imagine he must be fairly sizzling by now."

"He's not the only one. I make it six Turpin incidents in a couple of weeks, and we're not into summer yet. When the real tourists start arriving, we'll have even worse problems if we haven't caught the blighters. I had real hopes of Miss Seeton, but . . . " Brinton's voice tailed off as he watched Delphick carefully remove three sketches from a large cardboard folder and lay them on his desk. Two of them he recognised: the third, he stared at.

"She's muddled the two cases together, poor old biddy," he decided after a cursory glance. "It's all getting too much for her. She's beginning to dwell in the past the way a lot of these lonely old folk do—the way they like to get chatting to complete strangers just for the company," with a reminder to his visitors of the official reason for their visit. "Which the Sherry Gang are all too ready to exploit, and their luck's holding a sight too well for my liking. If people only read the local papers and used their noddles, we might not have two more unhappy old ladies this morning, and one of 'em in hospital, poor soul. She'll live, but it was touch and go for a while, the quacks tell me. I'd love to feel their collars, but without any sort of clue . . . "

He looked again at Miss Seeton's sketches and sighed. "Pirates and the second world war," he muttered. "Poor old biddy."

"If Miss Seeton suggests there's a connection between the two cases, I'm inclined to believe her," Delphick said. "And I'm sure there's a clue here, somewhere. She's never let us down in the past."

"When she was younger, perhaps. But everyone starts to tail off after a while, Oracle—you and me and even your young giant here," with a brisk grin in Bob's direction, "as the delights of married life begin to wear him down and the price of booze, as he's already discovered, keeps going up and up, and it costs him more to forget his misery. Maybe Miss Seeton isn't completely gaga yet, but just look at the way she's just taken elements of the two cases and muddled them together. A jolly enough picture, I suppose, but . . ."

"*Muddled* is the word she herself used, so it shows your minds are working along the same lines," Delphick said with a bleak smile. "And *together*, yes, but it's not simply the two original sketches combined. There's no air-raid shelter this time, for instance—"

"Hardly surprising, on board a pirate ship."

"Since when have Miss Seeton's sketches ever been noted for verisimilitude? They display nothing so much as her own peculiar logic. According to her lights, this does all make some kind of sense, if we could only interpret it. She must have *felt* there was a good reason for altering a few of the details, for instance, even if she doesn't *know* what it could be." Delphick remembered the adjective applied by his Ashford colleague to Miss Seeton's third sketch. "This ship is flying the Jolly Roger now, whereas before—"

"By heaven, so she is!" Brinton reached forward and snatched up the third sketch, examining it closely for the first time. "The Jolly Roger. Oracle, make Miss Seeton my apologies, because I think the old girl's got it! You were babbling earlier about your sergeant's views on the cost of booze—saying it must cost 'em a fortune to buy the stuff if they're chucking away a full bottle each time—said it would be cheaper by the case than by single bottles, didn't we, and wondered where they got the stuff from.

"There is a pub," said Superintendent Brinton in a voice that throbbed with suppressed excitement, "called the Jolly Roger— and they have a large off-licence trade. Booze by the bottle or crate or case, sale or return . . . And there can't be too many people buying sherry by the case, if you ask me. But the one who'd know for sure," he burst out, and leaped to his feet, "is the landlord. Come on, what are ycu both waiting for? Let's go and buy Miss Seeton a bottle of her favourite tipple, and toast her success!"

# chapter
## -21-

"ARTHUR," SAID MISS Treeves, "I have just come from the post office, where I heard something rather foolish. Now, I know you'll say—" the vicar's sister spoke drily—"that foolish talk is nothing unusual in this village, but I do feel you should go over to Sweetbriars and see if you can put matters straight before it all gets out of hand. I'd go myself, but you know I have three committees today."

The vicar regarded his sister with awe. The Plummergen Church Fete, the Flower Festival, and the Best Kept Village competition would involve much feminine feuding and argument with which he knew himself to be incapable of dealing. But Molly, bless her, understood how to deal with this monstrous regiment of women who (the Reverend Arthur admitted, to his secret shame) intimidated her bachelor brother so greatly. And how pleased she was to have made such an ally—such a good friend, the vicar corrected himself, *ally* carrying connotations of warfare—of Major Matilda Howett, the new head nurse at Dr. Knight's private Home, recently retired from the Army and, Molly had said in high approval, running the place like clockwork. Although *army*, too, reminded the vicar of war—and the war, of course, had still its part to play in today's world, with the fund for the church roof and Dennis Manuden's bunker . . .

"Arthur," Miss Treeves said patiently, "do pay attention and tell me you'll go and see for yourself that Miss Seeton *is* Miss Seeton, and not an imposter. The talk is getting quite out of hand, and if I can report back at my committees that you have been to see her, and that she has neither been kidnapped nor is in league with armed robbers, it should put all this ransom nonsense out of people's silly heads."

"Miss Seeton has been kidnapped? But that is dreadful!" The Reverend Arthur, who tried to like everyone and in truth liked Miss Seeton, looked shocked. "Although whether it is advisable to expect me, Molly dear, to face armed kidnappers single-handed . . . Of course I am willing to do what I can, in Miss Seeton's best interests, but surely the professional touch is what is required? And as to the matter of ransom, the Archdeacon might be willing to let us sell some of the church silver to raise funds, but—"

"Arthur, please. Miss Seeton has *not* been kidnapped. Which is what I want you to find out for yourself, and then you can tell me. And I," said Molly Treeves triumphantly, "can tell the ladies of Plummergen, and we can start to mind our own business again. There is a great deal to be done, if we are to be ready for the Flower Festival or to stand even a chance of winning the Best Kept Village competition. The Fete, of course, should almost run itself, provided the regular stallholders are suitably organised. Matilda Howett will do splendidly there. But nobody will be able to think of anything except this nonsense about Miss Seeton, until we have ascertained that nonsense is what it is."

But even when she'd explained it all to him twice, very carefully, Molly Treeves was not entirely sure that Arthur had fully grasped the purpose of his visit to Sweetbriars to see for himself that Miss Seeton was indeed Miss Seeton. He left the vicarage with his head whirling, thoughts of ransom notes and robbery on the Queen's Highway and guerrilla warfare as practised by the Plummergen ladies tumbling through his mind with memories of the second world war and air raids and bunkers with tin helmets and ration books inside, as on display in the post office window.

The public house, situated next to a travel agency boasting on its pavement sandwich boards Luxury Coach Tours, was a scruffy, long, low grey building with its owner a scruffy, tall, grey-faced individual who looked less jolly than anyone Delphick had seen since he arrested Bernard Finchingfield, the celebrated bigamist, as he was about to tie the illicit knot with Artemis MacSporran, the madcap whisky heiress. The owner's name, however, turned out to be Roger: and he looked more mournful than ever as he admitted it.

"Everyone makes jokes about it," he said with a sigh. "Can I help it if I'm of a serious turn of character? Why should I laugh when they come in asking for a bottle of rum and then start singing 'Fifteen Men on the Dead Man's Chest' and expecting me to join in the yo-ho-ho-ing? I can't sing, either." He sighed again. "Sometimes, I wonder if I might have gone into the wrong profession, but my father used to run this pub before me, you see . . . "

As Roger shrugged helplessly, Delphick caught the eye of Superintendent Brinton, and stifled a grin. "I suppose," he remarked, "it's true that people generally expect publicans to be bonhomous in the extreme—but why not set a fashion? Every pub needs its gimmick. The Jolly Roger could have a weekly sweepstake in which of the regulars would be the one to make you smile, bonus points if you chuckle or laugh out loud. Proceeds to the charity of your choice, and a good time had by all. You might even develop a sense of humor," he added kindly.

Brinton had no patience with such whimsy. "What we're here about is no laughing matter," he said, darting a dagger look at Delphick and scowling at Bob Ranger, who had dared to snigger. "We want to know about sherry, and quick."

"Sherry?" Roger looked more alert. "What sort did you want? And how much of it?"

"How do you sell it?" countered Brinton. "Single bottle sales, by the case, in the barrel—"

"A cask of Amontillado, perhaps," interposed Delphick as Roger blinked at the superintendent's keenness. The gloomy grey countenance turned towards the Scotland Yard detective, and lightened fleetingly with a smile.

"I'm a great reader," Roger said. "In my spare time I'm writing a book—my autobiography. I've led such an interesting life, I'm sure lots of people would want to read about it. Some very strange things happen in a pub."

"Something very strange," hissed Superintendent Brinton between clenched teeth, "is likely to happen right now in this pub if you don't answer my question. Do you sell your bottles of sherry—Sergeant Ranger, could you let me have the sample, please— *this* sherry, in bulk?"

Roger peered at the label and admitted that he did, but not very often. *Quinta Phylloxera* was the cheap end of the price range, only drunk by masochists; from time to time, however, people with less discernment than he, Roger, thought proper, would buy sherry of this label by the case: twelve bottles at a time.

"They sometimes buy it for wedding receptions," he said, "when they get married at the register office instead of in a church." He shrugged. "They probably see it as a judgment on the bride for not being in, well, the proper state. And we have the Holdfast Brethren, of course. They bought a case only last week. They're teetotal," he explained.

Before Brinton could explode, Delphick, divining the real meaning behind Roger's strange utterance, said mildly: "They want to smash the bottles in one of their services, do they? Heaping imprecations on the head of the supplier, or whoever, meanwhile."

Roger nodded. "I believe they make quite a ceremony out of it. Cover the case with a black cloth, preach at it with chunks out of the Bible, then attack it with hammers blessed by the Senior Brother in the tabernacle. Rather impressive, I imagine, if a little messy, and dangerous, of course. One of my regulars works for the ambulance service. Apparently there's nearly always at least one torn artery or slashed vein when it's a Holdfast Water Festival day."

"And has anybody else," Delphick enquired, thinking it tactful to take over the questioning before Brinton really did explode, "bought a case of this recently? Someone not buying for a wedding or an otherwise smashing time?"

"Oh, yes." Roger nodded; Brinton and Delphick looked at him; Bob Ranger prepared to make notes.

"Old Man Buntingford's son-in-law bought three cases," said Roger. "For the funeral. He'd wanted a good send-off. Wrote it in his will, I gather, and left enough money to pay for it, too. Quite a party, they tell me—"

Superintendent Brinton was almost foaming at the mouth. "Anybody else?" demanded Delphick, beginning to lose control himself. "Anybody you'd never seen before?"

Roger frowned. He scratched his head. "I believe there was," he said slowly. "It struck me as odd at the time, but in this business the customer is always supposed to be right—goodness knows why. Few of them have palates, as I understand the word." He reeled back against the blast of fiery dislike that scorched from Superintendent Brinton's eyes. He rubbed the tip of his long, thin nose. "There was a man," he said at last, "dark, in his thirties, I suppose, and I'm almost certain I've never seen him before . . . "

"Then tell us," invited Delphick, "all about him." And motioned to Sergeant Ranger to take notes.

The vicar had felt decidedly awkward. When Martha Bloomer opened the door of Sweetbriars, he did not find it easy to ask her whether she was absolutely sure that the Miss Seeton in whose house she was cleaning that day was the identical Miss Seeton for whom she normally performed this service two mornings a week. Mrs. Bloomer, an expatriate Cockney with a quick wit and a lively sense of the ridiculous, would most likely laugh at him, and while in a good cause he could see no harm in laughter, he felt that some respect ought to be due to the dignity of the cloth. Or, mused the Reverend Arthur, ought it? In his particular case? He had long ago lost his faith, and though the bishop had assured him that it did not matter, he felt something of a fraud. As such, he must ask himself if the pretence under which he lived his life and pursued a no-longer-valid calling was indeed owed any dignity whatsoever. Yet, to all outward appearances he was still a cleric in holy orders, and therefore the office, rather than himself in that office, might deserve—

"Can I help you, Vicar?" Martha Bloomer was tired of holding the front door open while the Reverend Arthur stared at her. "Were you wanting Miss Seeton?"

"Oh. Er, yes." The Reverend Arthur, roused from his trance, looked wildly about him and tried to recall what had been his purpose in coming here. "Miss Seeton—yes. That is to say—Miss Seeton. It *is* Miss Seeton, Martha?"

If he was looking for old Mrs. Bannet, he was by several years too late. "Yes, of course it is, Vicar," Martha said, slowly and clearly, as if to a backward child. Poor vicar, looked even more confused than normal, he did, probably all this talk of the church roof and the raffle and the bunker had took him back in time to when he'd been a fair bit younger, and Mrs. Bannet as well. "Did you want to see Miss Seeton, Vicar? Will you come in?"

Mr. Treeves cast a haunted look over his shoulder, then removed his hat and darted into the hall. As Martha closed the door behind him, he gasped: "You may confide in me with confidence, Martha. You realise that, don't you? Unless you have been advised otherwise by the police, that is."

"The police? They were here earlier this morning, and they never said nothing to me about confidences. It was that young sergeant as married Anne Knight, and his boss—but they didn't stay all that long. Wanted Miss Seeton to do them one of her pictures, I think. But you can ask her yourself, if you like. I'll just call her—she's out in the garden."

"Hiding from me? She heard the doorbell," said Arthur Treeves, still clutching his hat. "Tell her—tell her, if you think it advisable, that I will say nothing. Nothing," he repeated firmly. Wild horses, try how they might, would wrest no part of the secret from him.

Martha wondered why, if the vicar was determined not to speak to Miss Seeton, he'd bothered coming to call on her: but everyone in Plummergen accepted the Reverend Arthur for what he was, and humoured him. "I'll just fetch her in from the weeding and you can tell her yourself," she said kindly. She gently removed his hat from his hand and set it down on the hall table beside the umbrella rack. "Come through to the sitting-room—I've already done in there."

Bewildered, he followed her, and tried not to listen as she opened the french windows and called, "Here's the vicar come to see you, and will I put the kettle on?"

"Mr. Treeves, to see me?" It certainly sounded like Miss Seeton's voice—but the police had doubtless chosen someone skilled in mimicry to play such a dangerous part . . .

"Why, Vicar, how nice." A figure which also looked like Miss Seeton had appeared in the french windows: and, it had to be said, it still sounded like her, even close, too. Why was Molly so sure this lady was an imposter? And why should she wish to tell the Fete Committee and the Flower Festival people this remarkable story? Would their time not be more suitably employed in thinking of other ways to raise money for the repair of the church roof?

"Martha is just making us a cup of tea, if you'd care to have one," said—yes, the Reverend Arthur was almost sure—Miss Seeton cheerfully. "We could take it out to the garden and sit in the sun, such a beautiful morning for being lazy if the right excuse comes along. I have been waging war on the weeds, but it will be lovely to stop for a while."

Ah yes, the war. How it did seem to keep cropping up in conversation. Mr. Stillman's window, no doubt, and of course the raffle for opening Dennis Manuden's air-raid shelter, brought back so many memories, not all of them distressing. As a minister of the church, he'd played his patriotic part by becoming one of Plummergen's air-raid wardens: in a pleasing personal version of the swords-into-ploughshares text, his tin helmet, upturned, now housed seedlings in the vicarage shed. "Geraniums," said the Reverend Arthur, with a smile. He might be able to work this into next Sunday's sermon.

"Such very bold, colourful flowers." Miss Seeton, the perfect hostess, was always willing to adapt to the wishes of her guests. If the vicar had come to discuss his garden problems with her, however, he would be better advised to speak to Martha, who could pass on a message to Stan, who knew all anyone could wish to know about horticulture. Or should she offer to lend Mr. Treeves her copy of *Greenfinger Points the Way*? "One cannot easily mistake them for weeds," said Miss Seeton happily. "The leaves, so distinctive, and delightfully shaped, as well. I sometimes used them when I wished my pupils to draw a floral still life—the generous curve, and the zonal markings, so attractive. And I believe one can also eat them, although this is not something I have ever tried."

No doubt about it, this was Miss Seeton. Molly really should make certain of her facts before even thinking of spreading wild rumours. He would give his sister a little scold when he went home, though not until he had jotted down his notes for the sermon, of course, lest he might otherwise forget them. "Pruning-hooks and spears," mused the Reverend Arthur as he gazed vacantly at Miss Seeton. "And my trusty helmet . . . "

"Of course, you were an air-raid warden too, were you not, Vicar? Such a coincidence," smiled Miss Seeton. "How many nights I spent fire-watching on London roofs, I really could not say. Not that I begrudged the time," she hastened to assure him, "nor the lack of sleep, but one was relieved when the Blitz was finally over. Yet so sad to see all the dreadful damage, so many fine buildings lost, and the lives, which goes without saying. Many of them one's friends and colleagues," she sighed, shaking her head.

"Comradeship," said the vicar, recalling more wartime emotions and making mental notes for his sermon. "Everyone banding together against the common foe . . . " Should he emphasise the desirability of community spirit, he wondered, now that the Best Kept Village competition was under consideration? Plummergen, his home for so many years and a place of which he could not help but be fond, nevertheless had, he knew, from what Molly told him, some regrettably partisan and argumentative citizens. "A return to those dark days when England stood alone," he murmured. "This was their finest hour."

"Indeed it was," said Miss Seeton fervently, her eyes bright with memories. "Indeed it was . . . "

And then Martha destroyed the mood of reminiscence by clattering in with a most un-wartime-like tray. Tea, milk, and sugar in generous quantities, three sorts of biscuits, and several slices of her freshly baked rich fruit cake. "You take it into the garden and enjoy the sun," she said briskly. "Vicar, do you think you could carry the little table outside for us?"

The Reverend Arthur came back from his excursion into the past and leaped to his feet. "Certainly, certainly," he said, and waved away Miss Seeton's protesting outcry. "Only too delighted to be of assistance," he assured her truthfully: with something to do and someone to instruct him on how to do it, he felt entirely at home. He forgot the reason for his visit, and settled down to enjoy himself.

# chapter

## ~22~

HE LEFT FORTY minutes later, having indulged in an orgy of reminiscence with Miss Seeton and Martha, who had been a girl during the Blitz and could swap stories of close shaves and doodlebug bombs with the best. He also indulged in an orgy of biscuit-eating, and wolfed down, urged on by Miss Seeton, the remainder of the packet of chocolate wafers which Martha had intended to last the rest of the week.

"I will go and buy some more," Miss Seeton soothed her. "I had planned to drop into the post office anyway, to see if Mr. Stillman stocks indian ink. On such a fine day, it will be a pleasure to walk—and to escape the weeding for a little longer," she added with a twinkle.

Martha twinkled back at her and suggested adding the purchase of some gingerbread to her list, seeing that young Bob Ranger was so fond of it and staying in the village for a few days. "The size that lad stopped growing at, he could eat an entire week's ration in a day and still be hungry," Martha pointed out. "With a few more like him, we'd have had that rat of a Hitler on the run a lot earlier, mark my words."

As she made her way to the post office, Miss Seeton had to smile at the picture which came unbidden to her mind: Bob Ranger, all six foot seven of him, in full football gear, his mighty hand clasping the collar of a weedy Adolf Hitler he'd scooped from the ground and was shaking as a terrier shakes a rat. She chuckled: she would sketch out her idea as soon as she arrived back home, and if it turned out as well as she hoped she'd give it to Anne, as a companion for the other sketch she'd drawn with herself as

155

the Red Queen dragging Bob into the unknown. She wondered how Bob would have fared in military, as opposed to police, uniform—not that he wore one. Detectives didn't; plain clothes was the order of the day, or should one refer to it, or perhaps that ought to be *them*, as mufti. Yet Detective Constable Foxon from Ashford always seemed to wear the most un-plain clothes Miss Seeton had ever seen: flared trousers, pink shirts, floral ties of the shape that used to be called kipper, worn by so many of the spivs and black marketeers during the war and just after, when things were in such short supply . . .

Really, there was no escaping the war, it seemed, even so many years later. Almost thirty. Miss Seeton sighed for the memory of her young womanhood, although perhaps not as young as some, spent in the shadow of, first, the threat of war, and then in the relief of knowing what the worst could be, bad though it was. And surviving it, as so many less fortunate had not. Did this young woman, she wondered, have any inkling of how much worse things would get before they improved?

Miss Seeton blinked, and stared, and pulled herself very sharply together. For a moment, she was back in the war and yet somehow looking in on it as an outside observer—which, she had to admit, was often how she saw herself in relation to life—observing the young woman with the scarlet lips and shoulder-length pageboy bob who was coming along the road. How rude it must appear, having one stare at her in such a fashion—Miss Seeton found herself staring again, and with a frown forced her glance away— and yet, how . . . discourteous, perhaps, was the word, of the young woman to stare so very sternly back at her, without a word. Miss Seeton dropped her gaze, and hurried into the post office, out of which Betsy Manuden, in her old-fashioned costume of seamed stockings, fitted waist, flared skirt and squared shoulders, had just come.

And as soon as she entered the post office, everybody stopped talking and stared at her.

Miss Seeton had no idea whether or not she had been the subject of their conversation. She smiled a general smile, and asked where the end of the queue might be.

"We're in no hurry," said Mrs. Spice, after a pause in which she, too, stared hard at Miss Seeton. She spoke for them all. "Just having what you might call a friendly chat. You go right ahead."

Everybody else murmured their agreement, and Miss Seeton nodded her thanks before approaching Mr. Stillman to ask for the gingerbread and biscuits she required, and to learn, to her disappointment, that he did not stock indian ink. Miss Seeton, he suggested, would do better to try in Brettenden: lucky for her, if she was in a hurry for the stuff, the bus would be leaving in about twenty minutes.

Miss Seeton thanked him, collected her packages, smiled round at the kindly neighbours who had allowed her to jump the queue, and departed.

Leaving everyone inside to start gossiping about her—if indeed it *was* her, opinion was sharply divided—to their hearts' content.

"Spellbrook's rang while you were out," Martha informed Miss Seeton upon her return, with a sniff. As Miss Seeton handed over her confectionery booty, Mrs. Bloomer took it, but did not carry it through to the kitchen nor make any remark about healthy appetites. Something had annoyed her.

Not that it would be wise to comment on it directly, as Miss Seeton knew very well. With dear Martha, normally the most sunny-tempered of people unless she was in one of her Grand Slams around cupboards and shelves, it was far better to let her calm down by herself, because then one would be told what the matter had been without any embarrassing or impertinent questions.

"Martha dear," said Miss Seeton, "something has annoyed you, I can tell. What is the matter?"

"Oh, they say the van's out of order and won't be over this area again for a while. All that long time without a hoover, and the charcoal being trod deeper in the carpet every time you look at it. A crying shame, I call it, your lovely Wilton, and never mind saying you won't walk round the back of the sofa for another week, because I know you."

"Oh, dear me. Yes." Miss Seeton had to agree that once or twice since the demise of the vacuum cleaner she had, but only when essential, walked around the back of the sofa and perilously near the charcoal smudge.

Miss Seeton brightened. "Mr. Stillman had no indian ink, which might well be called providential. If I make haste it will be leaving in about ten minutes—the bus, I mean. For Brettenden. And while I was there I could enquire about a suitable delivery service—perhaps a taxi—"

"Six miles!" protested Martha. "It'll cost a fortune!"

Miss Seeton smiled gently. Dear Martha, always so kind and concerned for one's welfare, but for what else did one have a pension? And the police, so generous with their fees for her IdentiKit services as well as the retainer they paid—and one could always argue that the charcoal had been dropped in the pursuit of one's professional duties, which would justify the expenditure of clearing up the mess. Not that it was much of a mess, but since Martha was troubled by it, then something must be done.

"Something must be done," said Miss Seeton firmly. "I'm sure Mr. Spellbrook will know of somebody who could help, if I explain the circumstances. But if I am to catch the bus, I must hurry . . . "

It was the familiar red and green of the Crabbe livery which awaited Miss Seeton and the other Plummergen shoppers outside the garage. In some ways, Miss Seeton was relieved not to have to face again the driver who must have been—although far too courteous to say so aloud—irritated at one's non-arrival on the last Brettenden excursion, even if the circumstances had to some extent been beyond one's control. Yet it would perhaps have been the opportunity to apologise in person for one's tardiness, always supposing it had been the same driver again. But here came Jack Crabbe with a broad smile, nodding to all his friends, gloating over his dictionary in one hand, and the keys to the coach in the other.

"All aboard for Brettenden! Here, let me give you a hand up with that there wheel-basket, Mrs. Blaine."

And a hand, literally, was all it took to heave Bunny's wicker trolley on wheels off the pavement and up into the luggage-well at the front of the coach. Jack was by half a head the tallest of the Crabbes, who were as a family built along lines almost as generous as those of dear Bob Ranger. In such fine weather, Jack wore no jacket; Miss Seeton was quick to admire the shape of his muscles beneath his shirt, and the way he settled himself in the driver's seat as if he felt completely at home with the vehicle and the job. What a study of contentment he would make, Miss Seeton thought: a pencil in his hand, a dictionary at his side, the coach keys thrust into his shirt pocket to show the dual nature of his character—such a very helpful, kindly young man.

And Miss Seeton began to wonder whether she might dare to trespass on his good nature by asking him to assist her in the matter of the vacuum cleaner for Martha. Perhaps he would be prepared to come with her to the shop, and carry it back to the coach. Of course, she would offer to pay him for his trouble. But, knowing Jack Crabbe, he would refuse payment, which would be kind of him, but embarrassing. And what a pity to take him away from his crossword puzzles when he had so much missed them while the bus was not running . . .

Then Miss Seeton recalled that vacuum cleaners, in order to be easy to push across pile carpets, have little wheels underneath. Surely it should be a simple enough matter for her to collect the cleaner from Mr. Spellbrook and at first carry it, then if it grew too heavy push it, through the streets of Brettenden? Brettenden's pavements are smooth, and level, and its citizens are helpful and friendly . . .

And Miss Seeton felt sure she had found the solution to her problem. How pleased and surprised dear Martha would be—especially when she learned that it had not cost one penny extra to bring the new vacuum cleaner home today . . .

# chapter

## -23-

THE LUGUBRIOUS PUBLICAN had been induced to attend Ashford police station at his earliest convenience to look through a selection of mugshots, which, coupled with the description duly noted by Sergeant Ranger, would at least give the beat bobbies something to go on.

"But not much," muttered Brinton as the three detectives headed for his office and a brew of strong, sweet tea with sandwiches. "The Invisible Man, that's who we're dealing with, plus two invisible women we're got no real description for barring their ages, which nowadays you can never be sure of. And there's always Miss Seeton's sketch of one of 'em as a pirate chief, just to add to the fun." He sighed. "If I get time, Oracle, remind me to indent for a bottle of hair dye; I'm going greyer by the minute. Every time anybody so much as mentions Plummergen, my heart misses a beat, and add the words *Miss Seeton* and it starts doing a wardance."

"I'm still convinced," said Delphick, "that those three sketches of hers hold the key, and all we need to do is work out how to turn it, then bingo."

"All!" snorted Brinton, as his friend brushed sandwich crumbs from the cover of the cardboard file and opened it. He took out Miss Seeton's offerings and set them out on a clear part of the desk, studying them thoughtfully. "Three people, or six? Two women and one man, twice over, or the same lot using different techniques for the variety, and to keep us guessing—I wonder. We've started things moving with the Sherry Gang, but whether or not they're the same people it wouldn't do any harm to try

160

homing in on the Turpin crowd. A pincer movement, as you might say. It may interest you to hear my sergeant's suggestion, Superintendent Brinton—don't blush, Bob. I thought it was quite bright, myself. No need to be so modest about it."

"Modesty be damned," said Brinton, regarding Bob with a suspicious eye. "Out with it, lad—unless it's anything to do with Miss Seeton, in which case don't. My nerves—and my hair, what's left of it—couldn't cope."

"Well, sir," Bob began, then looked towards Delphick and said, "I'd rather you explained it, sir. It might not sound quite so—so—well, I'd rather you explained it, sir."

"And direct the wrath of Superintendent Brinton against myself instead of you?" Delphick twitched a quizzical eyebrow at the blushing Bob and suppressed a chuckle. "I told you, I thought it was quite a good idea. But we'll see what Mr. Brinton thinks—especially when he hears how you came to think of it."

"Sir!" protested Bob, but Delphick ignored him.

"If I'm to do your dirty work for you, Sergeant, let me at least have some fun while I'm doing it. The suggestion, Chris, arose from Miss Seeton's little mishap of climbing on the wrong bus yesterday—" Brinton groaned, and made clutching movements at his hair. Bob winced. Delphick carried on firmly—"and the good sergeant here wondered whether the same basic idea could be used in reverse, as it were. Have the Turpins holding up the wrong bus—a bus crammed to the rafters with plainclothes people, and the driver armed with a radio. He could be broadcasting his route through as he drove, and as soon as he said he'd been held up the patrol cars could join in the action. Roadblocks and so on. How many people could you spare for a stunt like that?"

"Not enough to fill a coach, that's for sure. Besides, how many days would we have to keep it up before they had a go at us? Decoys are all very well if you've got unlimited time and manpower, but—ah. From the way you're shaking your head, you've got an answer to that objection. Go ahead—no, let me guess. Miss Seeton's going to wave her magic umbrella in the air and conjure the Turpins to appear out of nowhere. Right?"

"It pays to advertise," said Delphick smoothly. "We've assumed, haven't we, from the locations of the various hold-ups, and the almost miraculous way they vanish before we can catch them, that the Turpins must have their base somewhere not too far from here. Definitely local knowledge, and very good knowledge, at that. Every coach they've ambushed has been worth the effort.

They've never gone for the likes of Jack Crabbe's Plummergen service, for instance."

At the mention of Miss Seeton's village, Brinton almost groaned, but stopped himself just in time as the Oracle went on: "Perhaps we ought to start asking how they can be so sure the coaches and buses they ambush are worth the effort. Each of the tourist parties booked through different travel agents, who used different coach companies, so it can't be anything as simple as a booking clerk tipping the wink to his mates. But, as my sergeant pointed out to me while you were off arranging the sandwiches—these travel agents are quite likely to work to a similar system, aren't they? It was the sandwiches, I gather, which inspired his flight of fancy. You see, if the system includes, as we saw this morning, sandwich boards standing free on the pavement for all and sundry to trip over—and to read . . . "

Delphick waited while his colleague made the connection. It took about five seconds. Brinton stared, first at his friend and then at the blushing Bob. He thumped his fist on the desk. "By heaven, it might work! I could spare a group just for one day. We'll swear a travel agent to secrecy and ask 'em to invent a tour package the chummies won't be able to resist, plaster it on a poster where nobody could miss it and date it a few days away, give the Turpins time to come in once a week for their shopping, or whatever. The travel agent can tell anyone who walks in off the street that it's so popular it's already fully booked—that way we wouldn't risk members of the public getting clobbered if the chummies pull the trigger this time. And if they don't bite after all, what have we lost?" Brinton answered his own question. He grinned at Bob Ranger. "A couple of handfuls of coppers will have lost a morning's work, but they'll have had a nice ride round in an air-conditioned coach goggling at the view. Of course, we'll have to find the hire cost, but I dare say we could wangle something. I'll ring Harry Furneux over in Hastings and see if I can't twist his arm to make Sussex go halves. This is just the crazy sort of notion that would appeal to the Fiery Furnace. And, who knows? Maybe it'll produce results. Nothing else has, after all."

"Not yet," Delphick reminded him, tapping Miss Seeton's handiwork with a thoughtful finger. "I'm still hoping."

"I'd rather trust your young giant here," Brinton said. "At least it's something *practical*, and I can understand it. Those scribbles of hers are your pigeon, Oracle. I should have known better than to try and make head or tail of 'em." He reached for his desk calendar. "Whit Monday's no good, we'd have to pay 'em overtime, but round about then would be time enough to get things organised. I'll have a word with Omney, Crabbe, someone like that, about hiring a bus. Mind you, I won't tell 'em why, in case word leaks out. I'll say it's for training coppers out of feeling travel sick. D'you want to come along for the ride, by any chance?"

Delphick noticed the eager look on Bob's face, and was considering the superintendent's offer when Brinton added: "On second thoughts, not Crabbe. With him being based in Plummergen, I don't think I could cope with the Seeton connection, and you needn't try telling me she wouldn't get involved in it somehow, because my bones tell me she would. Brolly and all. She can't even do the round trip from Brettenden to Plummergen without being hijacked. That woman is a walking threat to civilisation. I feel sorry for Crabbe if she's on his bus service into town today. She may start out intending to do some shopping, but you can bet there'll be trouble somewhere along the line . . . "

The late May sun scorched the Brettenden streets. Awnings were pulled down over shop windows to keep as much of the fading glare as possible away from their contents; some of the glass was lined with cellophane, yellow and wrinkled like a jaundiced old woman.

In the street—better not to try in the shops any more, too many people to notice now the word'd had time to get around—was the woman, not old, not jaundiced, with her weather eye open for a likely prospect. Looking for someone frail, elderly, in need of help. In a wheelchair, perhaps? Maybe not—it had been a close thing before. You never knew what drugs they were taking, or how they'd mix. But find someone who'd be glad of a friendly chat, and grateful for any offer of assistance—someone by themselves, then easy enough to establish in the preliminary sussing whether there'd be the risk of anybody rushing to the rescue back at the house. Where they'd be pleased to offer a drink, on such a hot day, to their kind new acquaintance who'd helped carry that awkward parcel for them . . .

And along the road, panting a little in the heat, came a prospect who looked weary of carrying the parcel that seemed not so much awkward as heavy. Even before she came level with the watching woman, she had adjusted her ungainly grip on the parcel twice; and now looked ready to do so again.

If she'd been with anybody, they'd never have left her to struggle about by herself carrying such a weight, and her no bigger than a child. An easy choice, this time . . .

And the woman switched on her anxious, neighbourly smile, stepped forward, and said:

"Oh, dear, you do look as if you're having trouble with your shopping. Would you like me to lend you a hand?"

Betsy Manuden was nagging at her husband. "She stared right at me, Den, and then she *smiled*. Almost like she was gloating. She recognised it was me from the holdup, never mind we was wearing masks and the motorbike gear, unisex or not. I'm smaller'n you, and it was me as went round collecting all the stuff from the punters. I got much closer to any of 'em than you ever did. And she knows all about art, teaches it or something. She's got an *eye*, Dennis, and she clocked me, all right. I'm sure she did."

"But you said," her husband objected, after a pause, "you said as how she just nodded at you and carried on into the post office." He scratched his head. "I don't understand—why didn't she raise the alarm then and there, if you're so sure she knows?"

"Probably wanted to enjoy herself gloating a bit longer, the old witch. That's what some of the kids in this village say she is, didn't you know that? Witches like to have power over people." Betsy shuddered. "Blackmail, that'll be her style, mark my words."

This was an idea Dennis Manuden understood well. "Then you reckon we should pull out, do you? Before she gets the chance to say anything?"

"We can't do that! Not without asking Mum. You know how mad she gets if anyone upsets her plans."

Dennis Manuden nodded. "And her plans've been working a treat, so far. Pity to spoil everything." He brightened. "And you might be wrong, at that. She could've been smiling about what a nice day it was, or something."

"She *knows*, Den." Betsy was positive. "And I reckon as Mum oughter know, too. She'll tell us what to do."

"I suppose you're right, she's gotter be told, but she's not due to phone for a couple of days when she's sussed out another good prospect." Dennis frowned as he thought, for it was not something he often did. His wife and mother-in-law handled that side of his life for him: it was rare for Betsy to be the one asking advice. "We did really," he said at last, "oughter drive into Brettenden and talk to her—"

"She said not to! You know she said we wasn't to get in touch in case people saw us together, not unless . . . " Betsy hesitated. "Well, I reckon this oughter be enough of an emergency even for Mum and her wanting us to stay away. But she always does the shopping in the afternoons when we're not, well, busy, so's she can suss out the likelies and save time. We didn't oughter hang about outside waiting for her to come home, and if we go looking for her and they see us together in Brettenden . . . "

Her pause was meaningful, and Dennis took her meaning. He nodded. "Bad news. We'll just have to hope Miss Seeton don't tell nobody before your mum's decided what to do."

"Yes, but I been thinking. We gotter decide quicker'n that! She might be on the blower to the fuzz this very minute, and us not able to let Mum know about it."

"You said—" and Dennis shook his head—"you said she'd gone into Brettenden on the bus. How could she be on the phone to the cops?"

"Oh, don't be so daft!" Betsy did not often snap at her husband, but today her nerves were frazzled. "All right, so she's not on the phone, but she could be walking into the cop-shop this very minute, couldn't she? I tell you, Den, we're not safe while Miss Seeton's on the loose!"

"Well, I suppose not," said Dennis, after another pause. He looked hopefully at her. "What shall we do?"

"Shut her mouth," said Betsy firmly. Dennis gasped, but had no time to say anything before she went on: "We know when the bus is due back, so all you've got to do is break into her cottage, easy enough now her burglar alarm's busted, and then wait for her and bash her on the head—"

"I'm bashing nobody's head," exclaimed Dennis in horror. "I've never killed nobody yet, and I ain't starting now."

He was seldom stubborn, but Betsy knew that on occasions when his eye gleamed in that particular way she would not be able to change his mind. And, on second thoughts, maybe he was right. Better not to have murder on the charge sheet if it came to an arrest. But something had to be done to keep the old bag quiet . . .

"We'll kidnap her," she decided. "Half of 'em think that's what's happened to her anyway, you should heard 'em when I was in the post office, made me quite surprised to see her trotting along so calm like she did—until she started that staring at me. Bet she gave 'em all a shock when she hopped up them steps and through the door!" Even at such a tense moment, she could not suppress a giggle. She sobered quickly, though. "You can still break into the cottage and wait for her to get back from Brettenden, then you hit her on the head—just enough to keep her quiet," she said, as he started to protest again. "Shove her out of the way somewhere until it's dark, then we'll bring her here and stick her in that bunker. Instead of fairies at the bottom of the garden," she said with a grin, "we'll have a witch!" But she could not help looking over her shoulder at the last words, and a little shiver crept up her spine.

This wouldn't do, letting Den see she was worried, when he was relying on her and so was Mum, though she didn't know it yet, being out of touch as she'd chosen to be when they first set up this scam. But now Betsy had the chance to show how she could cope, she wasn't going to pass it up.

"The vicar wants a prize for when the bunker's opened," she said, grinning again. "Well, he'll have one—he'll have Miss Seeton! We won't starve her or nothing, we'll just keep her nice and quiet in there till Mum says we're ready to leave, then we'll give the keys to the vicar, and Lady Colveden will draw the winning ticket—and Miss Seeton will be there when they open up the door, and we'll be miles away by then!"

Dennis was glad to see her looking so pleased, but only managed a weak smile himself. He did not relish the thought of hitting an old lady on the head and kidnapping her, not that he believed this village rubbish about witches exactly, but you could never be sure . . .

Betsy looked at her watch. "Bus'll be back in half an hour or so. Martha Bloomer only does mornings, so there'll be nobody in the cottage. You can just break in round the back. Climb over that low wall at the canal end—she'll have locked the side gate—and you just wait for her to come inside. Then a little tap on the head, and tie her up, and everything'll be fine, Den, won't it?"

And she gave him an encouraging hug before pushing him out of the door.

# chapter

# -24-

MISS SEETON, HER umbrella over her arm, paused at the front gate of Sweetbriars and smiled at her friendly escort with the awkward parcel.

"So very kind of you, and such a great help. In this hot weather, too. I had no idea that something which seemed so comparatively small would be so difficult to bring from one place to another. But the sunshine is of course most welcome. If it had been as large as a washing machine, or a refrigerator, it would not have surprised me so much." Miss Seeton smiled. "No wonder Mrs. Spellbrook had such a twinkle in her eye when I told her I proposed to wheel it through the streets of Brettenden to the bus!"

"You'd have worn the rubber off before you'd been going five minutes, if you ask me. Lucky I spotted you. Easily pulled a muscle or something trying to carry it like that."

"I expect you're right to scold me. Mrs. Spellbrook did, as well, and made me promise to look for a taxi, after I refused her kind offer to telephone for me. I thought she had enough to worry about, poor thing, her husband's van in that dreadful accident and, even though he wasn't badly hurt, such a great strain for her. Besides, I was sure I could find the taxi rank, you see, and then, once I had considered the problem, it hardly seemed much farther from there to the bus station."

"You're probably right, but I still say it was lucky you met me. Nice new hoover like that, you wouldn't want it all messed up before you'd used it, would you?"

Miss Seeton smiled a guilty little smile. "Dear me, no. How

upset poor Martha would have been! But now, with your kind assistance, how delighted she will be, I feel sure. It is exactly the model she asked me to buy, and what a lovely surprise for her when she next comes. Such a shame she will have already gone." Miss Seeton smiled more brightly at her escort. "She was baking a fruit cake when I left, and her cakes are delicious. Would you care to come in for a cup of tea, and a slice or two of Martha's best?" She twinkled again. "Had I made it myself, I would not have issued so confident an invitation. It would be ungrateful of me to return thanks for all your kindness by offering you a taste of my efforts at home baking! But Martha's cakes, you know, always turn out well."

"I wouldn't want to put you to any trouble, Miss Seeton, but I have to admit I'm tempted, thanks very much . . . "

"Good," said Miss Seeton, and smiled once more. "That's settled, then." And, tucking her umbrella beneath her arm, she held open the gate for her hoover-burdened companion to pass through; turned to close the gate; and, fumbling in her handbag for her keys, led the way up the garden path.

On Superintendent Brinton's desk, the telephone rang. With all the sandwiches eaten and the mugs drained of their tea, he and his Scotland Yard colleagues had been brooding on the two cases which Miss Seeton, by her sketches, had predicted would become somehow linked—or perhaps were linked already. Brinton maintained stoutly that either way his digestion, as well as his hair, would suffer.

"There's no peace for the wicked," he grumbled, reaching for the receiver. "Brinton here . . . Who?"

The earpiece of the receiver quacked again. Brinton's eyebrows shot up, and he said, "Have you, indeed? Are you sure? . . . I see, yes. So what did you do then? . . . Oh, did you? Carefully, I hope—we wouldn't want him to spot—oh, you did, did you. Good . . . Good . . . Just a minute . . . " And he jotted down on his blotter what looked to Delphick, trying to read it upside down, like a car registration number. "And can you give me a description of the vehicle?" Brinton asked, darting a quick look at his colleagues. "A *what*?" And as he jabbed his pencil down to write, the point broke off. Clearly, this was momentous news he was hearing; and before he had time to snatch another pencil from the tray in front of him, both Delphick and Bob had reached into their pockets and whipped out their own ballpoint pens. Without a word of thanks, the superintendent took one, and asked the telephone to repeat its information, please.

"A black. Ford. van," enunciated Brinton, writing these words in very large letters, while Delphick and Ranger gave muted cries of excitement, hastily suppressed. "Heading where, did you say? . . . And you're sure he didn't spot you keeping an eye on him? . . . That's a fine piece of work on your part, sir, and we're most grateful. Thank you very much indeed."

When he'd rung off, he turned to the Scotland Yarders. "That," he exulted, "was our friend Jolly Roger, the gloomiest barman in town. He's seen the man who bought the sherry—he's sure it was him—and followed him back to the car park. Where he got into a vehicle I gather you've both recognised, judging from the racket the pair of you kicked up—a small black Ford. A small black Ford van . . . "

"And drove off in it, from what you said," Delphick told his colleague, who was looking almost cheerful. "Did Roger say where?"

"Heading south out of the town centre on the Lydd road—that's all he can tell us. He was on foot, saw this chap in the high street, and decided to do his civic duty by finding out what he was up to. Detective stories, he likes reading, he said," said Brinton. "Ringing from a call-box—didn't waste time going back to the pub. We could do with a few more like him, if you ask me. He may be a Friday-faced beggar, but his head's screwed on the right way."

"And, talking of ways, now you know where he was heading, you can put out an alert for the van, can't you?" Delphick said, even as Brinton was reaching for the telephone again. "Sorry to try to teach you your business, Chris, but . . . "

"But you're thinking the same as me," the superintendent finished for him as he dialled another number. "There's an odds-on chance—yes, Brinton here. I want an alert put out to all cars, to keep an eye open for a suspect vehicle . . . " He gave full particulars, then hung up, breathed deeply, and continued talking to Delphick almost as if there had been no interruption. "A chance, and a good one, that there'll be another Sherry incident today. And this time we want to catch the blighters in the act—oh." A wary look crept into his eyes. Delphick leaned forward.

"What's wrong? Nothing serious, I hope, now we seem to have made a breakthrough at long last."

"Depends what you mean by something wrong," Brinton said in a doom-laden tone. "I should have thought—no, I should have *known*, when Roger said he was headed south out of town on the

Lydd road—because that road," and he sighed, "goes slap bang through the middle of Plummergen . . . "

"Where Miss Seeton lives," concluded Delphick, and tried not to look pleased. Chris Brinton might be driven crazy by the Seeton connection, but even he must surely admit that, once the connection was made, things certainly did seem to happen a lot faster than otherwise. And, with luck, if Miss Seeton waved her brolly at the small black Ford van as it drove past her door, perhaps it wouldn't be too long before the Sherry Case, at least, was cracked.

Miss Seeton was still puzzled that Martha, who was normally so very careful, seemed to have left the back door open when she left. Not that one was worried about burglars, or being molested in the safety of one's own home, for Plummergen was the most delightful village where, fortunately, nothing ever happened of a disagreeable nature. The papers—Miss Seeton shook a sorrowing head as she briefly considered the tabloid press—were always given to exaggeration on such matters, almost making it seem that it was unsafe to open the door to a stranger or to invite anyone into one's house. Which was, of course, quite untrue.

But the open door—well, never mind, for on such a hot day there was no risk, surely, of rain. "The fresh air, so very welcome," murmured Miss Seeton, savouring the draught from the sunny out-of-doors as she cleared away the tea things into the kitchen. Above the clatter and chink of china, she heard the chickens in their hen-house at the bottom of her garden squawking: they would be enjoying the sun, of course. In broad daylight, it would be foolish for anyone to attempt to, well, steal, one had to use the only honest word, eggs by climbing over the low wall which bounded the canal. The wall which sometimes, Miss Seeton knew, proved too much of a temptation to Plummergen youth—so mischievous, daring one another to clamber over and, and take what was not rightly theirs to take . . .

Yet not all young people were so lawless and wild in spirit. Young Jack Crabbe, for instance: how kind, and how very helpful he had been, insisting upon carrying the vacuum cleaner through the Brettenden streets for her—teasing her by saying he guessed she'd try to prove her strength and he had followed her just to keep an eye on her—even driving the coach past his grandfather's garage and right up to her gate so that he could spare her the brief journey down The Street, and only coming in for a cup of tea once he'd gone back to the garage with the bus and returned with a set of screwdrivers and an assortment of fuses. How pleased Martha would be to know that Stan would not have to come and fit the electric plug—to know that she could begin to use the vacuum cleaner as soon as she next came into the house.

Her washing-up done, Miss Seeton, leaving the kitchen door ajar—the sunshine, so glorious—moved back into the hall, and stood looking thoughtfully at the vacuum cleaner leaning against the hall table. "There's a bag fitted too, I checked, so you're all ready to roll," Jack Crabbe had said before taking his leave of her. All ready to roll—it sounded so easy. And wasn't that what Mr. Spellbrook had told her, when she first chose the cleaner in his Brettenden shop? "I wonder," murmured Miss Seeton. "The very latest model, and so much easier to use, he assured me."

While she nerved herself to plug it in and switch it on, she did not notice how the cackling of the hens had stopped. Either the sun had gone behind a cloud—or whatever had disturbed them had moved away . . .

"Perhaps just a little push up and down the hall," Miss Seeton told herself, "but no farther, or when Martha arrives it will not feel so much like a brand new machine. Not," she said firmly, "that I suspect Mr. Spellbrook of having sold me damaged goods, of course, but it might perhaps do no great harm to check—to try, for a very short while," and, with a little gasp at her own daring, she bent down, plugged it in, and pressed the "On" switch.

Above the throbbing level roar of the vacuum cleaner as she began to push it warily backwards and forwards along the carpet, Miss Seeton failed to hear the creak of the kitchen door as somebody pushed it shut after having crept in from the garden . . .

Dennis Manuden hovered in the hall entrance, wondering how exactly to put Miss Seeton out of action. She wouldn't keep still for a moment, that was the trouble, pushing the hoover forwards, backwards, forwards, backwards, and yet so awkwardly that there wasn't any rhythm to it and he couldn't tell when she'd next come into range. Twice he'd tried, but she'd lurched sort of sideways and headed in a different direction, though always more or less on the same piece of carpet. Betsy never made such hard work of hoovering, he was sure of that, but Miss Seeton seemed to be having quite a time of it, with the flex getting in her way and the hall never seeming quite large enough for her to manoeuvre in.

"Oh, bother." Miss Seeton and the cleaner had collided with the table, bumping it sideways, knocking her umbrella out of its clip. She pressed the switch to "Off," stepped over the trailing snake of flex, and bent to pick up the fallen brolly from the floor.

And Dennis Manuden, who saw his chance, knew he had to seize it. With one of her own pillowcases, purloined from upstairs during his earlier prowling of her cottage which the arrival of Jack Crabbe's bus had disturbed, he crept up on the bending form of Miss Seeton, popped the pillowcase over her head, and knocked her off-balance so that he could tie her up with a length of stout rope he had found in her garden shed.

Superintendent Brinton had organised a wide-ranging watch for the black Ford van, and, though Delphick longed to make for the direction of Plummergen on the off-chance of encountering the suspect, suggested they'd be better off sitting quietly in almost the only police car—an unmarked one—which wasn't out on patrol, waiting for a definite lead.

"We've got one," protested the chief superintendent, but without much hope. He and Brinton were sharing this case now, but the territory was Brinton's, not Scotland Yard's. Just as—he smiled—Miss Seeton, whose sketch had provided the original lead to Jolly Roger at the off-licence, was the territory of Scotland Yard, not of the Ashford police. For which, he knew, his old friend Chris was heartily thankful.

"You have to admit she's done us proud," he murmured, as he contemplated, yet again, the three drawings. "The pirate business has made sense, as I always said it would."

"I hate people who say they told me so," Brinton growled in a halfhearted way, adding in more challenging tones, "I suppose you can't explain why she keeps dragging World War Two into it all, can you? Then we'd most likely have both cases sewn up at the same time."

Delphick studied the air-raid portrait of the helmeted young woman blowing her warden's whistle to direct everyone to shelter, and frowned. "Not yet, I can't, no. But when I can, I'll tell you. And I'm prepared to bet that the bunker we still haven't got to see is somehow involved. I think I shall ask for a warrant if the Manudens aren't there when we call on them again . . . "

Dennis Manuden made his stealthy way back over Miss Seeton's lower garden wall, leaving her neatly parcelled on her own bed, with a pillowcase gag in her mouth as well as another pillowcase, patterned with rosebuds, over her head. There was no chance she'd escape, tied up like that, he knew, and was proud to tell Betsy so once he was safely home again.

But his wife wasn't as keen to make a fuss of him as he had expected. Normally, knowing Den's limitations as well as he did himself, she was quick to praise him when he tried something out of the ordinary and succeeded. But now, as he recounted his triumph, he sensed her attention was wandering—which it undoubtedly was.

"I'm not so sure, Den, not now. Maybe we oughter have a talk to Mum about it after all. I mean, that bunker—maybe someone'll hear her yelling for help, or something."

"We could keep her gagged, like now," Dennis said, sure he could manage that task again. Surprised by his assault, Miss Seeton had hardly struggled: and she'd caught the side of her head on the leg of the hall table as she fell, and was stunned, though not seriously, as he proceeded to tie her up. Otherwise she would have been a far more awkward customer for him to deal with. Her yoga-imparted ability to wriggle and contort herself would have given Dennis a few uncomfortable moments, and she would not have submitted so tamely to being parcelled upstairs in her bedroom.

But Dennis did not know all this, and was certain of his ability to take, and keep, a prisoner. "We'll gag her, and tie her up, course we will," he told Betsy. "Easy, I'd call it. An old woman like her, no trouble."

But as his confidence grew, so Betsy's diminished. "She might have to stay down there a while," she said, shuddering at the thought. "That'd be cruel, underground, in the dark. Killing her straight out'd be fine, but not to linger like that. I've heard things from Mum, about people buried alive in them air-raids and not found in time. Horrible, it was. She'd say the same, I reckon. Mum didn't like the war."

"Don't suppose anybody did. Your Mum's not the only one to've had a hard time of it." Dennis scowled as he thought things through yet again. "I'm not killing her, Betsy, and that's final. Leave her tied up, we oughter stick to what we said first, keep her in the bunker till we go."

"I'd like to ask Mum." Betsy jumped from her chair and hurried to collect the car keys from their place in one of the mugs on the sideboard. In another mug, the key to the air-raid shelter glittered accusingly at her . . . "I didn't think it all out properly, before," she said. "But I have now, and I'm not so sure it's what Mum would want. But come on, and we'll go and ask her now."

And Dennis, always so used to doing what she told him, hurried after her as she climbed into the car and headed out of the gate towards Brettenden.

# chapter
## -25-

THE RADIO BEEPED in the police car. Superintendent Brinton grabbed it and pressed the switch. "Yes?"

"Suspect van spotted in a side road off the B2080," came the welcome news. "It's empty, sir. Should I take a look?"

"The Plummergen road, what did I tell you?" demanded the superintendent of Delphick, before telling the radio to go nowhere near the van, but to keep it under surveillance. He and his Scotland Yard colleagues would be along to take a look for themselves, and only if the driver appeared and was about to vanish in a whiff of petroleum spirit was he to be intercepted.

"We're on our way," he concluded and banged the handset back in its holder. It uttered a protesting little beep as it signed off, but everyone in the car was too excited to notice. Brinton tried to introduce a note of caution.

"They might not be on a job," he said, as he gunned the engine and the car leaped into life. "It might be where the bloke lives, and he's parked outside because it's such a hot day he doesn't see the need to use the garage. Can't say I blame him if that's what it is—"

"But you don't think so." Delphick sounded sure of his diagnosis. "You think, like me, that they're emptying a house right now, and that if we're lucky we'll catch them in the act. We're on to the Sherry Gang at last," and he spoke a silent word of thanks to Roger, the reluctant publican who was a great reader and an observant citizen; and to Miss Seeton, who'd directed police attention to him. "How fast does this thing go?" he demanded as Brinton, despite his enthusiasm, stuck strictly to the thirty-mile

175

speed limit. "How far is it to the house?"

Brinton muttered something about people keeping their hair on, but otherwise did not answer. He was too busy threading his way through the Brettenden streets, avoiding other vehicles and the unwary pedestrians who stepped off pavements in front of any car but a police car—and this, unmarked, did not look at all like a police car. He didn't want to be stopped by some over-zealous beat bobby and made to lose time, and possibly the villains, too . . .

"There it is!" His shout of triumph as he brought the car round the last corner had Delphick almost leaping from his seat before they'd braked to a halt. "No, Oracle, hang on a moment. Let's have à word with my lad over there."

The driver of the lurking Panda car came over to greet them as they emerged from the unmarked car. "No sign of life, sir, but I didn't want to get too close, like you said. Besides, I don't reckon I'd know who was meant to be here and who wasn't. These houses are mostly rented property, the owners live away and change the tenants every few months or so. But whoever they are, they're not moving now."

"Then we'll move instead," said Brinton. "I reckon we should take a look inside the house this van's parked outside, for a start, and find out if anything's going on. Four of us—three of them. Is there a back alley? You and Sergeant Ranger here can guard it while we tackle them from the front. We'll start," said the superintendent, "by ringing the doorbell, to see what, or who, gets stirred up. Shall we go?"

They stood for a moment by the car, which Brinton had brought to a stop just in front of the black van to block, if it became necessary, any speedy escape. Bob Ranger looked about him for any indication of the back entrance he should be guarding. From his height of six foot seven, he could see over hedges easily; by normal standards, the other men were fairly tall, and they, too, easily scanned the scenery for any sign of a rear alleyway.

A small car, driven quite fast, turned the corner; and at the sight of four large men, obviously policemen from the size of their boots, braked sharply, hesitated and blocked the road briefly, then reversed with a screech of brakes and vanished in the direction whence it had come.

"Didn't fancy the look of them—guilty conscience, I'd say," Brinton said, adding, in a roar: "So just get after them, lad!" The young Panda constable rushed across to his waiting vehicle, leaped into the driver's seat, and switched on the engine.

The car stalled. The driver cursed and tried again. Meanwhile, Brinton had charged back to his own car, and was leaning over the radio. "Hello, hello—attention, all cars. Did anybody see the number plate?"

"Dark red Mini, sir, but I didn't get the number," said Bob Ranger.

"Two people inside, man and woman," said Delphick. "She was driving."

Brinton was relaying this information to all patrol cars as the Panda, with a frantic gunning of the accelerator, burst into life and sped off down the road with a further screech of tyres. Then there came a scurry of feet from the nearby house, and three people—two women, one man—rushed down the path to see what had caused the recent commotion. Over the high hedge, only Bob could see them, and he shouted a warning to his superiors. Everything happened very fast after that. The three heard his voice, looked at one another, then plunged on together towards the black Ford van, with such a turn of speed that they almost reached it before Bob leaped upon the man, Delphick and Brinton upon the women. Firmly but warily these two held their suspects; Bob was able to exert rather more restraint upon his captive. He shook his collar gently—the man collapsed, a near-dead weight; this brought Bob off-balance, and as he stumbled the man jerked himself upright, yelled: "Come on!" to the women, and they, as the attention of their captors was drawn to the tumbling Bob, wrenched themselves free, stabbing with elbows and feet in vulnerable places. While Delphick and Brinton gasped and Bob was still picking himself up off the ground, the black Ford van screeched off up the road in the same direction as the dark red Mini, and was gone.

Without waiting to ask, Bob grabbed the radio and broadcast a call, in Brinton's name, for all patrols to watch out for a small black Ford van with three people in it, driven by a man. Then he turned to assist Delphick and Brinton, who were rubbing their eyes and swearing, to their feet.

"Well done, lad." Brinton nodded his approval of Bob's quick thinking as he regained sufficient breath to speak. "We'll never catch 'em now. Best leave it to the others. They can't get far."

"We'd better check inside the house," Delphick said as he, too, breathed normally again. He led the way through the gate and up the path to the front door, which stood open to show a narrow hall with several cardboard boxes, crammed with an assortment of items, on the floor.

"The swag," said Delphick. "Ready to load into the van once they'd collected enough. Some of it's good quality, but perhaps not up to their usual standards." He examined a glass vase thoughtfully. "Reproduction, not original, one of a pair, I think—but if there's only one, it's obviously not worth as much."

He rose to his feet. "We can worry about that later. See that parcel on the hall table? Brown paper, string, one of those list labels with incomprehensible writing—it's a load of laundry, and now we can guess how they wormed their way into the house. But the question now is, is the owner of the house all right?"

"Through here, perhaps," said Brinton, leading the way down the hall and into the room at the end. "Yes—there's someone asleep in an armchair here . . . "

He dropped his voice as he moved towards the sleeping woman, who did not stir at his approach. On the table beside her was a bottle of Phylloxera Sherry, almost full. "Should we try to wake her, or not? How strong d'you reckon those pills are?"

"Wake her," said Delphick and took the woman's wrist to feel her pulse. "Sluggish, but regular. She won't come to any harm." And he shook her arm a few times before raising her head to slap her face.

He did not slap her face. He stared at it, instead. So did Brinton, as his friend cried: "I don't believe it!" And so, too, did Bob Ranger . . .

For the face of the sleeping woman was the face portrayed by Miss Seeton in her sketch of the air-raid.

"I don't believe it," breathed Brinton, while Delphick, coming to his senses, began to slap the woman's face gently, ordering her to wake up. "She—she *can't* have known!"

Delphick spoke again to the woman, who emitted a little groan. Her eyelids fluttered, and her lips moved. As she returned slowly to consciousness, her features firmed, and her age became apparent: she no longer seemed as young as she'd at first appeared—as young as Miss Seeton's sketch.

But the resemblance was still remarkable.

"How could she have known?" Brinton demanded, scowling at the woman. "It's—it's uncanny. No wonder some of 'em say she's a witch," and he glanced over his shoulder. But all he saw there was Bob Ranger, who in his turn was staring at the woman Delphick was slowly bringing back to life.

The chief superintendent was doing much furious thinking even as he cajoled the unconscious woman in the chair. What had prompted Miss Seeton to draw the sketches she had? What was the connection between the two groups of three, one man and two women, which she had shown? And why her insistence on the World War Two connection? Was it just the Manudens' air-raid bunker and the raffle prize?

One of these questions, at least, he could answer: maybe inspiration about the others would come as he spoke now. "I think," he said, standing back to watch the results of his handiwork, "that this is another victim of the Sherry Gang. She's not very big—probably why she's taking her time about coming out of the drugged sleep—and I bet she was struggling with her parcel of laundry, and that's how they picked her up."

"Makes sense," said Brinton, "though she's younger than their normal victims, isn't she? Fiftyish, I'd say."

"But hampered by a bulky parcel on a hot day," Delphick reminded him. "The poor girl in the wheelchair was thirty-something, wasn't she? Anyway, we can ask her when she wakes up—and we've got a few other things to ask her, too. Because I'm betting on Miss Seeton again—and I'm guessing now that what we have here is not only a Sherry Gang victim, but one of the Dick Turpin crowd."

The exclamations of the other two made the woman in the chair open her eyes briefly and groan again. She breathed in deeply, then blinked, sighed, and closed her eyes once more. Delphick spoke quickly, to forestall her proper awakening.

"Yes, she's a Turpin type. My guess is that she drives the car that blocks off the back end of the bus, while the other two, and I'll guess again that they were in that dark red Mini that didn't like the look of us, prance about at the front with shotguns and masks. Another guess is that she's the brains behind it all—that it's her local knowledge of the back lanes that ensures the gang always escapes before road blocks are set up."

"A lot of guesses," muttered Brinton, although he'd been watching the face of the woman who was no longer as asleep as she'd earlier been; and her expression had been anxious enough, as Delphick spoke, to make the superintendent wonder if his friend's theory might have some truth in it.

"I've even more guesses to make," said Delphick airily, and looked towards the woman in the chair. "I think that if we were to ask Betsy Manuden—we'll continue to call her by that name, though I don't know if it's correct—if she'd mind standing slap up close to this woman here, we'll find a remarkable likeness between them—because they're mother and daughter, and it's the daughter Miss Seeton has seen out and about in Plummergen, dressed in her wartime fancy dress and reminding everyone about an old scandal so that they'd never dream of a new scandal arising in the same place.

"Oh, yes," said Delphick, as Brinton and Ranger looked at each other and exclaimed again, "I'm hazarding my final guess on just one fact—courtesy of Miss Seeton, bless her.

"That this woman here," he said, "lived right through the war and remembers it well, and didn't die in an air-raid—and was known, to her friends, as Susannah Dawkin . . . "

# chapter

## -26-

"I DON'T KNOW how she does it," moaned Brinton, clutching his hair. "Two police cars written off, Brettenden town centre closed to traffic for an hour while everyone sorts out the chaos—it *would* happen in the middle of the evening rush hour, of course—and PC Potter in hospital with concussion, and Miss Seeton not even near the place!"

"Be fair, Chris." Delphick grinned at his anguished colleague. "On the credit side, we've got six people in custody and cleared up two cases, all thanks to her. We've seen the end of both the Sherry Gang *and* the Dick Turpins."

"Says you. The Sherry lot were singing like canaries, but we didn't get much out of your Turpins, did we? Every time I hear someone asking for a solicitor, my heart sinks—shows they know too many of the ropes for my liking."

"Susannah seems to have taught them well, I agree. But she couldn't resist boasting a little before we took her in, could she? Which ought to be enough to hold on suspicion, until we can dig out some proper evidence."

Brinton snorted. "That old swapped-identity-discs story—has anyone ever really known it to work?"

"According to Susannah, it worked for her. Certainly it was believed in Plummergen that she'd died in an air-raid—except the people who thought she was buried in the bunker, of course." Delphick chuckled. "We'll have to check it out for evidence now, won't we, which is going to put paid to the vicar's plans for a raffle prize. Not so much a time capsule as a robbers' cave. Maybe we should make a donation to the

Church Roof Fund, just to show willing."

"After what we'll have to pay out to get that pair of Pandas repaired, we won't be able to afford it." Brinton's eyes closed as he relived the memory of recent traumatic events. The dark red Mini, driven by the Turpin daughter Betsy Manuden, had bolted away from the police car outside her mother's house back towards Plummergen, with the young Panda driver in hot pursuit. Meeting on the road the patrol car driven by PC Potter, minding his own business, the Mini jammed on its brakes, turned tightly, and, evading the Panda, turned up the side road towards Woodchurch.

Such guilty behaviour, especially with a colleague of his chasing them, caused Potter to make it his business to join in that chase, and he stepped on the accelerator. But the Panda was attempting to turn to follow the Mini, and there is little room to manoeuvre on the Plummergen road. Potter, skidding round the Panda, drove into a ditch and lost his part of the action. The Panda driver radioed for help, then roared off up the side, turning after the Mini . . .

Which had reached the Woodchurch road in safety, only to meet another Panda, driven this time by someone who'd heard the general alert put out by Brinton. The Mini spun round yet again, with Brettenden the one route left, and fled in that direction with both Pandas in pursuit.

Meeting, at the crossroads, the black Ford van driven by the Sherry gang . . .

"Two cars written off," repeated Brinton, in a stunned, wondering tone. "Potter'll survive, thank goodness. They want to keep him in for observation, that's all. But she's done it again, Oracle, hasn't she?" He shook his head with a despairing sigh. "What was I told you once? Four things in life you shouldn't try to buck, and one of 'em's fate. But Miss Seeton," he sighed again, "is certainly the other three . . . "

"If we're lucky," said Bob, as they trod up the path of Miss Seeton's cottage, "there'll be a cup of tea and a slice of Martha's fruit cake on offer. I'm starving, after all that excitement."

"We are here simply to report to Miss Seeton," Delphick reminded his sergeant primly, "the success of her sketches in the capturing of not one, but two, criminal gangs. And to tell her the story of an exchange of identity discs, and a life spent on the fringes of London's underworld . . . which will, I grant you, be a long tale to tell, and thirsty work, on a warm evening like this." He grinned as he rang the doorbell. "I wouldn't say no to a cup myself, if I'm honest—but we'll wait for her to offer, Bob. No heavy hints from you, adopted nephew or not."

"I wouldn't dream of it, sir." Bob grinned in his turn. "I wouldn't need to—she'll offer at once, you see."

Delphick frowned. "What I see right now, Bob, is nobody coming—and Dennis Manuden did mutter something about Miss Seeton before he remembered to shut up and ask for a brief. I hope everything's all right." He rang the bell again and hardly waited for an answer before trying the door.

It opened.

"No alarm," he said, urgency in his tone. "Something's wrong, Bob," and there was a brief skirmish on the step as they worked out who was going to enter first.

Bob, being bigger, won, and stood listening in the hall for only a few seconds before pointing towards the kitchen. "That's too heavy for Miss Seeton, sir," he hissed, and in a sudden rush flung open the door and threw himself upon the man inside.

Who uttered a yell of surprise and dropped the tea caddy he'd just picked up. The lid burst off, and little dark brown leaves flew everywhere as Bob wrestled him to the floor. "What the hell—!" he exclaimed through mouthfuls of dried tannin.

"Get off his head, Sergeant," commanded Delphick, trying not to laugh. "I think there's been a mistake. Suspicious this character may be, but not *that* suspicious."

"Thrudd!" cried Bob, releasing his captive at his superintendent's command, and recognising Thrudd Banner, world-famous freelance reporter and friend of Miss Seeton. "I'm sorry, but I thought—Miss Seeton, we were worried . . . "

As Bob babbled, Thrudd clambered to his feet and dusted the tea leaves from his person. "Hope she's got another packet somewhere," he said, "or we'll have to go without, and Mel's sure to blame me."

"Mel?" exclaimed Delphick, who had a warm regard for Thrudd Banner's liberated ladylove, *Daily Negative* reporter Amelita Forby. "Is she here, too? Is this some kind of journalists' jamboree?"

Thrudd had finished tidying himself and was shaking Bob Ranger by the hand. "No hard feelings, Bob. Guess you were rushing to the rescue, so I don't blame you. Pity Mel and I arrived half an hour ago and beat you to it, though."

"The rescue? Miss Seeton—there *was* something wrong, then. Is she all right?" All other considerations vanished from Delphick's mind. "What happened?"

"We've been abroad for a couple of weeks, first holiday I've had in years," Thrudd said. "Mel nagged me into taking a cruise, says you can't beat it." Delphick nodded understandingly. "No newspapers on board, she said, and a proper chance to relax—which is why we'd got no idea there'd been all this highway robbery stunt right near where MissEss just happens to live. Odds on, we told each other once we got back home and caught up with the news, that there's a Seeton connection in it somewhere. The geographical coincidence'd be too much, knowing what she's like."

"I believe," said Delphick, as Thrudd paused and fixed him with a quizzical eye, "that Superintendent Brinton of the Ashford police would agree with you there."

Thrudd grinned. "Good man, Oracle—I knew you wouldn't let us down! I'll get Mel to twist your arm for the details—no use telling me by myself, or she'll never forgive me. Besides, you want to hear what we've been getting up to."

"At a guess, you called on Miss Seeton to learn what you could, found her tied up or otherwise rendered helpless, and rescued her." Thrudd grinned and nodded.

"Heard muffled sort of yodels coming from upstairs when we rang the bell," he said, "so in we went, and Mel charged to the rescue while I was still catching my breath. What a woman," he added in admiration. It was not clear whether he referred to Mel Forby or to Miss Seeton.

"What a woman, indeed," agreed Delphick, while Bob asked for further details of Miss Seeton's pillowcase predicament and demanded to know where she was.

"Mel's taken her to your father-in-law for a checkup," said Thrudd, "not that she needed one, from what I could see. She bounces back every time, our MissEss does. But Mel started fussing, so to keep the peace Miss Seeton said she'd go along—and they left me," he concluded, "to make the tea ready for when they get back." He looked down at the floor and shrugged. "Lost in a good cause, I suppose."

"I thought—well, I'm not sure what I thought, but I'm glad I was wrong," said Bob. "So long as you're sure she's all right—"

"See for yourself," suggested Thrudd, as the sound of female voices was heard in the hall. "Mel's going to kill me for lounging about in the garden instead of doing what I was told and making the tea, so I'd be grateful if you'd do a bit of fire-drawing and ask her to tell you the whole tale without letting on you've heard it from me."

"We'd certainly be interested in Miss Forby's opinions," Delphick said, smiling as the subject of their conversation entered the kitchen, with Miss Seeton close behind. "Hello, Mel. You have a story to impart, we're told."

But Mel was staring at the little brown specks on the kitchen floor. "Guess we've suddenly been overrun by large families of mice," she murmured. Miss Seeton gasped.

"Mice? Oh dear, Martha will be so upset, though living in the country one expects these little incursions from time to time. Good gracious." She stood beside Mel and stared at the tea-littered floor, too surprised even to greet Bob, who was blushing, and Delphick. "Good gracious—surely no mice could have done all this!"

"One large rat, actually," Thrudd told her. "*Very* large—I believe you know him?"

And everyone began to speak to everyone else, delighted at the reunion.

When she learned what had happened, Mel took it upon herself to order Thrudd and Bob down The Street to the post office to buy a fresh packet of tea, and they returned with a fair selection of cakes in addition. Everyone else was by this time sitting in the garden of Sweetbriars enjoying the evening sunshine, and Delphick had complimented Miss Seeton on her recovery from bondage as well as her sketching skill. Thrudd and Bob, the married man, brewed tea in the kitchen and carried out laden trays to the table, which Delphick and Mel had carried into the flickering shade of an apple tree; and for Thrudd's benefit, Delphick went over both cases once more. Miss Seeton smiled and looked pleased, while Thrudd took notes and Mel watched him fondly; Bob drank tea and ate quantities of gingerbread; Delphick talked and recounted in full all the police had managed to learn about the Sherry Gang and the Dick Turpin highway robbers.

And at the end of the second telling, Delphick regarded Miss Seeton kindly. "There'll be a cheque in the post just as soon as I can stir the Accounts people into action," he said, "and well deserved, too, every penny of it."

"An entire Seeton adventure," mourned Mel, "and neither of us anywhere near. That's the last time I take a holiday, Banner, and don't try to change my mind. Cruises, yet!"

"Everyone needs a little relaxation, my dear," said Miss Seeton. "All work and no play—I'm sure that the saying is true. Do you not feel refreshed after your fortnight away?"

"Refreshed," said Mel, "in spirit if not body," and she winked at Thrudd before adding hastily, "and ready for your next excursion, Miss S., so spill the beans. When is it, and where, and what? In Plummergen, or somewhere else? What's going to happen?"

"Why, nothing out of the ordinary," Miss Seeton assured her. "Village life will continue just as it has always done. The Summer Fete (for the Church Roof Fund) and the Flower Festival—and of course the Best Kept Village competition, which is a new interest this year, and seems likely to bring many visitors to enjoy the area. Which is as it should be. Sharing our privileges with those less fortunate, you see."

"I see," said Mel. "Carloads of complete strangers all over the place, and neighbouring villages trying to do the dirty on Plummergen so's they can win the cup, or whatever, and squabbles about who arranges what flowers where . . .

"I think," she announced, "that I'll change my mind about not taking another holiday—but I'm not going abroad. I'll be staying right here in England—because I've got a feeling things will fairly start to hum once the summer has properly come along . . . "

Only Miss Seeton had no inkling of what she meant.